# Trust in Princes

# The Cause of Hamlet's Lunacy

A Novel by

Julian Marck

To Deb,

Kathy sends her love, and hopes that
you will enjoy this "humble offering."

Julian Marck (aka "Mark")

Fulton Books
Meadville, PA

Published by Fulton Books 2023

ISBN 978-1-63985-874-3 (paperback)
ISBN 978-1-63985-875-0 (digital)

Printed in the United States of America

February 19, 2015

To my two audiences,

*Trust in Princes* is my offering of a look into the youth and young manhood of Hamlet, prince of Denmark. In writing it, I kept two audiences in mind. Well, my primary audience was my wife, but after that, the world is welcome to it as one or the other audience. It is a simple division, really. One audience is comprised of those who are not familiar with the play or who have a bare understanding of the plot, to wit, murder, lunacy, treachery, more lunacy, and more murder. To these people, I hope that *Trust* will be an interesting introduction to the characters they will meet in the play. In addition, I pray that it will whet the appetite and cause them to view one version or other of the play for they will not encounter it here since *Trust* ends only two scenes into the play.

My other audience then is comprised of those who know the play intimately, well enough to "mouth" at least half of Hamlet's lines and a decent fraction of Polonius's inanities to the discomfiture of those seated around them in the theater. What I hope these people will enjoy are what I call the "proto-Shakespearian-isms"; that is the half formed but not quite stillborn emergence of lines that later appear in the play in their mature Shakespearian form and some interesting— possibly ironic—parallels to events in the play. Additionally, I hope to give them a thought-provoking look at Hamlet's relationships to the other characters before he becomes so thoroughly disillusioned with them. They will, I hope, enjoy Yorick's banter and gentle mentoring, and they might be surprised to realize that Hamlet admired Ophelia's brother, Laertes ("What is the reason that you use me thus? I loved you ever" [act 5, scene 1]). Their reading of this then might also send them back to the play as to one visiting an old friend but with a mind to discovering something new in them.

Wherever you land, *Trust in Princes* has something for you, even if it is meet food for criticism, so enjoy!

# Introduction

# Hamlet as the Ill-Made Knight

*April 3, 2019*

In his work *The Once and Future King*, T. H. White presents the idea of Lancelot as the *chevalier mal fet* or the "ill-made knight." As simply as I can put it, he describes Lancelot as a young page possessed of what we might call nowadays as "poor self-image." What we are given for this is the fact that he is "ugly." The focus of his story then is Lancelot's reaction to this circumstance.

Significantly, rather than turning this failing into bitterness and an "ugly disposition," Lancelot shows his true nobility by determining that he will make up for this deficiency by becoming the best knight in all Christendom. To this end, he pushes himself to the limits of martial ardor, spiritual purity (we presume because White does not explore this aspect in a directly spiritual way), and moral correctness.

In time, he quite honestly achieves the ideal without compromise. Yet his self-perception keeps him humble. In his estimation—and regardless of what others may think—he will never truly meet the ideal. As sympathetic onlookers, we could readily declare him a saint and move on to other, more troubled—and therefore, more interesting—characters.

Unfortunately, what we begin to see is that this effort, even in its successes, produces a tension as Lancelot must not only strive to achieve the ideal but also maintain an increasingly untarnished image against a secret and growing love for a married woman—Queen Guinevere, as it happens.

This need to maintain what has now become a pretense of perfection—though he is still impossible to defeat in the field—brings this tension to high pitch. It ultimately intensifies the effect of his fall when it eventually happens and brings himself, those whom he loves, and the dream they had hoped to create to utter ruin. Such is the theme of Camelot.

In *Trust in Princes*, I wish to explore this same idea in the character of Hamlet; that he is also an ill-made knight of sorts. He is not ugly, to begin with. His fatal flaw is that he is too much the idealist. What begins to happen is that his concept of the ideal and his quest to achieve an ideal self—which he believes he must attain if he is to be a "good king"—begins to erode his self-image from the inside as he recognizes and tallies his own shortcomings. What his shortcomings are in detail, we can only guess at. His self-accusations in the lines following "get thee to a nunnery" in the play (act 3, scene 1) might be a good start point. For the most part, let us assume them to be a weakness for lustful thoughts.

In my story, a youthful Hamlet unexpectedly encounters an image of womanhood, and it will not let go of him. Here, I hope the story will connect with boys and young men of today who are bombarded in the media with images designed to arouse first sexual curiosity and then sexual desire, especially those who recognize that this is a deeply moral dilemma. In this respect, Hamlet moves from being a literary curiosity who challenges categorization and becomes *everyboy*.

These thoughts—which wash up against the pedestal on which he keeps all women, especially his mother, the queen; and Ophelia, the love of his life—constitute the start of this erosion of self-image. He possesses a nobility of sorts that stays him in moving from sexual thought to sexual action, with the possible exception of self-stimulation. Yet he believes his thoughts condemn him in any case.

He has read his Gospel, "If any man looks on a woman with a lustful eye, he has already committed adultery with her in his heart" (Matthew 5:28), and he believes that so long as his thoughts continue to master him, he is not eligible for God's grace. He is essentially experiencing Paul's dilemma as it is expressed in his letter to the Romans (Romans 7:15–24): "I do not understand what I do" but without the answer given to us in verse 25, "Who can save me… Thanks be to God who delivers me through Jesus Christ." Hence, Hamlet remains self-condemned and captive to his thoughts.

I want to add to this another dimension to complete the "cause of Hamlet's lunacy." Since he fails to see the shortcomings in others—especially those he admires—in his thinking, they meet his ideal where he does not. He then believes that he must maintain a pretense of the ideal that he hopes for and yet despairs of achieving someday. The success of this pretense becomes the key to sustaining the wonderful and intimate relationships in his life.

The tragedy behind the tragedy of the play is this: Though none of his shortcomings is fatal in and of themselves, yet we fall back on the demi-soliloquy that begins "So, oft it chances in particular men" (act 1, scene 4), and we begin to see even more clearly that it points not to Claudius but to Hamlet himself. In addition, though each of these shortcomings is easily overcome in the power of the resurrection (Ephesians 1:18–19), Hamlet's reliance on these personal relationships and on pretense to make up for his shortcomings, or at least to mask them, does prove fatal. Lunacy becomes both the path he takes and the gauntlet through which he must run.

These relationships have become so important in his need to maintain the pretense to the ideal that in the events that follow his father's death—at this point, we are beyond the scope of this story and into the play itself, and as the idealism of these relationships is shattered by the natural failings of these people, Hamlet is thrown into severe disillusionment, e.g., his father and Yorick—whom I have made a confidant to Hamlet in the story—are only mortal, his mother is not faithful, Ophelia is not a strong support to him, Rosencrantz and Guildenstern can be bought, etc.

It is this disillusionment built on the first premise of the *ill-made knight* and all the faulty thinking that proceeds from it that sets him reeling from one situation in the play to another, and that, of course, leads to its tragic ending.

It is my intent to use the story, *Trust in Princes*, to illustrate these falsely idealistic relationships of his youth as both the goal of his pretension and as the unwitting foil to his true redemption. I conclude with an excerpt from my notes on Hamlet's relationship with an added minor character, Fra Ignacio, the castle chaplain, who is meant to represent in part the spiritual antipode to his other relationships.

Hamlet's greatest failing is, in essence, a neglect of the spiritual foundation. As the play (not this story) unfolds, we will see how all of his relationships—with the exception of Horatio—fail him for the same lack of a spiritual basis. They fail him so utterly that his actions in the play and especially his lunacies—both feigned and real—can be seen as the result of severe disillusionment. Here I have taken my cue from A. C. Bradley's *melancholia* theory and added a rationale for the significance of these failed relationships. For I think that *they must have been strong indeed* for such failures to have sent him so close to madness.

So my title follows the biblical injunction "Put not your trust in princes" (Psalm 146:3) and at the same time treats of Hamlet's own trust in ideal relationships, i.e., the trust that is in this prince.

# Act 1

# Chapter 1

The yard of Elsinore Castle resounded with the exuberance of warlike practice. Two youths faced each other under the careful direction and scrutiny of a seasoned man-at-arms. Before each iron-clang echo of connecting blows had opportunity to die away in the angle of the castle yard, the students would disengage to resume their close regard, each of the other.

The older, and naturally bigger of the two, was a muscular yet nimble boy with long dark locks and heavy brows that most readily gave expression to his thoughts and emotions. These brows were raised now above a confident smile. Could he read the other's mind exactly, he would not be more certain of his opponent's next moves. His successful responses to the other's attempts thus far seemed to bespeak a gift for prophecy. In truth, he merely followed a wise course. For the moment, he fought on the defensive, allowing the younger to wear himself down in a succession of aggressive thrusts. 'There will be a time,' he thought. 'The readiness is all.'

The blond-haired younger, a wiry youth of medium height for his twelve years, sported an eager grin beneath his bright blue eyes. These eyes signified both intelligence and energy. A quick analysis of his opponent, some two years his senior, led him to an equally quick decision in his next move. He would affect a bold beat to his left to clear the other's blade, followed by a swift extension directly toward the chest. Confidence shown in his face as well. This, he felt sure would be the end of matters. He had the move clearly in his mind. It would be irresistible.

In the event, the elder easily—let us also say artfully—parried the thrust and the two returned to *en garde*. The clanging of metal on metal continued in almost pure notes through a dozen more attempts of the younger to beat and lunge successfully. Despite the clamor, the few attendants present in the yard gave only occasional fleeting glances toward the fighters and then went about their tasks.

After a half dozen more similar attempts at getting inside the older's guard, the younger began to understand that age difference and a corresponding difference in his opponent's height and size left him overmatched. He simply had neither the strength nor yet the proper technique to beat his way past the other's defense in single blows. He also realized that he had been timing his moves with a predictable regularity. Hence, the other was always ready.

'Perhaps,' he thought, 'it is time to throw caution to the wind and shift to a strategy of relentless battering.' He envisioned something akin to the freewheeling melees he had witnessed at tournaments.

Forcing a slightly high-pitched impression of a war cry, the younger jumped to a renewed offense. It was a brave show of battle lust, and for a moment, it pushed the older boy backward with some display of concern—or was it annoyance at a deliberate lack of form?

Any discomfiture on the older's part was only temporary, for soon the moment came. The blows began to weaken. The cries of "Ha and ha!" came between gasps for air. The younger shifted his focus to the other's blade rather than his person. He swung his sword in shorter and shorter arcs, like someone hacking desperately with a stick at a tree. He was forgetting to thrust. It was time.

Feigning an opening by leaving his sword wide, the older let the other step in with an extension but then beat his opponent's sword near the hilt, knocking it completely out of hand. Instantly, the older extended his own arm, bringing his point to a spot just below the other's rib cage. Had he driven the point home, even blunted as it was, it would have been fatal.

The disarmed younger arched his back like a cat on its hind legs, barely avoiding the point. He found himself staring down at the other's blade. For a moment, he stood poised as he considered the import of his predicament: the loss of renown, the loss of a kingdom, and the loss of life. He had but one weapon left. Resorting to it, he raised his head to fix the victor with a disarming smile. Both boys regarded each other, panting as the older traded a look of intense concentration for his own broad grin. He dropped his sword arm out to the side and made a slight bow.

"Well done, Master Laertes!" judged their trainer from off to the side. Receiving a grateful acknowledgment from him, the master-at-arms turned to the younger boy. "Lord Hamlet, you are improving."

"Laertes?" Hamlet looked to his sparring partner with admiration in his eyes.

"Indeed, my lord, you moved me from my place this time. You are gaining in strength, to be sure, though your ending technique was something out of fashion."

"Out of fashion." Hamlet let that sink in.

"Your fervor undid you in the end," the trainer appended the other's comment. "Impetuosity may give strength to your blows, but want of technique renders them futile in the essay."

"Yes, I see that now," responded the young prince with no loss of enthusiasm. "Thank you, Marcellus." It was clear that Hamlet coveted Laertes's approval over that of his trainer.

Marcellus, a stocky man-at-arms, studied the sky to discern the hour. "That, it seems, is your lesson for this day. Let us see how well you remember it on the morrow."

Both boys surrendered their weapons to an obliging page. Laertes walked off with Marcellus through a doorway at the near end of the castle yard. Their conversation turned on the qualities of various types of swords.

Left to himself, Hamlet slowly pivoted, gazing about the yard with a puzzled look. The simple folk continued about their business. One or two of the men dipped their heads in acknowledgment and respect as his gaze met theirs. These he returned with friendly regard. Everything under his survey was as it should be except someone was missing.

"Now where did he go?" the prince muttered to himself, picking up his step as he moved across the yard in the direction opposite to that taken by Marcellus and Laertes. He strode toward the short tower near the postern. Continuing to look about and still somewhat reluctant to quit the yard, he entered the tower and ascended the steps.

As with many castles of the day, Elsinore was a composite structure that had grown over the decades as necessity and resources dictated. The ongoing result was a curious hodgepodge of twistings and turnings to the wall segments that showed no discernable pattern. Some elevations followed the contour of the ground itself. Other extensions merely added angles designed to cover perceived blind spots in the existing walls. With the growing strength of the kingdom and the necessity for more armed retainers, a concurrent need for additional barracks and storage rooms added to the construction.

Contemporary defenders of its works appreciated the way such a plan—or unplan—could break up and compartmentalize the fighting should an assault breach the battlements. This would allow massing for counterattacks and buy precious time for relief efforts. To a boy of Hamlet's age and power of imagination, it served a different purpose in offering a setting to excite fantasy and give flame to heroic doings.

Continuing up through the tower, he envisioned an intense melee played out desperately on the stairs above and below him. Emerging out onto the first platform, he saw himself leading a small but significant counterattack of knights and men-at-arms across the open space to restore the defense, perhaps even to rescue his father who had been trapped in an isolated portion of the ramparts. Mentally, he picked his way over the bodies of slain warriors, friend and foe alike—but of course, more of foe than of friend.

The thought of dead fighting men put him, as was his habit, unto a new line in his imagination. He recalled a freshly told tale from the night before in the great hall at dinner when an itinerant troubadour spoke of a ghostly knight, the victim of a murder by a rival at love, who walked the battlements of his castle in search of revenge. This thought brought Hamlet up short as he faced the next set of steps leading up to the ramparts from the far end of the platform. These steps entered the wall itself and so were covered, making the entrance something like that of a cave or tunnel. The stairs turned a few times in the dark and were illuminated but dimly by light shining diffusely down through the gratings.

Hamlet's friend Horatio had termed it a "ghostly light" when he first encountered it in an early explore of the castle. Hamlet remembered the darkness then, and seeing it now framed by stone, he thought of how he had stared into the hearth of the great hall during the exposition of the bard's tale. The flames danced to words that spoke of one whose wicked heart propelled him stealthily through the castle halls to carry out an evil plan.

> 'Twas love for his fair lady kept
> The knight unarm'd 'gainst evil's sway.
> Thus, unforewarned he blithely slept
> When poison found its prey.

The poet went on, his words twisting and wrenching in and out of meter to paint the images that Hamlet saw in the fire. It was a tortured telling, and perhaps it was meant to be. Yorick, the king's own jester and storyteller, grimaced at every strained line. But it caught the young prince's imagination as he watched the sparks fly up into the darkness, the pop and crackle of dry wood punctuating each image like the cackle of a witch.

> The fable goes beyond the grave
> For, justice to a vengeance calls,
> And blood for blood will have
> Ere walks again a peace unto these halls.

Hamlet had tried to affect a casual interest as he approached Yorick that evening about the truth of the story. In private, Yorick could always be counted on to dispense with his usual antics and provide wisdom in addition to his father's pointed observations of life to an heir apparent. He could be trusted for explanations that expanded on, illuminated, and/or mitigated matters in question. Yorick had seen through the mask of nonchalance and did his best to make light of the tale. Hamlet believed him and slept with untroubled dreams that night.

He believed Yorick still about the ghost as he faced the present darkness. But that darkness now brought back to his mind the images he had conjured from the story. A son of the knight encounters his father's ghost in full armor on the ramparts at night and is driven nearly insane with muted revelations of eternal perdition and the ghastly truth of his father's murder. It was these very stairs that framed the setting for Hamlet's inspired vision of that meeting.

He saw it all again: he, the son, transfixed with terror while his own father in fearsome panoply towered above him on the steps vaguely illuminated, mostly in silhouette, but decidedly substantial all the same.

Reminding himself that he was the prince of Denmark, someday to be its fearless ruler, and that he had better start working on the fearless part now, Hamlet swallowed and stepped into the opening. He studied the stairs as they rose into shadow. The sounds of work from the yard below faded to nothing, leaving only the whispered draft that whipped past him, almost pushing him to the ascent, like fingers of a cold hand to prod him.

Deprived of light, he amplified his other senses and noticed two sounds as he moved. The first was his rushed breathing. Well, after all, he had nearly run up the first steps in the old tower and dashed across the platform as well. The other sound was his echoing footfalls. Though their source could be identified, neither was a comfort to him.

Turning the first corner plunged him into deeper darkness. It was almost absolute. He climbed on, left foot, right foot, and so on. One more turn, he knew, and he would be able to see light from the opening at the top of the stairs. This thought quickened his pace and threw him off his guard. Just as he turned the corner, a silhouetted figure loomed above him on the steps. It held a sword point toward him.

"Have at you!" a youthful voice yelled in a manner calculated to startle. Hamlet's heart went to his throat. He flinched backward, almost stepping back into the dark. But recognition of the voice recovered him quickly.

"Horatio!" he almost screamed his friend's name hysterically. "By the Mass, you gave me a fright, such a fright!"

At this, the dark figure dashed up the remaining steps giggling and disappeared into the light. Hamlet pursued him up onto the ramparts to find that his friend had turned to face him. He held two wooden practice swords, one in each hand. He tossed the one in his left hand to Hamlet as the latter came up.

"Defend yourself, sir knight!" Horatio called, coming to *en garde* as Hamlet caught the proffered weapon and assumed a similar stance.

"Assassin!" he yelled, advancing to fighting range.

"No, a Saracen!" responded his friend with adventure lust in his voice.

Hamlet moved to the attack with energy despite the exertion of his previous sparring against Laertes and his hasty ascent of the stairs. Aroused and somewhat piqued by the surprise he had just suffered, Hamlet struck with vigor and force though not with anger. He was ready for any game.

Remembering his lesson, he focused not on the opposing blade as before but locked his gaze to his friend's eyes as he drove him back. Here the tables had turned; the younger, shorter, lighter Horatio gave ground more easily than Laertes and was soon backed against the crenellations of the parapet.

"Yield!" cried Hamlet with an almost squeal of triumph that surprised even himself. In his mind, it was not Horatio but Laertes he had bested. There was a breathless moment. Then Horatio chuckled and parroted Laertes's downward turn of his sword arm, this time in token of surrender.

"I yield, my lord!" he exclaimed with gleeful admiration. Horatio was happiest at his friend's good accomplishments, even those that elevated Hamlet over him. Both boys understood that Horatio's presence at court was not so much for knightly training or even for the prince's companionship but for insurance of his father's loyalty to the king. This knowledge affected their friendship in no negative way and only made it more firm. Hamlet accepted Horatio, the token of loyalty, as loyalty itself. For his part, Horatio nurtured loyalty into true friendship.

Hamlet now studied his friend. Horatio was a year younger and possessed a slight build. His oblong countenance—a pleasant oval— still bore much of the softness of late childhood while his bookishness confirmed itself in deeply set, sensitive eyes that matched the dark brown of his hair. One would have to search thoroughly to see in him the warrior who was in truth the least part of his dreams for the future. But always, when next to Hamlet, this dream grew and came to the forefront of his more practical visions, making it almost a plausible aspiration. He did not diminish before the promise of Hamlet's greatness but rather shared unreservedly in it. Such was Hamlet's intent for his friend.

Hamlet accepted Horatio's proffered homage with the broad laughter of life at its full. He tossed his own sword in the air so that it flipped end over end once before he caught it cleanly by the handle. Looking around for the next thing to do, his imagination worked quickly to a plot—never mind that it was a well-worn plot. He pointed with his sword toward the tower that rose highest above the battlements.

"To the tower! Rescue the king!" With that, he was off closely followed by his friend. They raced along the parapet, ascended a half flight of steps that rose with the battlements, then advanced along to the door of the tower, stopping every few paces to impale an imaginary foe and pitch him over to a fatal fall.

Once in the tower, they sprang up a series of uneven spiral steps—perish the thoughts of the ghostly knight and the dark places between windows now. With much shouting, grunting, and slashing of their notched practice swords, they finally emerged into the open air of the broad tower platform.

A young man-at-arms stood posted there, gazing steadily out over the surrounding countryside. He had heard the approach of the two boys from the time they entered the tower below. It was nothing new to him. He had witnessed the saving of the castle many times by these two. He smiled thinking of his own youth.

"Bernardo!" cried Hamlet, gaining the opening first and recognizing the man instantly.

"Ola, Bernardo!" echoed Horatio as he emerged from the dark well of the stairs.

"Good day to you, Lord Hamlet, Master Horatio," he said pleasantly yet maintaining an official tone as his duty required.

"*Sir* Horatio," Hamlet corrected. "I've just knighted him." Horatio beamed though he did not seem to recall any such ceremony in their play as yet. "What news? How stands the watch?" Hamlet asked the soldier with the acquired confidence of a prince.

"All is secure, my lord," reported Bernardo, keeping his gaze to a sweep of the horizon. Though his watch allowed him to pass pleasantries with visitors to the tower, yet it would not do for him to relax his surveillance.

"Hm. No Nordics of Old Norway nor pirates about?" Hamlet scanned the horizon himself. "Hm. Not even a rebellious Dansker!" The young prince crossed to the other side of the tower and peered down into the castle grounds.

"Desire no such disruptions to our state, my lord. The countersign to my watchword is 'Peace to this land.'"

"'Tis so indeed. 'Tis so. I have heard it spoken at the gate," Hamlet returned with a slight drop of his shoulders. He continued his survey of the inner yards of the castle. "And here is the fruit of that peace, Horatio. Look where my father takes his rest." He motioned his friend to the edge of the battlement and pointed to a portion of the castle that formed a small terraced garden behind the royal apartments. At the end nearest the keep, a short portico rose on a dais above the garden by way of broad steps. Between the columns of the portico, they spied a couch on which reposed the king.

"By my faith and my own father's report, that's his daily custom. Is it not?" asked Horatio.

"To be sure. To be sure."

"The Lord let him long keep it then, if it is the signification of our peace."

"Aye, for the sake of peace, but he should not keep it overlong, else we'll grow soft for lack of use at arms, and eyes covetous of our state essay a test of combats to our embarrassment and loss. Besides, each prince must have his go at glory."

"You still have your training, my lord."

"Hm. Yes, there is that as well, and I must one day best Laertes. It is my goal."

"That would be a goal worthy of the effort," broke in Bernardo, still gazing outward. "I have seen his skill at arms and heard it well pronounced by the Master of the Sword."

"I will have him one day but only by gleaning the best at his hand. And then together, we will attempt Young Fortinbras of Norway. Set your imagination to it: myself, Laertes, and you, Horatio, at my side!"

"I, my lord?" Horatio sounded doubtful. He thought wistfully of his own lack of martial talent, which suffered all the more by reason of his penchant for bookish study.

"Aye," Hamlet reassured his friend. He was aware of Horatio's self-doubts. "Well, you will be my *stratego*, as the Greeks style their generals, and devise for me and my host brave stratagems to make our successful warlike labors less yet seem to be more in the eyes of the world. You have that strength of mind, I know." He was well pleased with this arrangement and turned once again to look outward toward the countryside.

"I suspect you will still have old Polonius, Laertes's father, to plan your wars," mused Horatio as he watched his friend cross the space.

"Perhaps, perhaps—if we intend to subdue our foe with weighty words. I heard him once launch a string of adjectives that, harmless in themselves, was like to bowl a stalwart yeoman over. The man is pregnant with potent predicates as well!"

"Indeed, my lord. He could out Laertes's sword with words, even hold back the invader with deliberations unto doomsday!"

They both laughed awhile at this, and even Bernardo had to wipe away a mirthful tear. Horatio joined Hamlet at the battlement, and the two friends resumed their scan of the environs, looking earnestly for they knew not what perhaps the approach of a new adventure. Hamlet was first to break the silence.

"Father says I think overmuch, but then, as if bursting the chain of thought that shackles deeds with indecision, I give over to action that sometimes hath no thought in it at all. I saw that today in my bout with Laertes." Horatio pursed his lips and looked aside over a different stretch of land, avoiding his friend's perusal. "Your silence brooks assent." Hamlet sighed. "Well, it is so." Then speaking softly to his friend, he said, "How my well-formed thoughts should birth such half-formed deeds is—but you must help me to a correction ere I become king."

"In all my best I will, my lord."

"I will hold you to that, Sir Horatio!"

The two remained in the tower until dusk obscured the landscape beyond discernment. Only then did they descend to dinner with many mock battle honors added from the day.

# Chapter 2

Hamlet rose early before the servant entered to stir the fire. This he did himself by design and with more enthusiasm than Odain, the young drudge whose job it was. In this morning, there was something about blowing life into the ash-covered embers and building them into a flame—first with kindling, then with solid wood—something that spoke to him of calling forth life more fully from a dormant existence. At first, he fed the tiny flames as one might feed an infant, adding just what was needed and with both infant and feeder fully absorbed in the process. He was in no rush though the drafts did chill his backside until the heat could build in the room.

As the flames grew, he mused further that each piece of kindling was a thought to feed a hungry young mind. The flames were his mind, and he would not choke out the former with too-fast feeding nor his mind with too-fast learning. Not all of this was original in his thinking. In truth, it was his father's lesson from the day before. Hamlet had asked in passing why he could not attend the council of the king's chief ministers held each morning. His father answered with a description of meticulously building a fire, assuring him that such heady business as was conducted there would be to his education like attempting to bring an ember to flame with but one huge log.

Hamlet accepted the answer yet longed to test the metaphor. He had gone to bed the night before with a mental library of theories about how he would conduct this investigation. Now he rejoiced, almost giggled to himself, to be able to affect his experiment and see the metaphor leap into flame, as it were.

Something else. He marveled at how, in all his twelve years, he could let such a daily practice go unnoticed, taken for granted by him, its lesson veiled in his experience until now. He thought also about how, on the other hand, Odain no doubt considered stoking the fire a tedious chore, one to be avoided, if possible. Yet here he was so focused in on the act that he felt he could go on feeding the fire through the whole day.

This was the working of his mind; that it could be bounded in a nutshell and yet find room enough to reign like a monarch in a kingdom of thoughts. Only with great effort could he pull himself away from the hearth. Rather, it was the heat now that pushed him back away from the happily glowing fire.

The metaphor complete, Hamlet took a taper; and from his new creation, Prometheus-like, he brought some flame to his bedside candle. By these lights, he finished dressing. When Odain did finally enter the room, he was not in any way surprised, except perhaps to see his prince in some natural employment. There had been other early morning experiments that often took some explaining. Little did he care. But let us not paint Odain so ungrateful as to lack in appreciation for this one chore done and to near perfection at that. He simply asked if there was anything else needed. Upon receiving a cheerfully negative reply, the servant withdrew, leaving Hamlet to his kingdom of thoughts.

*****

Hamlet's father, however, was having second thoughts over this same metaphor. Following breakfast, he summoned Hamlet to his apartments. The young prince arrived post haste to find his father standing in the center of his antechamber, reading over a parchment document. He knew to stand silently until his father acknowledged his presence. The king did so only after concluding his study of the sheet. He meant no slight to his son by this. For he, too, was capable of focusing on matters at hand to the exclusion of all else about him. Now he looked up at the presence that he had perceived while reading. Looked and smiled broadly.

"Hamlet, my son. You are well come. I have given more thought to your question of yesterday. In this I have set it down that while it is not yet time for you to make regular attendance at council, still it is meet that you should at least be witness to the proceedings for the day."

"Yes, Father!"

"I choose this day because in it, nothing remarkable is to happen. You may as well learn now that being a king is simply a heightened form of tedium. Monarchs are not free agents. We are bound to our people and their needs. We pay sorely for our rights and privileges in the hours we spend regulating the daily rise and run of our state. It is a drudgery of the mind at times more undesirable than that of the hand or the body. Yet to rule justly in the framing of a fair law or the redressing of just grievances can be, to a goodly king, a sort of reward. This, I hope, you will witness in the day's proceedings."

"Yes, Father."

"We will convene within the hour. I expect you to attend the entire session, and"—he chuckled—"as we were wont to say at tournament in my youth, 'still be on your feet at the end.' 'Tis a figure." He waved off Hamlet's perplexed look. "You will be seated, like the rest of us, but off to the side. The trick, you will see anon, is to stay awake throughout. Have you had good sleep this night?"

"Yes, Father."

"Splendid! Now come give us our morning embrace ere we each go on our way to dress and to take up the less personable robes and roles of public royalty." The king spread his arms to receive his son's affection.

"Might I bring paper that I may take notes?" he asked after pulling away from his father.

"It is meet you shall. But take care lest Polonius find you drawing caricatures of him and think you doodling elephants again." He laughed heartily at this, and Hamlet joined him.

"By your leave, sire, I go now to make preparation."

"It is granted. When you come, enter the council chamber through my rooms here, as you are prince."

"Yes, Father."

Hamlet returned to his room, nearly bursting with anticipation of learning what it is to be king.

*****

At one hour into the council meeting, Hamlet could well appreciate his father's admonitions to stay awake. He was already seated when the council members entered the chamber. They all rose for the king who brought notice that the prince was present to witness the workings of "good government." His presence seemed to please the members. At least, they smiled to him and then to each other as though enjoying a private joke. Now he was beginning to suspect himself as subject of that joke and his endurance in this business its substance. Yet he would not show these men that he was not yet up to the strain of "good governance."

Hamlet marked time by taking notes. Mostly, they were questions about the proceedings that he thought he would ask his father about afterward. Chiefly though, they were a pretext in the fight against tedium.

As anticipated, the chief adversary in this fight turned out to be Chancellor Polonius. Newly established as the head of the council after years as a member only, he used this opportunity to wax eloquent at every turn of the law. But even Hamlet could see that this eloquence consistently drew his verbal arrows wide of their mark. His parenthetical asides allowed him to "condense" five minutes discourse into fifteen. Tedium indeed.

Soon the margins of Hamlet's "tables," as he called his personal notes, were filled with "Blah, blahs" and attempts to capture the serpentine twistings of Chancellor Polonius's eyebrows as they added expression to his otherwise banal words. The chancellor was speaking now on the current property tax that by tradition or common law was based on the number of rooms within a domicile.

"And, my lords, as I have previously ascribed to you all, both in private session and in public council, prior to this and as I shall continue to ascribe so long as the skies hold their constant blue even above the heavy clouds of winter, when its native hue is hid so long

17

from our eyes that we are apt to forget its blueness had we not the seas to remind us, eh, except when they themselves assume a sickly gray green—eh—so long and so often and so continuously shall I hold to this position, my lords, that the common law, which was born in generations past out of the necessities of the time and which over these same generations has so well served our state as to resist, shall we say, amendment, continues to this day to serve this state to its uttermost good, and therefore, by reason of this time-honored and time-proven longevity, need not be yet amended in this our generation, however, much we, as an august body of politicals, may have grown in wisdom above our illustrious ancestors, who not only with wisdom and knowledge but also with divine grace, hath 'stablished this decree which we here bring into question."

"Lord Polonius?"

"Yes, Your Majesty?"

"A word more from you, and then need we move on."

"Yes, Your Majesty?"

"Do you, therefore, say yea or nay toward the motion?"

"It is a decided nay, Your Majesty, as I have endeavored, *sans* all rhetorical devices, to make clear."

"Thank you, good my lord. We ever marvel at how your wisdom comes through your words."

"My thanks to you, Your Majesty." Polonius bowed and resumed his seat.

Hamlet had to dip his head and screw up his face in an effort to refrain from bursting into insane laughter born of frustration over these past ten minutes of Polonius's declaiming. He was glad that he sat behind the minister, who thus could not see his efforts at restraint. At the same time, he was in awe that his father could keep his own countenance in uttering such a double-meaning compliment to the chief minister. This was likely the most important lesson he had learned in kingship thus far from the morning.

Lord Belmondo rose to address the next issue: a question of disputed fishing rights between two coastal villages that lay one within his demesne and one in a neighboring land. So it went.

*****

A short eternity later, Hamlet discerned that the council had come to and concluded the last item on its agenda. Over the previous thirty minutes, he had turned his mind to various strategies that he longed to try against Laertes at their next sword lesson later in the day. But as the ministers began shuffling papers in a way that Hamlet envisioned as knocking dust off themselves, the king lifted up his head and added a freshness and volume to his voice.

"My lords, ere we adjourn, there is some business that has come to our attention this very morning which we have held to the last as a matter of chief importance. We ask your kind indulgence in hearing this out. We know your warm lunches must likely serve you coldly even now. We intend for a short deliberation here then adjure you to consider upon our adjournment what our options might be in response. This evening shall we call you all to a special session to consider our course in these matters."

At this, the king pulled up the parchment he had been reading that morning when Hamlet arrived in his chamber. He recognized the broken seals that hung on ribbons from the edge of the sheet. His father extemporized from the text of the document.

"It says here from the Marcher Lord of Schleswig that he has sure intelligence of a plan wherein the Germans on his eastern border have conjoined in loose confederation with certain lawless tribes among the Nordics to venture an essay into his land. The latter are to savage his coastal habitations with plunder as their aim. The intent of this is to urge the Marcher Lord to throw the major half of his puissance into the fray against this effort, leaving his border towns to the east but lightly held. Against these, the Germans will move, whose purpose is to overrun his lands for the settlement of their own people."

At this, the tenor of the whole meeting changed; it became almost electrified. His father's mention of the Marcher Lord of Schleswig put Hamlet on the alert. That lord was Horatio's father. As his father described the dilemma, Hamlet's thoughts fused into one: A campaign was afoot. His mind raced like a boy's to scenes of martial glory best left undescribed here.

As head of the council, Polonius held the right to speak first. Hamlet winced to think what a cold hash the man would make over such a clear issue.

"Your Majesty"—he rose and began—"as always, I have counseled how cautiously we should rouse the sleeping hounds of war. For many a kingdom hath sallied forth with its armèd might against a martial foe to its own hurt. Long could I hold forth with tale upon tale in example of such times as when kings in many lands have seen fit to hazard their realm in warlike contests for the sake of a crown imperial or, as in this instance, for the holding of an outland demesne which hath but variable worth in it. I think easily of Croesus, of that ancient land of Lydia, who went to war on the prophecy that should he do thus, a great kingdom would fall and was unwitting that the doomed kingdom was his own. However, as you have specified brevity to this council, for the nonce, I will be brief."

"Oh, good."

"The invader is at our doorstep, so to speak. Our doorstep call I it though it be the easternmost of our state and marcher lands at that. Still have I heard it said among the French, who are most experienced against the Germans in this matter and, therefore, in the exercise of arms, have a wisdom tempered in the fire of repeated trials though with varying success. For these same French, I have heard it said, declare that in holding Paris 'gainst the eastern foe, they should best begin their defense on the river which is called the Rhine. That is to say, well in advance of the homeland and with vast mountainous features interposed. This wisdom from them suits us well, saving the mountains, which we lack, in this our current instance.

"Now we have all heard, I am certain, of the great warrior, king of Brandenburg, who had this to say on the value of experience. It is reported that he claimed to have had two mules in service among his forces who had been through some twenty campaigns—but they were still mules! Howbeit the French, though mulish at times, can be said to have gained much in their essays against their many enemies. Ergo, I make bold to say that this infraction to our state cannot nor should not be ignored. We must address might with appropriate might and do so in lands far off before the hurt comes too near.

"Therefore, the issue in the course of war-making has always settled upon the threefold question of *cause* and *might* and *means*. It is clear that in the Marcher Lord's intelligence of this matter, we have our 'cause.' I shall let that rest. As to 'might,' that is a question best answered by the Lord Marshal of Denmark, who is not in presence here. It remains for us, the holders of the purse strings of the realm, as it were, to ascertain unto the 'means' of war. My lords, it is our duty in these deliberations which follow to consider well how we shall assess, and gather, and dispose of such means so as to make no undue encumbrance to our state, even as we supply the ravenous appetites of war. It is to this endeavor our thoughts must bend in pondering the possible courses ahead that we must not find ourselves embarked on too great an enterprise and have to turn back all for the sake of poor husbandry. I have concluded."

"Once again, we are indebted to your wisdom, Lord Chancellor. I assume by this, we are in agreement that our course must be to sortie out to the assistance of the Marcher Lord."

All heads nodded in affirmation.

"Splendid. It remains thus, whether to move all our force at once by sea or by some timed embarkation of our separate divisions, to assemble and move the length of the land, gathering more forces as we proceed. As the Lord Chancellor has adjured you, we, too, echo his words to consider by what means we shall the expense of this endeavor meet. In addition, we call you to secrecy in this matter until our devices can be safely made known. If there be no other point to call into consideration, we shall conjoin this evening, at which time we also expect to have heard from the Lord Marshal. We shall together provide you with the details of our hope in this."

The king stood followed by everyone else, including Hamlet. On exiting, he glanced over at his son and, with a nod of the head, indicated that Hamlet should join him in the antechamber. As the ministers took their leave, many of them also acknowledging the prince with a bow, Hamlet strode to the side door and went to meet his father.

*****

The flood of questions Hamlet had wanted to pose to his father—nearly all of them now hatched out of the news from Schleswig—had to wait again until his father spoke first. As he entered the antechamber, Hamlet saw that servants had laid out a lunch for two at a table that had been moved to the center of the room. His father was casting off some of the regalia and the outer robes of state to make himself more comfortable. He motioned his son to take seat.

When the king joined him at the table, he looked over the dishes, deciding which to apply himself to first. There were coldly carved meats, bread and cheese, and some fruit. His father picked up a small bunch of grapes and studied it in the light from a nearby window. Finally deciding on a particular grape, he plucked it from the bunch and then studied it with curiosity as well. Without taking his eyes off the grape, he addressed his son.

"I know I told you that nothing of consequence would be addressed in council this day. Such was my intent, but as the meeting wore on, I thought it best to send the ministers off to their lunches with the essential matters in their thoughts to begin bending their separate purviews to the task at hand." He popped the grape into his mouth and looked at his bright-eyed son. "You may eat, lad. Do not stand on ceremony."

"Yes, Father." He helped himself to some slices of roast. His stomach made a gurgling noise.

"Well, I'm sure you have questions."

"May I tell Horatio of this news? He is the son of the Marcher Lord in residence here." Hamlet did not expect his father to be familiar with all the royal pages.

"Hm. I think it's best to keep this to yourself for the moment. It is not yet known that we possess this intelligence of the alliance against our vassal, Schleswig, especially in such timely fashion as to intervene. Should the foe learn this, they might abort their scheme. I would like to give our enemies a chance to court disaster. It likes us well. They, the aggressor, attempt to fall upon us unawares and instead are met with adequate puissance to render them ineffective for any further ventures 'gainst our state for some time. But back to Horatio, he will hear soon enough as our preparations are made manifest. Next?"

"Will you go on campaign or send the marshal only?"

"I believe this circumstance warrants the royal presence. I have been too long out of the field. Sometimes an overlong peace leads neighborly kings to blur their memories and mistake the measure of the king of Denmark, leading to sadly unnecessary wars in trial of our strength. If the outcome of this impending venture is as foreseen, the result will multiply to our advantage. And it is time again that I lead my troops and sleep like a commoner with but canvas to shield me from the elements. Now shall I essay your next question?" he asked with a smile and a look from under his brows. Hamlet smiled too, thinking how well his father knew him.

"As you will, sire."

"It is this: 'Will the prince of Denmark join his father in this venture?'"

Hamlet laughed but also maintained an eager pleading in his eyes. "Will he? I mean, will I?"

"I think 'tis time. But now, expect not to be in any fighting. You and the other pages are still too green to wade into a mass of men-at-arms, especially such as are fully trained, experienced in battle, and earnestly desiring to kill you."

"Yes, Father."

"What I expect you to learn from this campaign are the disciplines of war, the rigors of camp life, and the hardships of soldiering in the field. It will not be easy, but I am certain you will make the best of it and take some measure of youthful enthusiasm with you to be tempered into true endurance. In this, you will also grow to appreciate more the demands of your trainers. For there is nothing arbitrary in their corrections, but all are born of the necessity both to defeat the foe and remain alive."

"Will Horatio also attend us?"

"He is junior to you, is he not?"

"Yes, sire, by a year."

"Then I think it meet he should remain here."

"Is this also for security against Schleswig's disloyalty?" Hamlet asked timidly.

The king studied his son almost in the way he studied the grape. In the silence, Hamlet wondered if perhaps he had pushed his questions too far in one direction.

"Say not 'disloyalty' for I know the Marcher Lord to be a true man. But even a king may falter and be enticed to settle with the opposing, if he thinks his state may gain by it. To that prevention is Horatio, and a few others, kept under our wing. He is a friend to you?"

"Yes, Father, and I would that I not be compelled to play him false in his concern for his family in times of danger."

"You will be able to tell him all soon. Meanwhile, remember that as firstborn of the Marcher Lord, he will be your ally someday. Hold his friendship in that tenor and in those terms always." His father finally seemed to cease studying him, leaving a decided look to his expression. "You have a shrewd eye, my son. 'Tis good in one so young, and it tells me that I must rethink the course of your education."

"Time to move beyond kindling?"

At this, his father smiled with broad satisfaction. "Exactly!"

As they continued their meal, they discussed the possible debarkation points along the mainland coast and land routes from them into Schleswig. His father produced a map and pointed these all out to him. In this, he was also preparing his mind for a later discussion with the Lord Marshal. Hamlet soaked up his father's descriptions of the land through which they would be moving. He began to realize how little of his own homeland he knew outside of his own elementary map studies. The king added this consideration to his mental syllabus for Hamlet's future education. Soon, Hamlet ventured intelligent questions in the supply of an army in the field. These pleased his father greatly.

The meal was long concluded. Hamlet was about to take his leave but turned to ask one more question.

"Father?" he hesitated.

"Go ahead."

"Why do you countenance Chancellor Polonius with all his... his..."

"Wayward phrases?" The prince nodded dolefully. His father paused to consider carefully his response. "Consider his comments on the question of Schleswig. Though there be a comic cut to his eternal delivery, which runs unchecked because he perceives it not, yet there is wisdom to be gleaned from his words. And whatever else he is, he is loyal both to our state and to our person—and, by default, to you as heir apparent. You must seek diligently if you would find another man whose self-interest is so completely subordinate. Meddlesome he is. Tiresome he ever shall be, but canny in his own interests he is not."

"Yes, Father. Thank you for your thoughts."

"One thing more. I have heard there is great promise in his son."

"Laertes? Oh, yes!"

"He would a good successor to his father on the council make."

"Or as marshal of Denmark for all his warlike attributes."

"I will keep that in mind. And do so you for it is likely he will serve you when the throne is yours. Now have you a sword lesson?"

"I have yet an hour, but I shall practice beforehand. It would not do to be constantly bested by my own marshal."

"It does not hurt a king to keep better than he about him."

"Yes, Father."

Hamlet quit his father's chamber and went to change into clothes more suited to sword practice. On his way to the yard, he felt his spirit blazing like the hearth fire he had built up that morning.

# Chapter 3

By afternoon on the day following the special meeting of the council, rumors had grown like a web to capture and hold every thought in the realm. For the next few days, only one thing was known for certain: The king was rousing himself and Denmark to war. It became clear since no preparations for defenses were undertaken on home soil that this was to be an outward move to some foreign strand, an expedition. Whither and to what purpose remained a tightly held secret.

Conjectures abounded, some near the mark, most fantastically wide of it. In one tavern, it was booted about that Denmark had rallied to the French against England. In another, the preparations for shipping were noted; ergo, Denmark meant to bolster England against the Scots. Some looked for news to confirm suspicions of a faithless vassal state that was shortly to be brought to heal. Schleswig popped up in one or two of these surmises, but for the most part, the eastern marches remained in the backwash of interest or suspicion of intrigue.

Ultimately, this talk grew to a buzzing that for all of its focus on warfare, feats of arms, and glory should prove a subject of interest to boys like Hamlet and Horatio. Yet Hamlet found this atmosphere of talk over war preparations oppressive to his spirit. Holding the truth secret from his best friend, Horatio, was the prime cause of this oppression. His mind was split. His emotions swung pendulum-like over the tenor of his time with Horatio. Like the war talk, he suffered contradictions.

On the one hand was his desire to maintain their constant companionship, but at the same time, there was an urge to quit his presence whenever the latter broached the subject of war. His every glance at Horatio brought to his mind self-accusations of disloyalty in his silence over the truth of the matter. He could not push Horatio away nor did he want to. Nor could he avoid the lad as thick as they were in their time together and their confidences. Anything, any response or reaction out of the ordinary could be seed to Horatio for suspicions of the very thing he was doing. Yet he would not betray his father's trust in his silence either. Indeed, he saw this as his first test of true worthiness for the throne that was in his future.

Disaster had already come courting a few times. Horatio, having cataloged the conjectures to which he was privy, had sought his friend's opinion. There was no intimation that he believed Hamlet's proximity to the crown had put him in the know. This was simple and innocent boy talk, as two modern youth might discuss the prospects of a season ahead for their favorite athletic teams. Still, Hamlet found it difficult simply to shrug his shoulders and apply his father's words to them both: that they would know "soon enough."

To escape the constant buzzing of voices over "this plot" and "that strategy" and to get Horatio away from a setting wherein he could not help but talk about the upcoming campaign, the boys took to horse and ranged the commons beyond Elsinore.

It was a grand morning. Every open meadow was an opportunity to initiate a charge of chivalry against an imaginary foe. They had even essayed an unpracticed bout or two of sparring at swords on horseback.

All four, boys and their mounts, were up in energy and like-minded in their play. Even as they turned their steeds homeward, there were still battles to be fought, fields to be coursed at a gallop, and, in the fashion of the latest *chanson de geste* from the French court, great quests to be undertaken.

Regaining the road in order to pass through a defile of thick woodland, the boys slowed to a walking pace—though their mounts, sensing the homeward trend, pulled to return to the stables. Riding abreast, the boys spoke of the supposed sensations of charging into a melee with leveled lance and to crash against an opposing knight. When Horatio began to muse on the pain attendant to being unhorsed and sent head over horse's rump to a dizzying plummet and an abrupt impact with the ground, Hamlet responded with "The trick then is to *not* be unhorsed."

"That's easy enough said, my lord. But where any two such knights do meet, one or the other must attend to a defeat."

"Is that a proverb of Schleswig, or have you gone to rhyming now?"

"The rhyme was unintentional, my lord, as is the fall. And so, one must be prepared."

"For rhymings or for falls?"

"Both, my lord, as they are both in the world."

"Then for rhyming or for fall, to the former only will I bend my all!"

"That's clever in the former, my lord, but is it clever enough to avoid the latter?"

"To avoid the latter, I must needs throw more practice into the matter! Ha, ha!"

"Well then, if the monarch of Denmark is to be a rhyming king, then how will he deal in verse 'gainst our southern neighbor, the House of Orange?"

"'Gainst the House of Orange, I'll thumb my nose—and—oh, confound you. There is naught in our native tongue to rhyme with 'orange'!"

"Neither with silver, my lord, which is why kings hold commerce most with gold."

"Why then you have, like a faithful minister, set me back onto my track for with the House of Orange I shall make bold!"

"I have no doubts, my lord."

Their laughter carried them a good while. As the castle came into view, it triggered again the boys' thoughts of the ongoing military preparations. They fell silent, Horatio to speculation and Hamlet to brooding.

"Think you, my lord, that our chivalry will be called upon to fight the French mounted phalanx in their battles arrayed or the English behind their hedgehogs thick with potent archers or 'gainst the fearsome blue-painted Scots with their swords and bucklers and their wailing pipes and fierce war hammers?"

"Oh, 'tis all one, all one, Horatio. When at last we stand behind the Danish array on some o'erlooking ground and see beyond our own lances and partisans, the banners of them who oppose us, then we shall know who is our enemy."

"We? Our? Are the royal pages to go on campaign as well?" Horatio both brightened and worried at this.

Here was clear example of how Hamlet feared the slip of an innocent comment, his own tongue witnessing against himself. He was quick enough to cover his words this time.

"I have voiced a wish and a hope only, yet it may be time," he quoted his father in part. Casting about for something else to do in order to change the subject, he spied a rise in the ground not too distant. He recalled that it crested a bluff overlooking a brook in a dale that ran to the base of the castle walls at its northern end. "Race you to the base of yon hillock. You set the mark, Horatio."

"Very well, my lord. Ready? On three—three!"

Horatio's cleverly gained advantage was short-lived. Soon Hamlet overtook his friend and reached the goal first. But then he drew his horse up short of the crest so as to prevent his plunging over to an uncontrolled and headlong dash to disaster down in the brook. Besides this, he had caught a glimpse of others down at the brook's edge, which put him in mind of a new plot. Thus, he quickly turned his mount back down to the bottom of the low ground a few yards short of the crest. Here he met Horatio just coming up. He signaled him to draw rein.

"What is't, my lord?"

"We must spy out an enemy encampment." Hamlet nodded toward the crest and spoke in a hushed tone as he dismounted. They set their horses to graze in the low ground and proceeded afoot at a crouch back to the crest. Just short of it, Hamlet went from a crouch to all fours. Horatio followed suit. Achieving a position where they could see clearly down the slope to the brook, Hamlet went prone.

"Observe, good Horatio," he whispered.

"A camp, you say?" Horatio glanced about up and down the length of the dale.

"Aye, 'twas my word."

"My lord, your imagination waxes greatly. I see but two people."

"Well, 'tis an outpost then."

Horatio knit his brows. "Where away, my lord?"

"By the willow that grows aslant the brook and the bank that stands hard by."

"My lord, you know I am for you in any adventure of the mind. But that seems to me that it should be the maid Ophelia, sister to Laertes, and her ancient nurse!"

"Aye, seems." He paused and then, with a short sigh, decided to drop the pretense. "Well, 'tis so then."

They continued watching from concealment. Horatio grew quickly bored, but there was something in the scene that had grabbed Hamlet from the moment he saw them from atop his mount. Ophelia had been standing near the willow. Her nurse sat a yard or so off on a spread blanket reading a small devotional. The girl turned circles to spread her skirt wide. She held her arms outward for balance. But to Hamlet, it was as if she could encompass all of nature to her embrace. The afternoon sun was at a low enough angle to catch her even under the willow whose tendril-like foliage grew mostly out over the water. There was something about the sun on her hair and face that struck Hamlet as a thing to be studied.

He had seen Ophelia numerous times before, usually in company with her nurse and among other ladies or with her father and brother. Her mother was long deceased. She was not a stranger to him. He had heard her speak before as well though she never passed a word with him. There had been no need to. He recalled now the few instances of her speech.

To her father, she was meekly subservient, as befitting a good daughter. To her older brother, she was playful in a way that he thought at the time was tiresome, even for a sister. But now, for some reason, he wanted to hear her voice again, especially in that playful, familiar tone. What was more, he wanted that tone to be directed toward him.

Why this sudden desire for her to speak to him, he could not begin to answer. Why he insisted on creeping up and watching unwatched, he had no idea. He began to doubt his judgment in this. Yet he remained to watch as though something remarkable was soon to happen. For the moment, even her slightest movements were for him a matter of intense interest.

As they continued watching, even these few minutes, she stepped up to a low branch that stretched out over the brook and inched her way along it until she was nearly lost to sight in the foliage.

"My lord." Horatio broke into his thoughts. Hamlet met his friend's quizzical look with a trancelike expression. He could not readily shift his focus. "Is there aught that ails you?"

Hamlet flopped over on his back, bringing his hands up to cup them behind his head. He stared up at the sky and sighed deeply. "Oh, Horatio. Wait but a year!"

"Is't Ophelia?"

"I fear it."

Horatio turned as well and lay on his back. "You speak aright, my lord. I think not on these things yet. To me, all is armor and horses, well, books really, or I forget myself. But things female—they are on the moon. And there they had best remain, never to descend earthward to muddy my thinking." He looked over at Hamlet, turned on his side, and raised himself up on an elbow. A near panic filled him at the prospect of what lay ahead for his friend. He addressed his friend earnestly. "My lord, think of it!"

Suddenly, they both heard three sounds nearly simultaneously: a splintering of wood, a short shriek, and a great splash. Both boys were up in an instant. They knew where to look. Below them, Ophelia lay on her back, floating on the surface of the water. Her nurse had risen in alarm but knew only to wring her hands and mutter something they could not make out.

Hamlet flew into action. "Here is a task for a water-born Dane. Horatio, I go. Bring down the horses. *Adieu!*" He had jumped to his feet and was already off down the slope, calling the last of his words over his shoulder. Mostly out of shock, his friend stood, watching

Hamlet all the way down to the water's edge before turning to the horses.

For his part, Hamlet came barreling past the nurse like a Scot charging into battle out of his highland fastness, giving her a second start. He jumped feet first into the waist-deep water, landing nearly beside Ophelia.

In his mind, that was a heroic thing to do, and so it would be were Ophelia in any distress. As it happens, she was laughing. For she had managed to fall flat and saw that her clothes had spread wide and bore her up. She sensed too that her hair must be fanning out across the water's surface. Her predicament seemed comical to her. She began to entertain ideas of floating away on her back down the course of the brook and out to sea. 'I'm a mermaid,' she thought. But long it could not be.

Ophelia sensed that she was sinking at about the time Hamlet's heroically abrupt entry into the water sent a wave over her and awakened her to her distress. Her next scream came out gurgled and then cut off as she slipped below the surface.

For the short instant she was submerged, she was cognizant of the sun's light creating a sense of distorted patterns of illumination above her. 'I'm drownded' was her chief thought. She thrashed only once before Hamlet's arms were under her, raising her back to the surface.

Her wild impressions continued as she came up in Hamlet's shadow and therefore perceived him only in silhouette. The disk of the sun behind his head glared so as to register to her as a halo. After being drowned, was she now to be escorted to heaven in the arms of her guardian angel?

'Funny,' she thought, 'he seems mightily substantial for an angel, and I still feel the physical sensations of my wetting. Clearly, this isn't Nurse. She'd never venture even into waist-deep water, even on my account!'

Yet someone was carrying her to the bank. It was a straight drop so that her rescuer could not step back up with her in hand. The water finally drained from her ears and eyes. She heard her nurse being directed by a youthful voice to bring their blanket to the edge.

Then she was gently laid on it. By now, her rescuer had turned so that the sun was on his face. Recognition came in a flood.

"Lord Hamlet!"

"You are safe now. Wet but safe."

She sat up and looked slightly down toward him. "My lord, how came you here?"

Hamlet almost said, 'I was spying on you from yon hillock and saw you take your fall.' Fortunately, he was quick enough to dissemble mildly to a slightly different truth. "Horatio and I"—he nodded to his friend who was almost upon them, leading the horses—"were resting our steeds on yon hillock and heard your distress. I think you are nothing more than wet and startled, perhaps a bit less startled than your good nurse. Yet I must ask, how fare you?"

"Well, good my lord. Thanks to you."

She, too, had the heavy brows of her brother which likewise gave expression to her words. That expression now was one of wonder as she explored his face with deep eyes. Hamlet could not take his eyes off hers. She was still so overcome by his opportune appearance in her time of need that she forgot her naturally demure self and continued to stare back with wonder at him.

"I believe you are in no great straits. We Danes are more than half wedded to the sea. However, I think it meet you should take my horse to convey you and your good nurse can ride Horatio's, whereupon we will lead you back to Elsinore castle ere you take sick by reason of the afternoon chill and your sodden attire."

"Thank you, my lord, but Nurse doesn't ride."

"Not since my brother, rest his soul, was thrown," cut in the nurse, still clearly agitated. "And I think your young horse, Master Horatio, would not gladly bear my ample self."

"Well then," Hamlet continued talking to Ophelia, "you must ride, and all we will walk. It is not good for the dust of the road to coat and cake your dress."

"Well, I—" she glanced nervously at her nurse who nodded encouragement.

"My lord," cut in Horatio, "Mistress Ophelia could take my horse that the two of you should ride together and return her more expeditiously to her servants' ministrations whilst I see the good nurse back afoot."

"Nonsense." He was still eye-locked with Ophelia. "Wait. Here's better. Nurse, if you could give Sir—I mean, Master Horatio some instructions for your servants, he could ride swiftly ahead, and they make preparation for your return: a heated bath and such other curatives 'gainst a chill-borne illness."

With this, he shot a look to Horatio, a look that warned him against helping fate too much. Horatio took the message, suddenly feeling himself a spare person. 'Wait a year, indeed,' he thought.

"Aye, my lord." Horatio turned to receive the nurse's instruction—which came out half muddled and had to be repeated.

Hamlet climbed out of the water and helped Ophelia to her feet. They were still studying each other's eyes when Horatio mounted and, with a salute that was barely returned, rode back up the slope toward the castle.

Hamlet gathered up their few things into a roll, then helped Ophelia up onto his horse. She managed to sit it sidesaddle. He set the roll across the horse's back. Taking the reins, he led them zigzag across the face of the slope to accommodate the nurse's slower pace and to stretch out their homeward journey.

*****

That night, Hamlet lay awake reviewing the day with a strong sense that everything in his life had changed. Yet try as he might, he could not identify the change. Outwardly, there was nothing new or different to which he could point. His thoughts kept circling back to Ophelia, not as the cause—not yet—but as the source or the center out of which change radiated. Had she changed? Certainly, girls changed into women similarly as boys change into men. That could be it, even though he did not think of her yet as a woman, not like his mother, the Queen, or any of the court ladies or the women of the castle and town. And he thought of them not at all.

His gaze traced the wall of his room. Absolutely, it had not changed nor did it feel different. Good. Perhaps he was beginning to settle back onto solid ground. Perhaps all this feeling of change was but temporary and would recede back to normal. How he craved normal on this night!

But as the flames died down in the hearth, he did perceive a change to the room. It had gone darker, an elementary observation to be sure. Was this truly change? Reason told him that the room remained the same, even in the shadows. So the change was perceived only as light, or the lack of it, permitted him to see or not to see.

'I'm on to something,' he thought. He considered the rest of the castle in its nightly aspect. In the darkness, he would see it one way. In the daylight, he would see it quite differently. Yet physically, it was unchanged. 'Perhaps the change is in the way I'm seeing things. The change is in my perceptions. It is in me.' That was beginning to make sense. Ophelia was not different, but after today, he had begun to see her differently.

'Funny,' his thoughts continued, 'it was the sunlight that made me see her differently. Or did it merely draw my attention to my different view of her? And just as the sunlight on her hair and face caused me to see her differently, is she—the thought of her—causing me to see everything else differently? What about Horatio? Now that was a change I could put my finger on.'

He recalled his return to the castle. After delivering Ophelia and her nurse to the gratitude of her father, he went to seek out Horatio in the stables. His friend seemed subdued, almost as he was on his first days at Elsinore just over a year before. He had confessed later, as his friendship with Hamlet had grown to confidence, that he had felt as though he was in everyone's way, a spare person who was caus-ing others—here he thought compassionately about the servants—to adjust their lives in order to accommodate even his meager needs.

'Yes, he was acting very much that way again, nearly all the way up to dinner. Was that change caused by Ophelia?' It took Hamlet most of dinner to turn his friend back to forgetful merriment. The saving grace to the evening was Yorick's account of the rescue inci-dent that he presented following the meal. Who knows where he learned of it! He showed true genius in rendering the event into a mockery of the French *chansons*. It was just what was needed to raise both boys' spirits. And even Hamlet could laugh at himself when his antics were disclosed to him in the light of humorous reality.

But back to his friend. Did his mood bespeak a change? Hamlet did not suspect jealousy in Horatio over the introduction of a girl into his life and her interjection into their friendship. He determined that the boy's dip in his spirits was merely perplexity, as of the uninitiated. But he did recognize that his friend was too easily withdrawn because of it. He resolved to have a care in the matter and not wax verbal over the girl in Horatio's presence. Henceforth, he would keep his feelings to himself and his questions about such matters to his own counsel.

But what was his own counsel? He turned his gaze away from the hearth, lying back to search the ceiling. In it, he saw a pattern that spoke to him of diverse ways. The planks ran perpendicular to the supporting beams. His duty was to mold himself for kingship—good kingship. This was also his desire, one of them.

His "crosswise" desire was that he wanted to think about Ophelia. He had almost an earnest prayer that he might dream about her. What *did* the *chansons* do at this stage in the development of their themes? 'Oh yes, a detailed catalogue of the beloved's attributes. Beloved? Well, that was a fast jump. All right, *beloved*. What was she like? Where to start? Physical features?'

He had no idea of how to describe her face. Certainly, it was beautiful—to his thinking, but was his thinking correct?—and what made it beautiful? He had not the skill to describe hair and eyes. Attributes of character? He barely knew her or her moods or habits. Habits of speech or doings that endeared her to him? Could all these be gleaned from his meager memories of her? And still, something would be missing. Of course, her response to him. There was nothing of that in his past, saving this one afternoon's encounter. 'All right. Let's start there.'

He reconstructed the events, highlighting those parts specifically involving her. *Her*. It was funny how that pronoun—third person, singular, feminine—should now have grown and become in his regard encased in an aura of almost religious import. This was heady stuff. Dare he proceed? Was there no other course but to proceed?

Could he even turn back, be like a boy and show his sail of great-ness to rouse himself—as Horatio had pointed out—exclusively to warlike practice and immersion in his books? He saw himself epi-cally risen above the silken dalliance of romance to stand noble and unwavering!

Yet even as he urged his thoughts away from the dark void of romance, love—a form of it—like a demon, laughed heartily, pulled to on the slipknot of his weakness, and told him, "You are lost, brother. Give over. Struggle not. There is a way. Think on Ophelia, pure thoughts no less. Batten on constructed memories. Live a sec-ond life within your thoughts of her. Two lives in one. Who is't can do that but a man in love.

"Your kingly preparations run like the ceiling planks, consti-tuting the most part of your existence—and the upper most part to be seen by all. But when weariness at war or study or statesmanship o'ertakes you, that life could be undergirded by the crossbeams of your inner thoughts. It would be an innocent indulgence, a waking dream to refresh you when the real world goes awry."

"No, no, no!" he called out, batting this line of thinking away. It was too complex. He simply wanted to think of her. Nothing more but to pass the minutes between waking and sleeping in pleasant notions. He thought back to the sunlight on her hair, to her smile as she looked down on him from his mount. She had told him her mermaid thoughts, and they had laughed—together.

As they had approached the castle gate, he listened to her con-cerns for her brother, who spoke of attending a knight as squire on the coming campaign. He wondered what her concerns would be when she learned that he, too, would march out in company with the armed might of Denmark. He must be sure to calm her fears for his safety on that account with the truth that a page's duty took him not near the fighting. He would not puff himself at the expense of truth simply to be enlarged in her concerns. Besides, that would encourage her to fret and grieve over much, which he saw as a cruelty to her sweetness.

He must remember upon his return from the wars not to give himself to boasting of exploits in order to magnify himself in her eyes. No, though prince, he was merely a boy going forth to the firsthand study of war. He knew not yet what wisdom he would take from this great lesson. But he was determined that he would not lose himself in trying to make himself. He would keep careful watch over his character. For he had already heard that some men of baser morals oft used the circumstance of war and of life on campaign to pursue their lusts to the full, discarding them along the way as they made their ways homeward. Safely ensconced with hearth and family about, they think all is forgot and neglect to find that their war-proof had left them deeper scarred in their souls than fleshly wounds. To this avoidance, Hamlet would keep himself near the king's camp and attend only to those knights whose chivalry was both true and deep.

All this was in the purview of Fra Ignacio, the chaplain to Castle Elsinore. Hamlet made a mental note to visit him on the morrow to discuss the temptations of the coming campaign. With these thoughts and not with thoughts of Ophelia, he drifted off to sleep. Neither, to his regret the next day, did he dream of her.

# Chapter 4

As planned, Hamlet made his way to the chapel immediately after breakfast, before he could be waylaid by Horatio to boyish adventure. The chapel stood as an appendage to the keep and had means of access both from the exterior and from the hall on the way to the queen's apartments. He took the latter route, approaching it from the great hall where he had enjoyed a modest breakfast. Rounding a curved stair to the first landing, he was happy to see the arched doorway widely open. Fra Ignacio would be in already.

Inside the doorway, there was a short passage from which two small rooms could be entered before moving into the chapel proper. The room to the left constituted Fra Ignacio's office and confessional. To the right was the sacristy. The doors to both of these were closed. Hamlet elected to proceed into the sanctuary itself.

The chapel was contained under a single vault with shallow niches between columns that buttressed the arched ceiling. Long, narrow glass-pained windows of no color centered in each niche of the exterior wall across from him, allowing diffused northern light at day. The altar stood on his right as he entered. It butted up against the east wall. A few benches ranged from it back beyond the left of the passage way, ending at the double doors which opened unto steps descending to the castle yard. The sanctuary was large enough for a score, perhaps a few more, of worshippers. It was not ornate, as some chapels were wont to be, but plain "humble as a mendicant friar upon a borrowed donkey," as Fra Ignacio would say affectionately.

The truth was, the austerity of the chapel decor was a sign that it was an almost neglected aspect of daily life among the members of the royal household. The king and queen practiced a faith that was "just enough," observing major holy days and attending Sunday Mass. They received the sacraments appropriately and made ample and regular provision for the needy through the chaplain. They trusted the Scriptures for moral guidance but left the deeper consideration of spirituality to men of the robe.

Hamlet had been instructed by both his father and mother that the teachings of the church were true and should be heeded in so much as the health of the realm rested upon the solid foundation of good moral tenets. The life of Christ was an example of humility and righteousness for all and of good husbandry for kings in shepherding their people. They conveyed a belief to him of the divinity of Jesus but failed to catch for themselves or ignite for him the spark of the Spirit.

Fra Ignacio was held out to him as a good counselor for questions of right and wrong. And so, Hamlet sought him out mostly as a guide to interpret God's moral will. Hamlet found the chaplain's demeanor to his liking, his teachings clear—though simple—and his corrections gentle. At times though, he wondered if there should have been more. He considered the large Bible that lay open upon the altar through the day. It seemed to him that God must have much more to say in so great a volume than had been conveyed to him in his lessons thus far. His active mind strained as at a leash when these thoughts came to him. But he possessed little or no assurance that the kindly and simple cleric would prove up to the depth of his inquiries. So as he grew, Hamlet adopted his father's stance and kept his faith, like the chapel, an appendage to a life focused elsewhere.

For this morning's meeting, Hamlet prepared himself by a review of his concerns from the night before, that is, the question of one's moral conduct when the disciplines of military practice seemed to be counterpoised against the laxities of camp life. He thought he knew the sort of behavior that was expected of him, but at the same time, he wondered about the unexpected. Toward this ignorance, he had decided to apply to Fra Ignacio for enlightenment.

Entering the sanctuary, Hamlet saw the chaplain on his knees before the altar in prayer. Some years back, he had taken a correction for interrupting a man at his prayers. It remained ingrained in him now to wait patiently. He spent the minutes studying the chapel. He was well familiar with its lines, but considering his wild thoughts of the night before, he also wanted to satisfy his mind that change had not come upon this edifice of faith. It was no long time before he had assured himself that all was not only as it should be but also as it had always been.

Fra Ignacio seemed to be dallying at his prayers. Hamlet was not one for standing long at nothing. He slipped quietly onto a bench and let his mind roam where it would. Naturally, it bended back toward Ophelia. Indeed, she had never really left his thoughts since his waking. Many of these thoughts were surmises about her doings simultaneously to his. Had she risen early? Did she take breakfast? What was the subject of her morning orisons? His thoughts settled there for a moment. Her prayers likely included her father and her brother, certainly the latter's plans to serve as squire and his safety in the war. Was she thinking of Hamlet at all? Was he in her prayers? She knew not yet that he was also bound for these same wars.

His own *Pater Noster* had been rendered to tatters by thoughts of her despite his struggle to focus. Were her morning prayers forcibly superimposed over the image of his eyes as his prayers had been over hers? Hamlet was not so self-assured as to think so. This caused him to sigh. The sigh was sufficiently audible to announce his presence to the chaplain, whose head canted slightly at hearing it.

"Is that you, my Lord Hamlet?" he said in an echoey and aged voice.

"Oh! My apologies, Fra Ignacio. I did not mean to disturb your prayers."

"I was just concluding. In truth, you have been much in my prayers."

"You always say that, good Seigneur."

"Perhaps that is because you are always in my thoughts. One cannot pray o'er much for he who will one day rule over the state." Fra Ignacio turned at the end of this, rose from his knees, and approached the lad. "Might I ask if that heartfelt sigh was the manifestation of an equally heartfelt prayer?"

"I was thinking more than praying. Is that wrong in a chapel?"

"Well, 'tis said that words without thoughts never to heaven go. But as far as thoughts without words, I suppose it depends on the substance. One would hope them to be godly thoughts?" It was an invitation to confess.

Hamlet was not yet sorted out in his thoughts on Ophelia, so he quickly looped over to his original purpose for this visit.

"It is conjectured that some of the royal pages will attend the king in the coming war. Were it so, I have good cause to believe I shall be among them."

"And are you thus troubled for your soul should you fall in battle?"

Hamlet was not sure if this was earnest inquiry or a prelude to condescension. He determined to give the cleric the benefit of the doubt. At this question, Hamlet suddenly realized that he had not given that matter any such thought. He was at the age when mortality is a remote notion. He sensed that an affirmative response to such a question would be seen as an invitation for a lengthy discourse from a man whose trade straddled both the here and now and the hereafter. He was not up to any instruction touching on eternity, not yet. No, it was wisest to give honest vent to his thoughts on the subject, especially since he had no intention to be open about Ophelia.

"Well, I know that pages labor in camp like the drudges of war to fetch and carry, to burnish dull armor to impossible brightness, and to replenish empty tankards. These are not perilous duties, save to those who habitually neglect them to their chastisement. I fear not battle death for myself though I would for His Majesty, my father."

"Still, there is death to disease, whose tally in protracted campaign shows it to be no respecter of king, knight, or page."

"There you speak truth, sir. But that is a death long heralded, leaving me time to prepare unto."

"So death is not the issue?" Fra Ignacio took a seat on the same bench as Hamlet used, with a comfortable distance between them. "What then is your concern, my lord?"

"I have heard that life in camp—uh—there are aspects that—" Hamlet's pleading look hung in the silence of his unvoiced thought.

"Ah!" At length, Fra Ignacio discerned the problem. "Yes, well, sure am I that you shall encounter some sights and sounds not meant for tender eyes and ears. In truth, the Lord's standard is but one for all, and so would the same be not suitable to any witness. Nevertheless, evil is in the world. However, you have been taught what is right and to distinguish it from that which is wrong. Likewise, have you been carefully instructed in the nature of sin.

"In general, consider that anything you might chance upon inadvertently should not be accounted to you as sin—should you turn away in good time, that is. Let your conscience rest easy—and be forewarned—on that one point. It will be good to remember that all we are commanded to flee temptation.

"To continue the thought, you must beget and nurture a care over those acts that you purpose to do. Choose your company well, and do not assume that the majority has the right of the matter. Reserve your judgment. If you have a purse, keep it close, and remember that it has a bottom too easily reached. Deal honestly with each man. Be sparing in your promises and fulfill them promptly and in good faith—not by halves.

"Keep in mind that the wisdom of God brings glory to him and edifies those who walk in that wisdom whereas the wisdom of man puffs itself and does so often at the expense of others. Hold all women as chaste, whether they be or no. For just as it is the groom who bestows beauty on the bride, so, too, man is the keeper of the chastity of woman. Above all, if you carefully establish the Lord *Jesu* as mediator not only betwixt you and the Father but also between yourself and aught of his creation—man, woman, or matter—you will then always hold it in the proper regard. And its proper handling by you would follow as surely as day follows unto night."

"Fra Ignacio, you have painted a campaign of war in the spiritual realm equal unto our efforts against any force of man. How shall we stand therefore when temptation's battalions sound the charge?"

"I do not think that temptations will come upon you pell-mell to unhorse you from your morals. You are too well seated for that. If I have read your nature aright these years, your defenses, in the form of your gentle predilections, are up and your conscience unassailable to mass assault. Rather, beware the subtle enticements, the single spies of Satan whose argument is 'Just this once' or 'What is the hurt?' or 'Who would know?' With these arguments, the decrepit shield of faithlessness is emblazoned for those who heed the call to perdition.

"Guard your thoughts, therefore. Make holiness your aim and purity not the aim but the measure of it. A daily diet of prayer—as you are in the habit—will burnish the armor of the soul beyond that 'impossible brightness' of which you spoke. Remember that if the spirit falters, the defense is breached, leading most certainly to the fall, first of thought and then of the body. Pursue no entreaties of the heart to a spiritual holiday however slight or short-lived the intent. Finally, to a second conclusion, train yourself to appropriate the power of the Risen Lord to cast down all strongholds of Satan, and be most assured that he and his will then flee from you."

"But are there no particulars of which I should know and thus be forewarned and forearmed?"

"There would be a whole catalogue of particulars, as many as are in life. For campaigning is but life condensed, and those who are facing death while yet in their strong years, think to taste as much of life in so short a time, that the life of the camp is but all life compressed into one or two mad throws of the dice, filling experience up against a sudden abridgment of that life. Such will find a spiritual death more instant and more eternally woeful than that enjoyment of life for which they chanced at dice.

"But to answer your question directly, I think there is nothing exclusive to the warrior's life that you would not find were you to go in search of sin in the very nooks and crannies even of this well-ordered keep. Fear not, therefore. You will not be cast adrift into Sodom's eager embraces."

"Will you attend us on campaign?"

"Alas, my old joints are too easily rheumatized by marching in the rainy field and waking to a tent of dew-dripping canvas. Besides, the marshal already employs a chaplain for the nurture of Denmark's levees. It were good you make his acquaintance and seek out his portion at each encampment. It will not be far from the king's pavilion.

Rest assured also that I shall, in this stronghold, marshal the prayers of the faithful and all the saints to your succor and your success."

"Could we pray now for such?"

"That is a fair request and a happy duty."

They both knelt, and, while Fra Ignacio led in prayer, Hamlet was able to concentrate fully. For the moment, he had forgotten about Ophelia.

*****

Hamlet's thoughts were not free of Ophelia for long. Leaving the chapel, he returned toward the great hall. He sought Horatio. As the hall was the crossing point of fate in the daily life of the household, it was most likely that he should meet him there, especially if his friend was looking for him as well. Hamlet had developed a new habit of walking up and down in the hall, reading from a book. In this practice he could pass the time, be available to his friends, and observe life unobserved.

Entering the hall, he did not have time to be disappointed at not seeing Horatio there. For he did see someone else just as welcome. Yorick often hung about the hall, sometimes to pace out the portions of his next entertainment, sometimes to trade quips with Hamlet, and most often to absorb the latest news in the daily life that might be meet subject for his essays of wit.

Seeing his other mentor, the man who made up for any deficiencies in his formal education, Hamlet's thoughts leaped to an opportunity that had only been in the back of his mind until now. But devilish habit overrode even his earnest concerns of the moment and an alternate plan formed for quick mischief.

Yorick stood between two long tables on the main floor of the hall with his back to Hamlet. The circumstance was inviting—no, it was irresistible. Without further thought, Hamlet dashed stealthily as he could across the hall, leaped up first to the bench, then to the tabletop, and threw himself onto Yorick from behind, landing piggyback on the man.

"Have at you!"

Yorick, a man of strength and stature, staggered but a little, stooped forward to hoist Hamlet comfortably higher on his back and reached around to catch his legs in his arms and keep him thus mounted.

"Ho! My lord. It has been some time since I bore you on my back. But it does make me feel younger to have you thus, though you've put some stones weight in your breeches o'er the months. I cannot hold you long nor prance about with you a-Yorick-back as I was used to." He laughed heartily.

"And it has been some time since I would kiss you ere I was carried off to the cradle to free you for riper reveling out of the hearing of the innocent."

"Aye, my lord. Time passes for us both." He let Hamlet down and turned to receive a playful embrace in which he lifted the prince a short inch off the floor, swinging him back and forth a time or two. Setting him down again and stepping back, the man studied the boy as though he had not seen him since those days of which they spoke. "How does my lord this day? Like all else, are you lost in war thoughts?"

"Can a man think of cold fish when there is the aroma of roast venison?"

"Ha! You are merry, my lord. It is other than war thoughts animates you."

"There you speak aright. I do have a question. Let us sit here." They each took seat on benches, facing each other. Yorick read the signs that something deep was in the offing.

"This is earnest talk. What is't, my lord?"

Hamlet crumpled his mouth in thought, knitting his brow to a commensurate wrinkle. It was as though he was holding his words back, building them to a pressure that would overcome reluctance and force them to utterance. Yorick dipped his head and raised his brows above merry eyes, inviting Hamlet to speak and ready to receive just about anything. When Hamlet did speak, he leaned forward and used hushed tones. Though no one else was about, he was careful of "ears."

"It is this, what can you tell me about women?"

Yorick leaned back with one quick guffaw. "Ha! Why, I can tell you that they are not men!"

"Ho! Scoundrel!"

"Let me speak on, my lord. They are not men, and therefore, neither do they think like men. In truth, I begin to suspect that we do not even share a common language with them. For what they say in words understandable still seems to convey a meaning all out of even the stretchiest nuance and comes out a mirror image, the reverse of its sense!"

"These are not hopeful words. How then do I speak with a girl?"

"Am I to understand that my yesternight's sung romance of your exploits in aid of the maid Ophelia was not too wide of the mark?" His eyes continued to sparkle, now with a knowing glee that merely remembered his own such boyish feelings.

"I pray thee, do not mock me." Hamlet started to brood.

"Forgive me, my lord. I meant not mockery but rather doctor-like to diagnose your particular ailment. There be some lads whose eye first falls upon a mature woman, and then there be others who prefer the innocence and tentativeness of one their own age. Each malady is to be treated with a difference. Would you have me—to carry forth the medical metaphor—to prescribe wrongly, say a tourniquet about the neck for a headache or a chicken broth for a severed arm?"

"No, but back to your buried question—yes, it is Ophelia. I have been unable to think of aught but her eyes and her smile and the sun on her hair."

"Oh, you are far gone, far gone!"

"What then is the remedy since you would style yourself a doctor of *loveology*?"

"For love on the wing, I am no true doctor nor have I ready remedy. For love is like unto the common cold. It must be endured in its season with little effective curative—in the main, dosages that address symptoms only—and suffered with good grace until it runs its course. And the affected youth must pray it leave no pocky marks, none to the public view, at least." He saw that his humor was not having its intended effect. He changed course.

"This I can tell you: Ophelia, what I know of her, is a demure maid. Ardor in the name of love may inwardly thrill her yet may outwardly evoke revulsion or flight. I would counsel a slow simmering of this pot. Be like the cook who seasons sparingly and tastes often."

"Fra Ignacio says I should hold all women as chaste, whether they be or no."

At this, Yorick sat up and cocked one brow. "Ignacio speaks too prophet-like unto a distant future. At your age, as this world goes, chastity is a given. And have no worries about Ophelia on that account. She is the court kitten, beloved by all the ladies—the queen included—as gentle and obedient as any of them could want in their own daughters. For worldly experience, you are both but runners still at the mark. Tarry there awhile. If it's 'her eyes and her smile and the sun on her hair' gets your blood up, leave it thus and cherish the charm of it. There will be time for country matters much, much later."

"But I go soon to war. Is there aught I should do ere I depart? Your *chansons* speak of tokens and stolen moments and pledges of undying love and—"

"Hold, my lord. I see now by the mirror of your plight that I have with my art plowed too deeply here." The bard scratched his whiskered chin. "I must make amends. Know you aught of her feelings for you?"

"She smiled, warmly I thought, when we parted yestereve, she to her bath and I to a sleepless night."

"Hm. We must have some closure in this lest you become a sleepless knight! Sorry!"

"I have not seen her since. Nor do I foresee any unforced occasion to see her. I presume she might by chance sail through the court here, a part of the fleet, that vast and formidable armada of court dames. There is no chance to speak with her then. It may be fated that until this proposed war is concluded and I am able to return home, I may only borrow for my own memory a handful of her farewell waves and blown kisses to her brother as we march out the castle."

"Hm. Borrowed kisses, eh? Would you have her know of your distractions on her account?"

"I see you do not call it 'love.'"

"Do you?"

"I know not what to call it. 'Distractions' is true enough. Schleswig is half way to the moon. Think you that distance and war-like activity will dull the tug of heartstrings?"

"Or make them snap. And by the way, you have just let slip the object of your father's preparations. Do we then move against the eastern marches? I would have thought them secure in their loyalty."

Hamlet threw his hands up to cover his face and moaned softly. "Oh, Yorick. I am undone by my own tongue! I knew this vexation over Ophelia would be the ruin of me." He uncovered his face to reveal an expression of deep anguish. "But I must tell more to correct a misreading of my slip. We march not against Schleswig but to her aid. That is all, and now must I swear you to secrecy."

"Fear it not, my lord. Though I am oft polled by those with itchy ears, and I have by many embassies been approached to 'spill my guts,' as it were for personal gain, yet I am a loyal and true Dane and can readily see the damage done to royal motives too easily disclosed. Glad am I for Master Horatio's sake that we go not against his kin. But back to you.

"I do not see that there is aught for you to enact toward Ophelia in these short hours unless your discussion here so far masks a less quiet desperation. It may be that this separation is but to test your true feelings. If the heartstring does not snap, yet it may find its true tuning.

"Could you keep yourself in the trial of those temptations sure to come in soldiering far from home and could you hold fast the smile and the eyes and the sunlit hair in your fond imaginings, then perhaps on your return, a more definite course of action will present itself. And you may begin to see what affection lies between you twain. For it may be that her thoughts of you upon your vacancy will magnify in the distance, and you will find in your homecoming a warmer smile and a heart made merry at your reappearing."

"It is my hope."

"In the meantime, cherish the innocence of the moment and live your soldier's life as though—a Michal to your David—she were looking on."

"Very well. I shall guard my soul for the sake of Ophelia, that I might return to her a Galahad of chaste conduct in my past and pure intentions toward her for the future."

"That's well conceived, my lord. And it may be that I will be the one to pen a true *chanson* to celebrate the historical love of Hamlet and his Lady Ophelia!"

"With couplets."

"With couplets."

*****

In the week that followed these interviews, Hamlet did have the occasion to see Ophelia twice at court. The first was, as Hamlet had described, a passing of the fleet through the great hall. At the time, he was crossing the dais at the end of the hall where the king and queen sat at table for meals. He was reading from his book and heard a rustle of skirts preceded by a scattering of giggles. Looking up from his text, he saw a dozen ladies led by the queen crossing the center of the hall and heading for her apartments.

Ophelia walked not last but in the rear third of the group. She was speaking or being spoken to by a lady who walked beside her in such a way that she could see past her companion and notice Hamlet. In the instant that their eyes met, she smiled but then so quickly lowered her gaze that Hamlet had but the slightest impression that the smile was for him.

The second occasion came with the arrival of another troubadour new to the court. Ophelia joined her brother and father, who had arranged for a special performance of a popular *chanson de geste*. It was a dramatic recital. The evening was comical only for Hamlet and Ophelia, who alternated their study of each other with cast down looks. Each quickly became aware of the other's perusal, and the exchange ended in smiles, letting Hamlet know that Ophelia had indeed "noticed" him and was pleased.

The happiest moment of his existence thus far was at the conclusion of the recital when, just before exiting the hall with her father at her arm, she turned once more to look for him and bestow one last smile. He resisted the urge to wave to her, but he did at least dip his head in salute and return the smile.

Neither of them had noticed that the subject of the troubadour's song was Galahad.

# Chapter 5

The queen took such a liking to the troubadour's verses that she requested a private recital for herself and her ladies in the terraced garden the following afternoon. The husbands and a few bachelor knights attendant upon the unmarried ladies were also invited, for such entertainments were not beyond the interest of men in those days. Learning of Hamlet's intent to join the king's foray south, the queen extended her invitation to him as well. This came in the form of an earnest entreaty for she desired to have some time with him ere he took his leave of her to become full-time companion to his father in lands far off.

Mother and son had always been close in their affection and time together with him reporting to her daily in her chamber to discuss his latest discoveries about life and wildflowers and crickets and such. But in the last two years, she had reluctantly stepped back out of the way to allow him time to break from the company of skirts and to learn the talk and manners of men. This distance, though not physically great, weighed on her and strengthened her need for time with him now in view of his impending departure.

For his part, Hamlet would naturally have agreed to attend the recital. He still thought tenderly of such times with his mother, and his own penchant for wordplay, nuance, and artful syntax made him an avid fan of the romances. Needless to say, his recent encounter with a pair of deep searching eyes brought him more in tune with the romantic themes themselves. We must, at this point, also unveil in the young prince a mercenary bent for the instant the queen's request reached his boyish shores, his mind ran to the following equation: "troubadour plus queen plus ladies equals Ophelia." To say he, therefore, pounced upon the chance may convey the strength of his response but falls short of the gyrations of his heart upon receipt of the queen's request.

"Tell you the queen, her entreaties are potent beyond need. I shall attend her as she were twice our mother."

The young servant skipped off with the good news.

Try as he might, Hamlet could not coax Horatio to the recital. He, too, was most appreciative of epic poetry, but with everyone more or less paired up—his mind conjured the same equation as did Hamlet—he determined, out of discretion, to flee any chance at an afternoon of emotional estrangement. As more than consolation, the friends agreed to meet afterward for additional sword practice and war talk. To pass the time, Horatio assured his prince that he would compose some overdue letters home. He would not waste away the afternoon.

Prior to the appointed time, Hamlet passed an unprecedented quarter hour becoming acquainted with his mirror image. He could not fathom what Ophelia might see in his permanently pensive countenance topped by such ruffled hair. The latter simply would not hold for all his exertions to keep it flat. His practice at a series of smiles: the knowing smile, the shy smile, cavalier smile, and so on; produced nothing to his satisfaction. Soon he quit the field of self-study, and, like a repeatedly unhorsed knight, he physically strode but emotionally limped toward the terraced garden.

At the far end of the great hall, he came upon the tail end of the exclusive audience as the couples were filing through to the open air. He did not readily see Ophelia, but neither did he despair yet. Rightly, the others would have made way for him, but he waved them on, deciding to enter last.

Benches from the great hall had been carried out and placed in a series of loose concentric semicircles about a single chair where the troubadour sat tuning his lute. He had risen at the entrance of the queen and her guests, but she bid him keep seat and continue his preparations while they arranged themselves.

Hamlet entered, nodding greetings to smiling couples. He approached the queen's seat. Near her, a few separate chairs had been placed for the more privileged guests. Suddenly, he mis-stepped while his heart spasmed, turned somersault, and then slowly settled into place when he beheld Ophelia seated at one of the chairs with only one empty chair between her and the queen. The chair on the queen's other side was already occupied. This was no incidental arrangement, given court protocol, and still it was too good to be true. Or did everyone know? Was this an ambush of sorts? Would all eyes be on him as he struggled with the joy of his fortunate proximity to Ophelia? He quickly looked at a few other couples seated near the queen. Their smiles betrayed no sense of teasing mirth.

"My dearest Hamlet!" his mother called to him as he approached. "We are so glad for your presence among us. I have saved you a seat by me." She indicated the empty chair. He looked across it to a smiling Ophelia.

Hamlet had to fight to keep from fixing his gaze on the girl. He did manage one quick smiling glance at her. Then he followed with a few of the same at others nearby, this to throw any suspicious noses off the scent.

"My thanks, dear Mother. Glad am I for the occasion both to attend you and to hear the good songster." He bowed to his mother and took the seat to her right. He also gave a short bow to Ophelia. His heart expanded with a desire to do more than simply bow, but he had no earthly idea what that more would consist of, saving perhaps a study of her face for the first half of eternity. Whatever unpracticed smile came out from him, it sat favorably with her for her own return smile radiated warmth and welcome. It was difficult not to lock eyes with her again.

"Of course, you are now acquainted with Mistress Ophelia having been her knight for a season, if Yorick's epic song have some truth to it." The queen's eyes were merry but again not teasing.

"Aye, Mother, saving the dragon, which was sadly absent in the reality." He looked back to Ophelia. "*All* else was true." He hoped the girl caught the emphasis to affirm by way of hidden message that Yorick's made up protestations of Hamlet's love for her in the song had a claim to verity.

"She sits here for her father as sponsor to Master Guilliame."

"Ah!"

"Lord Polonius could not attend, as he and your father continue their war preparations."

"I see." 'Well, that explains that,' he thought. He could now relax, somewhat, any fears he might have over suspicion of his feelings.

"The queen says you are to join the great expedition," Ophelia said softly. Was there something in her voice, some sadness or worry?

"Yes. I am to learn the art of war but at some little distance from the fray." He quickly added the last, staying true to his promise about not overplaying any advantage at the news.

"I would I could be there!" she said with enthusiasm.

"You do?"

"My brother."

"Ah, yes."

"Perhaps you will be companions in this business."

"It would please me. Yet if he serves a knight, his duties may call him to a different division of our force. But if you like, I shall keep an eye open for him though he is quite capable."

"He says you are gaining on him in practice at swords."

"Truly?" He could not have been happier with a free entrance pass to paradise. Here was news that his hero not only thought well of his skills but had communicated this good report to the girl of his heart. He was so filled with joy that he could have leaped down the throat of Yorick's fanciful dragon, hacked his way back out through the beast's innards, scaled and gutted it, and then served up dragon cutlets to all his friends. David's triumph over the giant of Gath would not compare.

"Yes, truly. You know he is bound for school at Paris upon his return from these?" Her tone saddened at her own news.

"No, I had not heard. I had hoped to learn more of the art of the sword at his hand." Here was the first dark cloud in the day.

"He is sure you will go on to excellence without his aide."

"That is too generous."

"He has a generous heart. As I spoke on our walk home together, I shall miss him."

"I have asked Fra Ignacio to pray for Laertes on your account."

"Thank you, my lord. I, too, have asked for prayers on his behalf. And I shall add you to mine. That is, I shall add your time in the wars to mine for you as well."

On these last words, Hamlet was nearly swinging from the branch that stretched across the garden above their heads. If he had read her words aright, she had just indicated that he had been in her prayers! Forget the troubadour; this was beyond joy! If only he could report all this to Horatio without causing a corresponding depression in his best friend. The whole world should share in this joy. Certainly, there was enough within him to go around.

"I shall remember you in all our doings on campaign, in my prayers, that is." An accusation of cowardice stabbed his heart as he amended his declaration with that last clause.

"My thanks to you again, my lord." Ophelia's voice dropped to a whisper, which cue she took from others as the troubadour rose to begin.

The queen took Hamlet's hand and gave it a squeeze. How he wished his free hand could find and hold Ophelia's, who saw the movement from the corner of her eye and smiled. Hamlet and Ophelia passed another look before attending to Master Guilliame.

Standing, the troubadour was as tall as Yorick, but there any other resemblances ceased. Yorick was a bear of a man, brimming over with life and energy, possessed of a demeanor that favored raucous tales and madcap antics. Hamlet remembered hearing of his doings one night at a local tavern where he poured a whole flagon of wine on one fellow's head when the latter insisted on singing along with him but was off-key. It was only his good-natured rhyming and his offer to pay for the wine that kept the man from laying him out with his fists, even as big a man as was Yorick. For the other, being a gravedigger possessed true muscle in his arms. Before the evening was out, the two were singing together though Yorick was hard pressed to carry the tune against the other's "accidentals," as the jester recalled the man's sour notes.

In contrast, Master Guilliame stood spare and somberly graceful. His light brows pitched to a soulful high center above sensitive amber eyes. Here was a poet. His art was in the words as much as in the subject of his tales. Hamlet regretted Horatio's absence for here, he thought, was a kindred soul for his friend's deeper thoughts.

"Your Majesty, ladies and gentlemen, I begin with a sad tale of the *Chevalier mal fet*, the 'Ill-Made Knight.'" With slender, graceful fingers, he strummed a progression of chords in the minor mode and then pulled from these chords some notes that were not yet strong enough for a melody, but they were as substantial as thought. He closed his eyes, and Hamlet had the impression that the bard was composing as he went along. He spoke but, lyrically, more than sang the following:

*The Chevalier mal fet*

Of heroes of old many songs are sung,
of valor and strength and noble heart,
of mighty feats, and purest love,
and tempered faith unending.
These men, who all their years throughout,
from youth to manhood, birth to grave,
their will did they tune to attain their best,
and gain a fame unending.

So too you gentlemen assembled here,
your minds and arms do labor long,
to steel the heart 'gainst any foe,
and stand though you the sole remaining
among your comrades fallen round,
whose fellowship you cherished,
whose lives, though not their friendships, perished,
and thus, great glory gaining.

You know what 'tis to toil and sweat,
to strive and painfully succeed,
to set the riches of the world at naught,
and seek that fleeting glory

to pursue relentless ever higher
in martial skill and moral might;
'tis you, you men with hearts of oak
will best perceive this story.

The *Chevalier mal fet*, he's called,
but neither village, castle, town, was of this
appellation wary,
nor aught of it knew family, friends, nor mentors all;
'twas in his thinking only.
Though outwardly his talents shown,
his graces and his gifts prevailing.
To others he was blessed indeed,
but inwardly was lonely.

What cause for loneliness was here,
in one so noble and so strong,
in one so fair and full of grace,
whose skill was daily growing?
The "ill-made knight," he styled himself
from self-assessment failing.
A greater doubt than glory spread
from seeds the Evil One was sowing.

Which seeds could so devour a man,
whose valor, strength, and mind were tested,
found never wanting, never bested,
from point of soul unto the hilt,
could so corrode the truest heart,
the noblest aspiration,
such a heart of solid gold,
to heart of wood encased in gilt?

'Twas guilt indeed began its work
when heart was young and hand was soft,
when faith was sure and trust was keen,

and promise still unflower'd.
Th' idyllic aim of this young knight
to see the world before him bright
and live this ideal strong and true;
'twas guilt his hopes devour'd.

Guilt o'er his thoughts of earthly things
that held him earthbound from his flights,
and thoughts and prayers
of true nobility ascending
that pulled him down and held him fast,
'til swelled with anguish, he at last
perceived himself, who should be knight,
into the night descending.

Yet outwardly he shown like light
in strength of arms, in depth of thought,
but humble, for he knew his heart
in private self-cajole unheeding.
Though failed of strength to inward fight,
the outward man rose in esteem
of those who saw not inward strife;
his endeavors all succeeding.

Proceed he then, in double life,
in inward thoughts and outward show,
in anguish, but with placid face,
too weak to fight pretension.
Ever higher rose his good repute
in efforts meant to compensate,
to break through sinful, lustful thoughts,
the heart of this contention.

His Gospel learning deep ingrained
taught him the lustful eye to pluck,
and suffer life the better, maimed,

than whole attend perdition.
And also, he who one law breaks,
the whole transgresses to his loss;
so he believed with breaking heart
stood beyond the pale of salvation.

Compound this with the added fear;
though he his thoughts did not enact,
and only nightly entertained
in private weakness yield to flame,
exposure of his "other man,"
unto a world that held him great,
should such a fall from such a height
lead him to the depth of shame.

The years have sapped his struggling heart
and brought him tearstained to the thought
of what was not but could have been,
a painful lack of fruit assessing.
Could he have caught God's grace and power
to wash the stain to white as snow,
a different song would then be sung:
a song of grace and blessing.[1]

In the abrupt ending of the song, Hamlet noted a universal hush among the audience. Almost as one, they expelled a breath. A few women applied kerchiefs to their moist eyes. Couples looked to each other and smiled wanly. He took advantage and glanced at Ophelia to see her eyes glassy with sentiment. She managed a brave smile for him. The applause began a bit tentatively but grew to a warmth.

"Your Majesty," said Master Guilliame, "I confess, such a somber start to these proceedings is unusual. In truth, this was a new

---

[1] The remainder of this *chanson* is printed in an appendix at the end.

composition of mine—first heard here—based on knowledge of a former patron who suffered the malady of the ill-made knight for many years and who asked me to tell his story. My curiosity to see it well received got the better of me. I promise the remainder of the program will be of a lighter and more adventurous vein." He bowed deeply.

"Your trust in our approbations is rewarded," replied the queen. "Though sad, there was in it good truth and a mighty lesson. For the rest, we do pray you will make good your promise, else our kerchiefs will not survive the soaking. What have you next for our ready ears?"

"It is an adventure of Sir Percival, Your Majesty." This announcement elicited a few "aahs" among the listeners. Ophelia squirmed slightly with glee. Hamlet sat up. Master Guilliame began.

*****

Following the recital, Hamlet, with a gallant display of concern, asked leave to escort Ophelia back to her residence. Inwardly, he congratulated himself that he could summon up the courage. He had to promise to return to the queen's chamber afterward for some needed time between mother and son. In this, he gladly acquiesced.

As Ophelia's nurse met them just outside the entrance to the great hall, there was not much opportunity for intimate conversation—he would not have known what to say along the lines of intimacy at any rate. They passed the too-short time discussing the merits of Master Guilliame and the high points of his various songs. Hamlet was gratified to be able to illuminate Ophelia on some of the finer points that she had missed. He basked in her gratitude for both the instruction and the escort before she and Nurse turned to enter their home.

Hamlet barely remembered the walk back to the keep and practically flew up the stairs to his mother's apartments, up the stairs and into her arms. It was in this embrace that he realized how much he had gained on her in height. Where he used to nuzzle comfortably below her breasts, he was now well above them. Perhaps the two years of intermittent growth was best served by this break in contact,

61

at least as far as awkward embraces were concerned. They swayed together a long moment.

"Oh, Hamlet," the queen sighed. "How many more such embraces from my babe ere you are too much the man for such displays of affection? I fear you will return from this warfare too ready for another's arms."

"Now, Mother. Father has foreseen this to be a campaign for one season only. Expect no stubble-chinned son to dismount a massive destrier and administer a crushing embrace."

The queen motioned for them to take seat at a small side table. She studied her son with admiration. "Are you happy, my son?"

"Why, what should a man do but be happy?"

"Liked you Master Guilliame's pieces?"

"They are a delicacy best ingested sparingly for all they are so rich. I thought his 'Ill-Made Knight' a shade too somber."

"Indeed, it put a chill in my heart that was only warmed nearly two songs after. But truly, you seem happy."

"Seem, madame? Consider, I am to go off with my father to learn both the art of war and some of his trade while in the field. I am well thought of by Laertes, my better at swords. This intelligence I had this day from Mistress Ophelia. I enjoy the friendship of good Horatio. My father is undertaking some refinements to my education commensurate with my growth. God's in his heaven. All's right in Denmark or some such saying. Why need you ask?"

"It is important to me that those I love are happy. Indeed, it has become my aim among the ladies of the court to foster joy among them. I abhor the intrigue of the seraglio and wish for peace to reign at court. We should all be merry."

"Then for your sake, dear Mother, and to give your mind good rest in this, I am merry. But I must point out, your ladies are hardly a harem."

"Of course, dear. I spoke figuratively. What think you of Mistress Ophelia now that you have come into her orb?" Again, there was no hint of any pointed question here. Joined together with the queen's previous talk about happiness, Hamlet took her question to be a natural inquiry into how well he passed the afternoon.

"She is—the fairest damsel I have rescued thus far!"

"I would have you know that she is sweet and likely to be a gentle addition to my ladies. I like her."

"That intelligence, I am sure, will be a great joy to her, and so you are consistent in meeting your aim. She enjoyed Master Guilliame, as I did. I believe the 'Ill-Made Knight' gave her a sniff or two of sentiment. In all, it has been a good day—oh!"

"What is't, my son?"

"I was to meet Horatio hereafter for redress of our lost afternoon." He affected a pleading look toward a dismissal.

"Well, go then, but return to me often ere you march away."

"Shall I come every day with bent wildflowers?"

"Yes, but leave off the crickets. They would get under the ladies' skirts and set them all to unseemly dancing."

"You would then be a step closer to that seraglio. However, I shall in all things obey you, Mother."

# Chapter 6

Sleep could not hold Hamlet long. The day of marshaling had come. There were few in Castle Elsinore who slept through this night. The constant bustle about the yard kept even the uninvolved awake. Hamlet rose after only three hours sleep, dressed, and then breakfasted with a number of soldiers in the great hall. Horatio joined him, and they spoke of what lay ahead.

Though the destination of their march was not officially published, it was generally perceived that the movement was to be southward to shore up borderlands. Hamlet had secured permission to let Horatio in on the essentials, that he should not fret an action against his own people and kinsmen. For the most part, Horatio seemed relieved not to be going off to war though he owned that he would miss his friend and something of life in camp.

The breakfast concluded; the two boys returned to Hamlet's room where he completed dressing for the march. As a page, he neither wore armor nor carried arms, saving a small dagger at his belt. Still, he made sure his tunic was as smart and as military looking as possible.

Odain took the last of the prince's accouterments and carried them down to a place on the wagon that would carry the king's effects. In all other matters, Hamlet was to associate himself with the four other royal pages selected to attend the march. Together, they remained under the charge of Marcellus, who was tasked to acquaint them with the menial duties of a page in the field. The lads were to continue their training at arms but also attend to the needs of the king's household as a page would attend his knight. The aim of this, for the prince included, was practical obedience and humility.

Laertes had found a position as squire to a knight in the division of the Lord Marshal. He had already marched off with the advanced guard. Thus, Hamlet despaired of the borrowed waves and kisses to Laertes from his sister, these already having been administered in private the evening before.

The boys now moved listlessly about the room. There was yet some time before the starting out but not enough to initiate anything of any great import. Hamlet simply stoked the fire and then sat staring into it. Through the window, Horatio watched the activity out in the yard. At length, he turned his gaze skyward.

"The dawn comes graying out over the sea, my lord. Yet there may be some rosiness in its cheeks anon." He moved to sit and also watch the fire.

"We march in rain or full sun and certainly all in between. That's the soldier's way and his lot. So says Marcellus and many others of our veteran ranks. I wonder what experience of events to come will season my speech upon my return. For 'tis certain a soldier's speech hath ready-made phrasings and short truths to fill the gaps of philosophical thought and make life the easier to bear. A soldier's talk is full of 'I remember when we were at thus and such a place, hard pressed by weather, hunger, marching and the like, by which the present discomforts pale.' And then follows the catalogue of names whose brave example bolstered weary souls and pressed the rank and file to great exertions in the service of the goddess victory. That's the nine-tenths part of history, Horatio."

"And the remaining tenth?"

"Oh, thus and such a ruling from such and thus a parliament of Polonius's ilk. 'Tis filled with corn laws and fishing rights."

"Is there no part for philosophers then, my lord?"

"Else they catch the conscience of kings—and with considered counsel—cancel coming confrontation—eh—they must their own books write."

"Or trust their students to enshrine them in the bindings, like our dear Socrates. Nice alliteration though, my lord."

"It needs a better conclusion. I'd work on it in the saddle, but I've lost the first part already."

"'Twas of no import. Do soldiers alliterate, I wonder?"

"I think their usage is something too rough. 'Tis possible I'll return with a few notches dinged into the edge of my speech."

"So long as you don't bowl your mother over with manly oaths."

"My mother! Oh! I am to see her ere I go. Come. Let's to her apartments."

"Let me decline, my lord, lest motherly tears set us all to blushing or bring to mind the parting endearments of my own mother and set a likewise spring to welling in my eyes."

"In the yard then upon our departure?"

"Sure, my lord."

Horatio left. Hamlet cast one studious look about his room, took up his cloak, and then made his way to see his mother.

*****

Once past the chapel entrance—he had no time for Fra Ignacio's counsel this morning—Hamlet continued up the stairs. As he approached the queen's antechamber, the sound of talk filtered through the curtained doorway which had been left ajar. He readily recognized his father's voice as well as his mother's. About to enter on them both, he thought it wiser to make sure their talk was not too private for his sudden appearance among them. In mind of Horatio's words, he thought there might be wifely tears to precede motherly ones. In short, he meant to listen sufficiently to determine the tenor of their talk but not to eavesdrop.

"Come back to us soon, my love," spoke the queen. "'Tis clear in the grayness of this morn, you are taking the sun with you."

"Two set forth with me this morning, perhaps, but only one 'son' will I keep to earn his spurs. The other 'sun' will likely burn through the overclouds and be reminder to you that no matter the distance, we stand beneath the same golden orb for warmth and light and beneath the blessings of the same God."

Hamlet thought that this was sweet and almost announced himself. But then, his father's voice turned official.

"Touching upon the regency, keep this in your counsel and write to me if aught falls out according to our doubts voiced of late. My brother is an able man. In our growing up, he attended jointly with me the lessons of kingship from our father. He has always been eager for the wielding of some machinery of government. He has proven himself over in the various offices and embassies assigned him. Though he revels overmuch for my liking once the sun is low and the great hall supper cleared away, yet he will not lose the grip of state. I have seen him follow a night of drinking with a day in the saddle alongside the most conscientious and sleep-rested of our lot to return successful from the hunt and, in the same stride, attend another night in the cups. His constitution is supportive for drink. My concern is not there."

"So you have said, my love. Why then the heavy brow?"

"His eagerness bespeaks some latent ambition, which in this opportunity may be too much a pull to carve some for himself. But even in this, I trust that Polonius's careful eye will be sufficient stop-gap to overzealous use of kingly authority. Claudius is a curbed tiger, content for the nonce to 'mounch' the morsels of proximity to the throne. I think he will be no trouble."

"That is good to suppose. Then it will go well here at court. The amenities will not suffer. I like your brother's company. And his presence will remind me of your own loving countenance."

"Truly? I have it from most hereabout that we are not brotherly bookends but more Jacob- and Esau-like though none have ventured which role is doled to which. To be sure, I am a man of the open field, and he is the more likely to have dwelled in our mother's tents—not to strain the meaning of the phrase. But with this difference that I cherish my birthright and am not disposed to barter it or my son's inheritance and the succession for a mere mess of pottage. Even should some untimely death take me, which the Lord forbid, this crown shall pass to the next Hamlet, saving some unforeseen undermining of his character as to render him unfit and undeserving, the which I immensely doubt."

"Such talk is ominous. Leave off, my love."

"I know it rubs against your new religion of happiness for all. Have no fear in this. Claudius and I do not flag in brotherly affection. My cautions and my words are not meant to be prophetic. They are as substantial as the words only to fly forth and dissipate into the air almost unheard. See, they are gone. And should you turn to your window, madame, you will see also that the clouds, too, are scattered to a dawn whose sun will smile upon us both and upon Denmark, even as I depart."

"Would that the clouds of war were as easily scattered, not calling you off to reassert the greatness of your reign above even these petty encroachments. I know 'tis time for Denmark to see her king once more in the saddle in her interests. And men must have their time in the field, else they come too close to loving their mother's tents. Be a king, my love! But when kingly calls are sated, return to my arms and be king over me only."

"Over you, most assuredly!"

"Oh, leave off, or the march will be delayed while watching eyes turn toward the queen's window, and dalliance become the foil to your hardly derived timetable. Kingdoms have been forfeited for as much."

"Well, I go to war then. But I plan no conquests until I return home!"

Hamlet heard his mother's laughter cut short by a playful squeak. He knew then that they would be locked in embrace. He had enough time to take a half turn back down the steps and thereby be seen to be ascending as his father came out from the room smiling.

"It is a good son who remembers his mother's arms in the excitement of warlike departures." He tousled the boy's hair and passed down the stairs. "Your mother awaits. Be merry and leave her not in tears," he called back, descending

"Aye, Father." Hamlet stepped to the open doorway. "Mother?"

"Hamlet! The other half of my life comes to bid me *adieu*." She held her arms out to him, and he embraced her warmly. "I know you go not to battle. But the chances of war still range wide of the battlefield. Keep close, my son. You have had all your instruction in this. Fra Ignacio hath said that you came to him wary of the pitfalls of campaigning. I will ask only that you let remembrance of your mother's loving regard also guide your steps."

"Aye, Mother."

"Remembered you your kerchief?"

"Aye, Mother."

"A scarf and something for your ears?"

"Aye, Mother, and I have packed Quickbeam along."

"Your hobbyhorse? Whatever for?" They both laughed heartily.

Then the queen sighed. "It is a mother's office to worry." She sniffed.

"For the composition of my kit, I have conferred with all the most sage campaigners, Marcellus and Bernardo especially. And I have been provided with a purse commensurate with that of a page of modest but sufficient means that I may make up for any unforeseen deficiencies from among the sutlers or the locals. I will sleep as well provided for as the king under canvas and rise to daily duties that will not leave me idle to wander into any wantonness that beckons. My deportment will be as kingly as a prince can contrive. And I shall make it a practice to launder my kerchief 'gainst an infectious sniffle. Are you thus happy?"

"I am satisfied but not happy." They embraced again.

From out in the yard, a drum beat an assembly. His mother strengthened her embrace as she moaned a single sob. "The tattoo summons you."

"The tattoo beats at evening, Mother. Would you have the soldiers jump back into bed?"

"You have learned your soldier's art well. There will be no maneuvering beyond your lines."

"And now, do you say to me, 'Come back with your shield or on it'?"

"I am no Spartan mother. Just come back."

"God willing, before the summer's out." One more embrace and Hamlet strode out the doorway. "God-be-wi-ye, Mother," he called over his shoulder.

*****

"Huzzah for the warrior prince!" This was Yorick's greeting as Hamlet entered the great hall. "If you conquer all your foes in like manner as you conquered that mince pie yesternight, the Turks and the Tartars, the Avars, and the Bolgars will tremble for their easternmost holdings as they fall back against the Great Khan!"

Hamlet waved off the jester's salute. Fresh from his mother's embrace, he felt that something more manly was needed here then his usual embrace from his mentor and friend. He approached slowly with a sheepish grin. Yorick read his thoughts aright once again and offered no accolade. They simply stood facing each other in wordless appraisal.

"If my election held any potency, I'd advance you for regent in our absence."

"Ha! Then we must take the name 'the kingdom of Bedlam' for our realm. And for holidays, never would we advance in the calendar beyond the Feast of Fools. And our years, therefore, would never move forward, and then we would live forever, my lord!"

"You will live forever. 'Tis certain. For I heard one of your riddles bandied about the stables the other day past. So shall your fame as a wit live on."

"It would live on in the stables. Aye, my words to comingle there with the ready muck, heavy, odious, and not easily to be shaken off when one comes unwittingly upon them."

"No, you shall live forever, just like my father."

"How shall you then become king, my lord?"

"I would gladly be prince eternal to an everlasting king like my father!"

"These are borrowed religious titles, if I be not mistaken. Do you deify yourself and your father?"

"God forbid! I meant no blasphemy. Only—I wish we could go on unchanging except perhaps—drawing closer."

"Hm. I hear a pair of eyes in your speech. How then, if you will not grow older in eternity, will you take to wife"—here, he leaned in and whispered—"a certain young lady of the court? Shh!" He raised a finger to his lips and made a show of looking about.

"In heaven, where all things are eternal, they are neither given nor taken in marriage. So says Fra Ignacio. What then do the bachelors and the maids there all the day?"

"They pray a lot, I hear, but for what, I know not since there are no marriages to be prayed for. And any undertaking betwixt them outside of marriage is not proper substance for prayer and, therefore, not meet for paradise."

"But neither is there 'meat' in paradise for even the lions will eat straw like cattle."

"Then you had best make me regent. For never would I aspire to make Denmark a paradise and turn our customs and our uses on their heads. 'Tis too unwieldy a concept. On second thought, it is best I not be regent, lest I back us into some eruption to our state by reason of a misapplied witticism. Nations do go to war on the grounds of insult. Statesmanship is such madness, I hear."

"Then should you be regent since madness is in your purview?"

"I am but mad two or three points off the compass. When the weather's up and straight sailing called for, I make correction and come 'round to true north. 'Tis madness in mirth only, my lord, never madness in earnest!"

"Then sure will I miss you on this endeavor for I foresee a dearth of mirth in't."

"There will be camp entertainment enough though some a little closer to earth than mirth and, therefore, best left in that dearth then in the abundance."

"Touché. But 'tis certain that I shall find your absence hard going for such puns will go wanting among my companion pages."

"Oh?"

"Olan and Fenris though they are my seniors by some margin, haven't the ready wit. Jürgen swears puns are 'gainst religion, and Osric thinks 'hawk' a pun for 'handsaw'!"

"Hm. Barren company indeed. A pity you could not stow young Master Horatio away in your kit."

"We essayed the idea in our thoughts but could come to no successful conclusion. I could get him to bend nearly double and look something in appearance like my sleeping roll—albeit an intelligent sleeping roll. But the exchange of the one for the other, leaving us both without warmth for the nights, rendered the plan… extravagant."

"Ho, you left me no word for punning. *Extravagant* is no word. 'Tis an icing."

"Then I leave you with the icing, dear Yorick, for the drums have sounded and our array must march off. Keep us in your layman's prayers."

"On my knees, as we do in the world, and not on my face, as they do in paradise. Else my cracked layman's prayers may crack the flagstones. But 'tis certain you will march off with all my good will and wishes attending. Eagerly will I wait to hear your stories upon your return. It will make up the first canto to the 'History of Hamlet, Prince of Denmark.'"

"Comedy rather. And I have just composed, extempore, your ending couplet ready served. It is…ahem: 'The princely page [or pagely prince] returned from war, in wisdom steeped—but saddle sore!'"

"It likes us well, my lord. Rest content that should your aspirations not congeal into kingliness, you would a princely jester make!"

"That is high praise from your lips. I am content."

They passed another moment in eye contact. Then Hamlet hit upon the manly idea of offering Yorick his hand. With a smile, the jester took it firmly—wrist to elbow—and, with his free hand, clapped the youth on his shoulder.

"Do the Germans your worst, my lord, so they make not a *wurst* of you!"

"And so I will." Hamlet strode out of the hall feeling a half-inch more the man.

*****

The young prince stepped out into the broad light of morning. The sun had broken the horizon but had not yet surmounted the battlements. He surveyed the castle yard and found it a match for his most adventurous imaginings. To his right, a formation of men-at-arms stood at ease. A few men entered and left the ranks either on errands or in remembrance of some necessary item left somewhere to be fetched.

Across the yard, toward the gate, a group of mounted knights also stood loosely together. Most of them were conversing with each other. He saw one or two who appeared to be at prayer, with heads bared and faces cast downward.

Immediately to his left was the king's guard standing near his mount. His father had not yet appeared. He stepped off in that direction, knowing that somewhere behind that group would be his own mount held by a servant from the stables. Rounding the king's party, he spotted his horse with Horatio standing for the groom.

"Have you cast off all lines, my lord?"

"All but one, and this one most reluctantly."

"Have no regrets, my lord. It should be that I shall be better able to apply myself to my studies since adventure comes not so readily to my mind as yours. And all our imagined foes may have a season of rest while you attend to true foes—if foes can be said to be true. I am content to remain here in my books though I envy you the visitation of my homeland."

"Yes. I have your letters in my saddlebag here. I shall deliver them along with good report of you."

"For that, many thanks, my lord."

"Well, to horse then." Hamlet offered his hand to Horatio in the same way he had to Yorick. Horatio clasped his friend's hand and held it for a single firm shake. Then he helped Hamlet to mount. After an exchange of salutes, Horatio stepped back into the small crowd of onlookers to wait the appearance of the king.

Hamlet looked about from his raised position. Beside him sat Marcellus with the rest of the pages paired behind them. Glancing back, his words to Yorick about his companions felt like prophecy fulfilled. At the rear, Olan and Fenris looked inert. Perhaps they were already feeling the lack of sleep. Next up, Jürgen sported an officious cast. No doubt he had ideas for the proper turnout of the pages, and the reality had not met with these. Beside him, Osric looked on the verge of giddy with anticipation. Hamlet refrained from any mental comments about him.

"Good morrow, my Lord Hamlet," offered Marcellus briskly.

"Good morrow, Marcellus. No swords today?"

"The first day on the march is always the longest. And there will be duties in camp as I have indicated in our earlier talk. Look not to resume our lessons until we establish our base at the other end of this. For the present, riding is the thing."

"Aye, well, you can help me pass the miles with recounting your experiences in past forays. I have a mind to make the most of these days."

"'Tis well, my lord. However, the king hath called for you to ride out at his side. And so should you expect to pass the first day at least, being thus introduced to your future subjects. Yet wait here until he comes. Then will he beckon."

"I see. For that good intelligence, I thank you, Marcellus."

"My glad service, my lord."

They did not have to wait long. At the sound of a pair of trumpets, all the separate conversations ceased while formations straightened themselves out. In the immediate silence, the king appeared at the doorway to the great hall. He did not bask long in the cheers that followed but strode quickly to his warhorse and mounted. Looking behind him, he called loudly, "Prince Hamlet, it is meet that you be at my side this day, that the eye of Denmark may behold her future king!"

Nodding to Marcellus, Hamlet led his horse to the position of the junior man, that is, to the left and half a horse length behind the king. Father and son regarded each other silently. Then the king raised his voice. "We go!" They started off to cheers from the crowd in the yard.

With the king and Hamlet leading, they passed into the short narrow street leading to the gate. The crowd was not great but was certainly more than the usual morning collection of servants and menials. In addition to these, there were the wives and women attached to the soldiers marching behind them. A few held the hands of small children. One or two held babes. Hamlet could sense that behind the cheers were the concerns of loved ones. There did not appear to be anything ominous in it. Yet he was glad to be sensitive to it, for he wanted to be a king who remained in touch with his people.

He smiled self-consciously at hearing a few of the women call out, "Hoorah for the young prince!" Their youthful feminine voices suddenly reminded him of Ophelia. He found himself surprised that he could have gone so long without a thought of her. He felt almost guilty. And here he was with her house just coming into view.

Hamlet had no expectation of seeing her since Laertes was long gone. Still, he looked the facade of their house over with a rising heartbeat. Suddenly, at an oriel window, he saw the sashes opened out to reveal her standing in a dressing gown. Her hair was down but neatly combed without any arrangement. She saw him easily and smiled. Hamlet could see her nurse standing behind her—probably frowning upon such an immodest display of sentiment, he thought. Her wave was broadly for all who were marching past. But her eyes and her smile were for him. He knew it.

So far, the king had acknowledged the approbation of the crowd with solemn but friendly nods of the head every so often. Hamlet tried to make his nod to Ophelia special, but he was not sure that was the effect that registered with her.

As both father and son were about to come abreast of her window, Ophelia leaned forward slightly so that the single wisp of the kiss she blew to Hamlet would not be observed by the nurse. Before he could stop himself, Hamlet touched his forehead in salute. His father caught the exchange and slapped his thigh with merry laughter.

Hamlet dared not turn his head around once past her and prayed she would understand. Two more houses and they were passing under the portcullis and out into the town. There he saw various companies posted at side streets, ready to fall in behind their force. Hamlet suddenly realized the extent of this expedition as companies grew into regiments. He was about to move into a bigger world. Yet behind him, probably closing her window and turning to start her new day, was an even bigger world for him.

# Act 2

# Chapter 7

Sea oats covering the top of the dunes dipped and swayed in the shore breeze that also blew against Hamlet's face. He breathed in the smell of the sea as he stood just behind the crest of the highest dune along that stretch of coast. Marcellus was with him, as were Olan and Fenris. They had been posted here as part of the watch over a selected region of the coast. This region, the king and his marshal had deduced, would be a likely spot for the Nordics to make their foray.

The march to Schleswig had been uneventful except for a day and a half of rain that had come in from the sea. It left him so rain-soaked that the young prince had begun to think he would never feel dry again. But he continued on as uncomplaining as his mount. Hamlet found the time on the march to be a vast expanse of "room for thought." Landmarks discerned way in the distance went by at a walking pace. Indeed, the slow passage of time seemed to him to be the true enemy in the campaign thus far. The threat of dulled senses outlasted both the damp of the heavy morning mists and the choking afternoon dust of the road. Marcellus's anecdotes were instructive, but all the campaigning events of his years of service, plumbed to their very depths, still could not fill up the time.

There was always Ophelia to think about. But even her search-ing eyes and warm smile began to blur as the distance between them grew. His feelings had not faded any that he could tell for he still recognized the sensation of warmth that thoughts of her brought. These thoughts then, he found both a relief and a drag weight on the passage of time. To be sure, the endless days of the march were the furthest thing to be had in the way of adventure. This he had expected. But added to that was now the growing sense that this whole expedition stood in the way of his return to her, and in that sense, time stretched in the passing.

He reminded himself that not so long ago, even the privations and the flatness of this eternal procession would have been filled with imagined adventure. And the rush and exhilaration of battle to be expected at the road's end was the stuff of his dreams. Now his dreams ranged elsewhere.

In this circumstance was formed the first of the great dichotomies that were to frame his life. On the one hand was his desire to experience this very military existence in all its facets—even the tiresome ones. On the other, he embraced the very gauntlet of emotions, of doubts to assurances, melancholy to elation, and despair to hope. These he ran by reason of his feelings for her—or was it unreason? And so, time slowed when weighed against his druthers to be again in her presence.

Sometimes though, his thoughts of Ophelia helped him to pass the hours in unexpected instances. He would look up from a thousand-mile stare at some point between his horse's ears and see that somehow the landscape had changed, finally. He filled the emptiness of his days with the same surmises of what her present activities were. It was a strange sort of comfort to him to think that while he endured this limbo of duty-filled time, she was living life for the both of them. He formed the habit of falling into thoughts of her as soon as his brain began to register any situation as characteristic of the word *misery*. So relentlessly driving rain, middle-of-the-night watches, footsore and saddle-sore miles, these and the many other miseries became invitations to muse and lose himself in thoughts of her.

This dichotomy could become, as now, the cause of conflict. Here at this post on the shore, the need for watchful surveillance over a figurative kingdom of near absolute stillness stood against the tug of his romantic druthers. Nothing had changed in the four days since their posting to this spot. Even the weather appeared to differ only by seasons. On this day though, the wind had shifted to blow in directly from the sea. Perhaps it would bring a change. For the unknownth time this morning, Hamlet surveyed the empire of his wasteland of thought.

Below them lay a fleet of three fishing boats, beached while their crews were tending to the morning's catch. The breeze caught the wisp of smoke that rose from their modest campfire and quickly whisked it away up the dune. Occasionally, he breathed in the smell of the fire and the cooked fish. It made him hungry. He let his gaze not linger here.

To his left, the coast stretched away in endless dunes exactly like the one on which he stood. To the right lay the mouth of a river opening out to the sea. It appeared from between two low green bluffs, at the base of which he could make out a few trees. This was a navigable river that led some four miles inland to a village of considerable size. This village stood as bait in the king's plans.

There were three such villages in this region. They sat farthest from the eastern border and were therefore helpful to the confederate's plan. Both the Nordics and Germans desired to draw Schleswig's main might farthest from the second and more fatal blow, which would fall against her lightly held eastern borders.

These villages were accessible directly by the river, walled with wooden palisades but lightly manned. The garrisons had been bolstered to a modest strength that should hold against raiders for a time sufficient for the king to bring his forces up in relief. Yet they were not so strengthened as to awaken suspicions in the raider's minds of any premeditated prevention.

The king had divided his force equally and encamped them, each division a short march from their respective village, out of the way and hidden. It was his intent that the raiders come up river, as was their wont, and find the villages assailable. Once they applied themselves to the task of taking the towns, the Danes would respond. With one subdivision of men, they would move to establish a blocking position against the raider's return downriver to the open sea. With the remainder, they would strike directly at the Nordics, either catching them between their own relief force and the walls of the village or directly reinforcing the beset garrison, whichever would be most effective under the circumstances.

In this way, Hamlet and his two companions along with Marcellus found themselves attached to the marshal's division at the northwestern-most end of the region in question. Jürgen and Osric remained under Bernardo with one of the king's divisions farther to the east. Each morning, the three pages and their mentor rode from camp before first light to relieve the night watch and stand in alternating watches through the day until just before evening.

At present, Hamlet and Marcellus had the post while Olan and Fenris passed the time either with hunting to augment the night's meat or with more sparring practice. Hamlet envied them the activity. A quick study of the land behind them completed the circuit of his perusal. Between them and the marshal's camp stretched over three miles of flat grassland growing tenaciously out of the sandy soil. Here and there stood coppices of stunted trees shaped by the winds into graceful but terrible forms that were beginning to fill the settings of his night dreams. He stifled a yawn and turned back to look seaward where 90 percent of his gaze rested.

"'Tis no wonder that soldiers rush eagerly to battle as a least means of bringing these doldrums to conclusion."

"Or to break them off for a time, my lord. For the battle concluded, a true soldier curtails his triumph and returns to weary watchfulness, lest complacency compounds with the enemy's rebound, effecting a reverse of that triumph."

"So battle is but a punctuation to the larger text of expectant waiting."

"Aye, my lord. It would seem so."

"And leisure is but enjoyed with one hand on the sword, as in Bible times."

"Aye, my lord."

"'Tis a wonder more soldiers don't turn poet. Had I my books, I could have, in these four days, composed a whole volume of sonnets."

"And the foe's strength come upon us as you battled with metaphors and nuances."

"Aye, there's the rub and the shame of it. For surveillance's sake, we must bend our all to catch the fateful changeover from endless nothing to the need for haste. We dare not miss even the passing second to idle thought. So need we must converse here, not face-to-face but companion-like, side by side as we study the great nothing together."

"You have it, my lord."

"The untried opus in verse is no great loss though. I perceive the larger half of that poet's volume would, in the end, be odes to sea oats!"

"To be sure, the world narrows under our watch. But soldiers are poets in their own way or troubadours of a sort. For at even' camp and at other times when personal surveillance is relaxed by faithful relief and there is time to idle about the cooking fires, the soldier expounds with a treasury of anecdotes to rival your court-born *chansons*."

"True enough. I have heard these tall tales, which often tell against fellow soldiers yet in ways not meant to damage the character. They are so steeped in humor, one would think a soldier's life the most jovial of pursuits and war not a horror but a comradeship of humorous mishaps. The biographer of these men's lives would from a wealth of tales mine a wealth in sales, of his opus, that is."

"Aye, my lord, but for one axiom that for impediment keeps the soldier from advantage in this."

"What is that?"

"To the reception of these tales, there are in the world but two types of ears to hear: the ears of those with similar recollections—fellow or veteran soldiers—and the ears of those who have not these experiences—wives and men of civil profession. This latter will never savor of the full episode, no matter how faithfully nor how artfully it is recounted. For they have nothing similar upon which to draw for empathy. They simply will not comprehend."

"And the former?"

"Being privy to the same dreads, drudgery, dangers, and deprivement, they do not wish to hear it!"

"Ha! So the soldier's life is in the main, unsung."

"Aye, my lord. In this, he is most godlike in the realm of blessings. In victory, as in the blessings, the gratitude is profuse and even heartfelt but short-lived. It dies just past the tongue and fades with the rump end of the triumphal procession. And when blessings and victories push long time between themselves, the author of them is forgotten entirely and even looked upon as unnecessary. The wealthy man sees no need of God, and the safe citizen bemoans the taxes that feed the men who with their service and their lives procure that security. Not to mention that pensioning is the forlorn hope of any state's largesse."

"Be this the reason so many of our old soldiers turn to beggary?"

"Aye, my lord, or to brigandage. For having spent their lives as soldiers, they are often at a loss for peaceful trade unless they pursue and occupy a tradeful niche in the camp—cooking or barbering. It is the rare soldier who can store up his wages and prize money against old age. Camp life encourages the wastrel's habits. 'Life is short and death is quick,' so goes the adage."

"Aye, but many are those who come back from the war young and useless with lopped off limbs."

"True, my lord. There's where the soldier must draw deepest from the well of courage. To die in battle is but the unfortunate matter of a painful moment. But to live a daily death to one's manhood and survive on the crumbs and occasional glory of recounting, 'I was in thus and such an action,' goes beyond courage."

"Hm." Hamlet nodded, feeling he had nothing to say.

"But perhaps there is a place in paradise for soldiers, good soldiers. For war brings out the beast and the best—"

Here Marcellus cut himself off as both he and Hamlet noted the appearance on the horizon of a flotilla of sails. These soon began to grow into full ship's hulls as they rounded the earth's curve on their way toward shore.

"Is't them?"

"Aye, my lord. The breeze brings them in. Now is that need for haste you spoke of." Hamlet turned to fetch his mount. Marcellus took his arm to stay him a moment. "Hold an instant, my lord. Let me compose." The man-at-arms thought a moment as he studied their numbers, direction of travel, and approach speed. "Ride you to the marshal. Tell him they come, some fifty or sixty vessels from the looks of it. I give them an hour to the estuary and then some short time up river. The wind favors their inland movement even against the current. Push your two companions of the watch up here. We shall spy them out, and when they enter the river, we will parallel their progress. I will send Olan or Fenris with any additional report as needed. You or the marshal's scouts will find me along the planned route. Now repeat all that back ere you ride."

Hamlet repeated the report exactly, then trotted down the slope to his mount. Halfway up a nearby gully, he found Olan and Fenris. Sending them on to Marcellus, he spurred his horse onto the flatland and headed for the marshal's camp. 'To catch that changeful moment from endless nothing to the need for haste,' he thought as he rode on.

*****

Hamlet took up a position not far behind the marshal as their force moved out from camp toward the village. His pulse, already quick, picked up even more once he saw his report translated to action by the beat of drums to assemble. Every man moved as if they were each as ready as he after these days of boredom. Now they were nearing the village by the planned covered route. More than the hour estimated by Marcellus had passed, and another hour followed. The blocking force had separated from the main and moved by guides down to its position.

Hamlet kept himself ready as a messenger either to the blocking force or back to find Marcellus. So far, he had not been needed. Yet he kept his ears and eyes open to be able to recount any situation by personal witness and without needing lengthy instruction.

Now Fenris appeared out of the tree line that was the last cover between them and the village. That told Hamlet that his friends had been able to follow the fleet all the way up without mishap. Fenris rode quickly up to the marshal and reported while both remained on the move. Hamlet could not hear the report, but he noted the lad's gesticulations in the direction of the village. Having completed his report, Fenris returned whence he came. The marshal signaled his lieutenants forward.

The knight whom Laertes served led the blocking force. From their encampment of that morning, Laertes rode off behind his lord before he and Hamlet could exchange words. Hamlet said a prayer for his safety, both out of friendship and for Ophelia's sake. Again, he realized that events had pushed Ophelia well out of his thoughts and kept her away from the moment of the alarm back on the coast until now. He commanded his thoughts of her back to the rear of his mind and found that compliance came easily when more urgent matters called.

The marshal completed his instructions to his lieutenants, who moved off to their charges. He turned and, seeing Hamlet, beckoned to him. Hamlet rode up quickly.

"My lord, the raiders have disembarked from their ships below the village, out of bow shot."

Hamlet nodded, remembering that the village wall ended at the river bank and that it was therefore open to attack on the water side. There had been a question of whether or not the attackers would come all the way in and risk their ships being fired by archers with flaming arrows.

"We will catch them between the walls and our force. There is five hundred yards distance from this last woodland cover to the walls. I have ordered our forces to traverse the wood in march column. It is quite dense, as you can readily see. We will debouch quickly on the far side, form our ranks, and advance with no delay. You may follow behind to witness these events, but under no circumstances are you to join in the fighting. This is your father's command. And I concur. I must ask if you understand this clearly?"

"Aye, Lord Marshal."

"Good. And it may be that similar action is unfolding in one or both of the other two villages on the coast for these sixty ships reported by you cannot be their full force. If all goes well, there will be more than one victory with which to amend our history and add to the Lord's credit ere this day is over."

"Aye, Lord Marshal. The Lord's arm strike with you."

"And keep us all for better days. Watch our deployment from the wood's far edge and bring me report later of what you have learned from it. We move as silently as possibilities allow and pray our thrashing through these parts does not raise the birds in alarm. Neither will we raise the cheer until the latest moment, so as to come upon them unsuspecting and thereby shorten the distance of our charge."

"Aye, Lord Marshal. I understand and will study its execution." Hamlet was grateful that this man of war had taken the time to explain matters and give his rationale. He supposed it to be a good use of the time while orders were passed down.

The Lord Marshal quickened his pace, and the army followed the scout's leading into and through the woods. The route followed a narrow footpath which the column took four abreast, making a tremendous noise in the breaking of dead tree limbs and the trampling of undergrowth. Hamlet had a side thought that the local peasants would welcome this artificial "windfall" for the supplement of their smoky peat fires.

The woods ran a width of about a hundred yards of dark canopy. Riding back out into the light, Hamlet quickly moved to the side to allow those behind him to pass. His attention was drawn to the scene below. Easiest to see was the town. It had not been fired and all appeared normal, except at its northern end. There he could see a large body of men gathered near the base of the wall. Scaling ladders had been thrown up against the wooden ramparts, and men were ascending under the cover of archers from below, who were keeping the defenders' heads down.

It was clear that without the marshal's relief force, the village could not hold. Farther to the left, downstream, Hamlet could also see where the raiders had beached their long ships. A thin stream of men moved back and forth like busy ants from them to the attacking force. Hamlet reasoned that these men were bringing up more arrows and any other needed equipment.

So far, the raiders were too preoccupied with their attack on the village to notice the threat gathering against them from the woods. Hamlet prayed this would remain so for a good long time. The relief force was nearly deployed when it appeared that the raiders had seen them. The marshal caught their reaction and ordered the advance without any delay. Not wanting to tire his men out with a five-hundred-yard charge, he advanced them at a brisk walking pace. Hamlet and a few other pages followed at a respectable distance. With less than two hundred yards to go, the raiders had changed front but were not as tightly formed as the Danes, and they had not had time to loose even one volley of arrows at the new threat before it was upon them.

A great cheer went up from the defenders and the relief force alike. It was powered by the giddy knowledge that they had their foe trapped between two fires. Everything was according to their plan. The marshal's line broke into a trot and finally a dead run in the last thirty yards. Hamlet could hear the clash of arms and shields as the two forces met. Archers from the walls now repaid the raiders for the damage they had done. Their arrows ate away at the rear of the raider's formation while the new front fought desperately against the Danes.

The noise of battle rose to include individual yells and grunts that gave power to the warriors' blows. Add to that screams of agony and rage. Hamlet tried to imagine the effect of these weapons on human flesh when they were wielded in frenzied earnest. He did not have to rely on his imagination for long.

Slowly, the line moved forward, eventually uncovering a scattering of felled bodies and the debris of battle. Only a small number of the fallen moved. Some of these, as Hamlet and the others came up, turned out to be the twitching of muscles still responding to the last messages sent from now dead brains. He also saw the lopped-off limbs of which he had spoken earlier with Marcellus. There were not a few, and he found himself having to take great gulps of air to keep himself mounted in a world that wanted to spin about him. He saw one of the younger pages on foot double over and wretch at the sight of one ghastly mutilation.

It was not long before the raiders broke and turned toward their ships. The battle now became a deadly footrace. Here the mounted Danes had the clear advantage. Hamlet saw the knights surging ahead of their own men-at-arms. They rode down the fleeing Nordics, hacking left and right with no lack of foe to strike at. The noise of battle lessoned, both in intensity and with the increasing distance as both forces streamed toward the ships.

Out of the body of warriors, the marshal rode back. His gaze quickly fell on Hamlet and once again he beckoned. Hamlet spurred his horse to try and cover the greater part of the distance and thus keep the marshal closer to his command. As he came up, the marshal called to him.

"Lord Hamlet, know you where the blocking force is positioned?"

"Aye, Lord Marshal."

"Ride you there and report to them what you have seen here. The Nordics have to their ships fled, and there are at least ten or a dozen pulling toward them. He is to fire them up as best he can according to the plan."

"Aye, my lord. Ten or a dozen ships to be fired according to plan."

"Good. Godspeed you on your way!"

Hamlet again gave spurs to his horse, making a straight line to parallel the river. As he broke clear of the end of the Danish line, he could see the ships of which the marshal spoke. They were already pulled away and making good way under oar power as well as using the current. He gauged that he would beat them to the blocking position, but it would be a near-run thing. His prayer as he rode included a provision that the blocking force had time to set fires to light their arrows.

*****

The blocking position was located where a patch of woods reached the river at a narrow point. Between it and the village, there were two bends in the river that favored the Danish side. Hamlet was able to cut across them and was soon out of sight of the retreating ships. On the last stretch, he took a chance and galloped across the open to a point of the woods almost where it came to the bank. He was able to get there before the first of the ships could round the last bend in time to see him enter the woods and be forewarned of the Danes' presence.

Once inside the tree line, he could see the soldiers, many of them archers, positioned and ready. He remembered then that dry wood had been stacked and prepared for firing two days before and that the force had planned to bring hot coals carried in gourds. The fires were ready.

"I seek Sir Hugh!" he called to the first soldiers he met. They pointed him out, and Hamlet recognized him standing by one of the fires. Laertes stood nearby. The undergrowth was thick here, so Hamlet dismounted and handed the reins to a soldier while he dashed up to the knight.

"Sir Hugh, I come from the marshal. Our surprise was successful, and in the main, we have them, but some ten or a dozen ships with their crews have slipped off and are coming downriver. They are not far behind me, as the current favors them. The marshal directs you to fire the ships according to the plan."

"My thanks, Lord Hamlet. We will give them a warm reception. Watch you here and be prepared to take back to the marshal report of our successes."

"Aye, Sir Hugh."

The knight turned to his lieutenants and bade them make ready. Hamlet took advantage and slipped over to Laertes.

"Laertes, how fare you in these?"

"Well, my lord. I have learned much and have a better measure of what I need to learn further."

Hamlet had to stop himself short from asking after Ophelia. He remembered that they would not have been away long enough for any letters to have come and so make his question a casual pleasantry.

"Shall we move to better vantage?" he asked Laertes.

"I have a spot all picked out." The boys made their way to Laertes's spot.

In less time than one could tell a hundred, the lead ship came around the bend. They all heard the pull of the oars. Over that, they could hear the voice of the man calling cadence. Though they were nearly half way clear to the sea, the voice betrayed an anxious strain. Hamlet realized that though cloaks had been staked to cover the enemy side of the fires, there was no way to disguise the flames and smoke completely. They all hoped the Nordics would think them the fires of woodsmen at their labor.

According to the plan, the first volley would be plain arrows in an attempt to disable as many oarsmen as possible. Then would follow fire arrows mixed in to continue seeking lives and to set the ships alight. On came the ships, one leading followed by pairs abreast. The marshal's dozen turned out to be quite a few, and though smarting from their setback, they still looked formidable. They were not limping away but came on with power.

Not waiting for the lead ship to come abreast of their position lest it slip too easily past them, Sir Hugh gave the signal to loose arrows as soon as it came in range. The first volley struck the crew of the lead ship completely by surprise. For a moment, the oars lost all cohesion. Hamlet could hear the solid *thunk* of the arrows and the grunts of their target victims. When the cadence resumed under a different voice, many of the oars did not move. This made it difficult for those who were still trying to row.

The second volley presented a fantastic display of arching flames that struck the ship at multiple points. Hamlet could see as many as three men stand up in the shock of the impact with a flaming arrow embedded in each of them. Other arrows struck the deck and two lodged in the mast where the flames took hold and climbed up it.

In a stroke of good fortune, the helmsman was hit and slumped against the tiller, knocking it to the side and causing the ship to turn its bow slantwise across the current and heading it almost directly for the men shooting at them from the woods. This also slowed its progress as it now drifted obliquely downriver. More volleys took a fearful toll as the archers could now engage down the length of the ship. The next two ships in line came up on the lead so quickly that they were unable to maneuver around it, and they became fouled in its idle oars. The three ships together were now drifting and nearly choked the river while the deadly rain of arrows continued with fatal effect. Likewise, the remaining ships slammed into these and into each other. Fires spread from ship to ship.

Some of the raiders jumped and attempted to swim to the far shore. Their chain mail hauberks dragged many of them down.

The few who made the far shore would not find sympathy from the people they had come to plunder. They would be hunted down in the ensuing weeks. Thus, they proved no threat. Others swam or waded to the near shore and stood in a knot awaiting the arrival of Sir Hugh's men-at-arms to round them up. Since they jumped ship without arms, they had no choice but to surrender. When the work was clearly done, Sir Hugh sought out Hamlet.

"My Lord Hamlet, you may report to the Lord Marshal that saving a score of bedraggled Nordics afoot on the far shore, whose effectiveness as fighting men is in serious doubt, there will be no return of this force to advise the Germans that they have picked, or should I say 'piqued,' the wrongest foe."

"I will do so, Sir Hugh, and will give you credit for the pun as well."

"A hearty thanks to you, good my lord."

With a salute and nod to Laertes, Hamlet made his happy way back toward the village. He had seen his first action and the success of it, and though he had done no fighting, yet his contribution as a messenger had been meaningful.

# Chapter 8

The marshal's prediction proved to be correct. The Nordic raiders had timed their strokes to fall simultaneously. The king's force met with and destroyed an attack against the village in his area on the same day as the marshal's battle for his village. In this action also, the chief headsman among them was captured and was now being held. A misfortune in the king's plan anticipated the third attack on a village different from the one where it actually fell. The force with whom Jürgen and Osric waited along with Bernardo continued to wait while the raiders struck slightly farther east.

Yet there was a good to come of this turn of events, and the king could still count his strategy a success. The marshal reasoned and pointed out to his sovereign Lord that this one successful foray of the Nordics would give birth to misapprehension among their enemies. Their leaders, unwitting of the other two failures for lack of witnesses, would report back to their German confederates a success on a scale at least sufficient to send the Marcher Lord's forces scurrying westward in response. Thus, it could be assumed among the invaders that the Schleswigers would vacate the eastern borderlands as desired.

In a counter-assumption that the seafaring arm of the enemy plan had done its part and that there would be no other coastal raids, the king could now collect his forces and march to the eastern border to await the planned invasion with some preparedness. Thus it was, that on the third day following the defeat of the raiders, the marshal's command decamped and marched for a designated rendezvous point near the eastern marches.

Over those three days, Hamlet had noted a relaxation of tension among the troops in camp. These were the immediate fruits of victory. The first evening following the action was marked by singing and an easier sort of talk among the men. There were already a few anecdotes born out of the modest engagement that rounded out the details for its participants with some humor. By the second afternoon, when the grim business of interring the fallen was concluded—presumably each man with the right parts reunited, as the story went—the atmosphere in camp was almost carnival. One of the anecdotes from that day told of an extra arm being found which could not be explained. However, as that was passed about by soldiers in their cups, its validity was questioned.

Despite the relaxation of tension in camp, surveillance and security measures remained as Marcellus had explained they should. Hence, Hamlet and the rest continued to keep watch on the coast in the day and return to camp ere dark for a rest. The young prince was glad enough that this duty, though dull with expended anticipation, excused them from details assigned to the collection and burial of the dead. His sympathies ran strong for a few of the other pages and squires whose initiation into this practice left them pale and shaken by the evening fires.

At their party's return on the second afternoon, the spirit of the camp was at its highest. To be sure, in all the days since the force arrived at this bivouac, with no hint of the length of their stay, there was every hope that there would be a long rest from the rigors of the approach marching of the previous weeks. It was in this type of setting that the vices of camp life began to make their appearance. Drink was available in abundance. Gambling proliferated, and the comforts provided by the usual camp followers—and a few of the daringly curious local girls—made the rounds from tent to tent. So long as no excesses materialized into violence or serious lapses of discipline, most of these practices were winked at by the officers.

Hamlet wondered that the marshal could be unaware of the situation. Marcellus assured him in somber tones that the marshal was too busy with the continuing concerns of the campaign to bother and that the modest amount of immorality was generally accepted as the price of keeping soldiers fit to fight and eager to respond to orders in time of need. Additionally, the policing of these offenses was too complex a matter when some of the officers themselves made provision for their own comforts. Hamlet reluctantly accepted this as a part of the unfortunate realities of war.

\*\*\*\*\*

On this second afternoon, Hamlet and Marcellus rode into camp abreast, as usual, with Olan and Fenris paired behind them. They had just passed the inner picket and were approaching the first tents. As royal pages, their own pavilion lay near the center of the camp, not far from the marshal's.

The lowering sun cast long shadows across the trampled grass and turned everything gold orange beneath a tired hazy sky. Small groups and individual soldiers were coming up from a nearby stream, carrying bits of their washing and armloads of wood or vessels of water for the evening cooking. Others stood about their tents chatting as they sorted out their gear for word had already passed that the next morning they were to move on.

From one of the tents, as they came up on it, issued the sound of raucous laughter, including the unmistakable laughter of females. Hamlet looked at Marcellus, who simply shrugged his shoulders. He meant to ignore the implications of this noise of unrestrained joy entirely, but the laughter drew his attention in curiosity. Thus, as he studied the tent, the flap was thrown open and out sprang two women gleefully shrieking. Both were in various stages of undress. These women were immediately followed by two jovial soldiers who quickly grasped them and pulled them, wriggling back into the visual privacy of the tent, where the sounds of laughter continued.

In this circumstance occurred Hamlet's first glance at the form of womanhood. Immediately any of his misconceptions of their private parts were set to rights. In the initial confusion of shock, he managed to be grateful, in part, to learn that his impressions were not too wide of the mark. Though the incident lasted but an instant and he and his friends rode on without comment, the image remained in Hamlet's thoughts. There they remained in a confused cycle of analysis well past their arrival at their pavilion and throughout the currying of their mounts. For a long time, try as he might to banish the image, it simply would not go away.

In the evening, when he went to their pavilion to announce supper to his comrades, he overheard Olan and Fenris within in what was perhaps their first profound conversation of the campaign.

"Which one did you fancy then?" Hamlet recognized the thin voice of Fenris.

"The one on the right for me," responded Olan in his deeper tone.

"Oh, that's only by reason of her being the most visible!"

"Not so! She appealed the more to me. Truly."

"Think you they were about it for wages?"

"Saw you the two men who pursued them?"

"I hardly noticed, being that my glance was otherwise occupied."

"Ha! But did you see that there was little to commend them?"

"Well, that, but what's your point?"

"Were I a wench, it was only the promise of wages would draw me to such as them!"

"Or to such as you! But I wonder what wages—"

"Counting the cost, are we?"

"Well—"

"I am certain it is beyond your purse and mine conjoined. We must content ourselves with the fortunate vision only, and there it rests. Or if your desperation waxes unto the duration of our service in these parts, find you out a country lass upon your return home and one not too bright or discerning at that."

"Aye—hey! Ah, I have it. From here on, I will strive to burnish up my service in these wars and look for a hero's welcome behind the homely haystack."

"'Tis a plan. Be sure to mind the pitchfork and the shadow cast by some *codgity pater* disagreeable to your romp, else you might woo for yourself a skewered rump!"

Hamlet had heard about enough. He was starting to feel as light-headed as he had at the sight of the corpse-strewn battlefield. Retracing his steps a few paces, he turned and reapproached the tent, whistling some snatch of a tune.

"Ho!" he called out. "Are you two hobbyhorses within? There's vittles to be had and a long march on the morrow!"

"Food!" he heard Fenris's response. "Now there's a dainty within reason of my grasp. You need hail me but once, my lord." Almost immediately, the two pages launched out of their tent.

"Once has come and gone then. And Marcellus advises that following our repast, we make preparation to decamp."

"Aye, my lord," said Olan. As they came past Hamlet, Olan started to ask, "My Lord, saw you those—" But Fenris elbowed him brusquely, cutting him off.

"Peace, brother!" Fenris hissed at his friend, who rubbed his arm where he had received the correction. Fenris thought quickly and attempted to finish Olan's question in a different vein. "Saw you those, eh, sugared raisins at the sutlers?"

"Aye, with the mind of my purse, which bends to frugality."

"But you've yet to celebrate our sure victory, my lord. After all, 'life is short and death is quick.'"

"That saying, I hear, was coined by a canny sutler. I'll refrain from what's good and even what is better and save against what's best—when I see it."

"I would I had followed that course earlier," bemoaned Olan. "Methinks I saw what's best sometime earlier this day!"

"Hush, fool!" hissed Fenris again. He took Olan's arm and pulled him away toward the marshal's mess.

Hamlet stopped to let them get ahead, out of hearing. "'Tis not the best," he said under his breath.

*****

Hamlet's thoughts bounced in multiple directions as he found himself once again riding in the long march column, heading first south, then east. He was grateful that the preparations for their departure had kept him late the night before. Finally lying down upon his sleep roll, he did not have to wait or think long before sleep took him. Fortunately, he awoke to a camp already bustling in anticipation of the day and with the attendants of the marshal's field household eager to strike their tent. Dressing, breakfast, and final preparations had also occupied his mind thoroughly until the start of the move. For all this distraction, he gave thanks.

But now, once again on the road, his mind was free to dwell on the day before. In doing so, his brain now fashioned the second great dichotomy of his life. Two camps competed for chief place in his thoughts. Into his warm images of Ophelia intruded the momentary but, oh, so lasting remembrance of those two women. He batted them away as often as they appeared while trying to hold Ophelia's blown kiss in the arms of his musing.

Now arose the first of three problems. He realized that his thoughts of the sweet girl he left behind were mostly static, portraits in the mind that suffered the blurring of distance and time. There were her eyes and her smile. Memories of her conversation with him were genteel and pleasant. Then over these would burst the shrieking and the laughter of the day before and, most of all, the imagery of movement. It was the motion of the body—that joyful wiggling— that he sensed made the images so strong in his mind. He could not forget the scene.

The second problem: This image evoked in him a different kind of exhilaration than the excitement of Ophelia's presence or her attention. Where the latter was warm and pleasant in all its aspects, this new feeling loomed with something dark and threatening in the distance beyond the immediate excitement and forbidden pleasure of the thought. It was also an exhilaration that had become oddly exacerbated by his shifting about in the saddle as he rode on. There was an uncomfortable yet somehow enticing stirring in his loins that brought with it a sense of pleasure and, because of its source, of guilt. The sensation, with its demands for immediate attention, was maddening. In this way, he measured the passing miles in inches.

The third problem: From somewhere in the deep reaches of his thoughts drifted up the suggestion that he attempt a synthesis of these two warring camps. It was the voice of Eros reemerging from that evening after Hamlet's rescue of Ophelia, the voice that had proposed an underlife in fabricated memories of her to fill his days. He had fled that voice once before and thought it was gone. But now it was back and suggesting a creative use of Hamlet's imagination, to consider the form of Ophelia's womanhood.

As soon as this wisp of a suggestion formed itself into the merest substantial thought, Hamlet flung it away with an audible growl that brought him out of his inner conflict to find Marcellus extending him a questioning look. He thought quickly and returned an exasperated countenance, and he winced. "Saddle sore!"

"So soon, my lord? We are but an hour upon the road with many more to tell ere we come to the end of this day—and more days beyond await us in the saddle."

"Methinks it is residual from the previous. Yet I will live and, at length, laugh at its memory. But I tell you truly, I wish we could lock certain memories away."

"But who would keep the key of it?"

"A trusted friend. Or failing that, as in the case of some memories, I would I could cast the key into the deep."

"Keys cast carelessly may yet resurface at inopportune times and in dubious hands, my lord. A trusted friend is better."

"Aye." Hamlet thought of Yorick, and now a second call to hasten home was born. Yes, Yorick would understand his plight and perhaps even be able to explain it to him. That thought cheered him somewhat and stole away the threat of endless perturbation. 'All may be well,' he told himself inwardly.

*****

After three more days of marching, the marshal's force approached the rendezvous where the king and his men were already encamped. The cheers of the civil populous over the victorious return of an army was one thing. But the cheers of comrades reunited after equally sharing in victory was like a welcome into paradise. Even Hamlet, whose spirits had been worn threadbare with cloaking his mental agitations, rose to the joy of the occasion.

Most of the marshal's men were turned off to their own portion of the encampment before they could become too mingled with the welcomers. The marshal, his chief lieutenants, and the pages contin-

JULIAN MARCK

ued on to a meeting with the king. The pages, of course, would be reattached to the king's household until it was decided how the forces would be newly apportioned for the tasks ahead. For them then, this was a sort of homecoming.

Hamlet was amazed at how he brightened at the familiar faces of the soldiers comprising the king's guard and even those of the stewards who helped maintain the camp. These were men he knew. Marcellus greeted more than a few comrades as they rode by well-established tents and pavilions.

"Are your goslings accounted for, Marcellus?" queried one old campaigner good-naturedly.

"Aye, and they return the more fledged, their flight feathers show promise."

"That's grand, *grand*. We'll tip a tankard together to their health once you see them to the roost."

"Aye, if you've left me any by then!"

They rode on to more such comments. As they neared the king's pavilion, the marshal turned and called to Hamlet. "My Lord Hamlet, come you with me while your friends stand down. I think you will not be long. I know the king, your father, would have earliest good news of your return, and I would you were present as I make my good report of you."

"Aye, Lord Marshal," Hamlet called back. He turned to Marcellus. "Do not count me out of the necessary duties, Marcellus. I'll not rest on princely rank when there is work to be done."

"There's not but to curry our mounts and settle in. Fear not, my lord. There be duties enough on the morrow."

"Enjoy your tankard then." He moved to the junior position behind the marshal.

There were more cheers as the king emerged from his pavilion to greet his marshal and his son. His face beamed in the sunlight of the midafternoon. A breeze had set the banners to a brave fluttering. Puffy white clouds drifted across a deep blue sky to complete the sensation of a world in joyful motion.

"Lord Marshal! Ever have you brought victory in your wake! You are well come!"

"My thanks to Your Majesty. I did but carry out your plans under the smiling face of God."

"The plan, as we recall, was more than half yours. But we'll not quibble over victories. We see that you have brought us back our son. Has he done you good service?"

The marshal dismounted, and Hamlet followed suit. They both approached the king, Hamlet still maintaining the junior position.

"We credit him with the timely receipt of our alarum and with swiftest warning to Sir Hugh at the blocking position to catch the defeated foe and finish him. He has a watchful and ready eye to events and their analysis. Besides, his grasp of the ebb and flow of battle bespeaks kingly promise."

Hamlet kept his gaze downward during the Lord Marshal's report. Though it cheered him greatly, yet he suffered a pang of sorrow because of his struggling thought-life for he felt that it robbed him of the most thorough nobility that should be resident in a prince who was destined to be king.

"Look where his humility sits like a denial of his good services," said his father in response. "Our anticipations wax full. We are pleased. At supper will we drink the health of Denmark's heroes, old and young. But for the nonce, there are plans to discuss. Our reunion here may be timeliness curt mantled. Come inside. And you as well, Prince Hamlet. It is meet you should witness how wars are planned."

"Aye, sire."

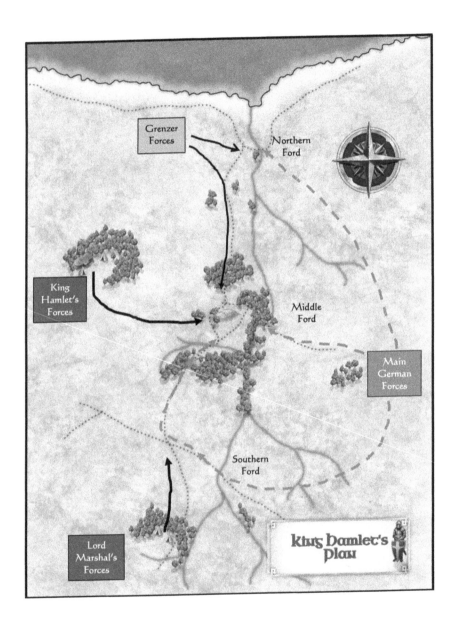

Grenzer Forces

Northern Ford

King Hamlet's Forces

Middle Ford

Main German Forces

Southern Ford

Lord Marshal's Forces

King Hamlet's Plan

They entered the king's pavilion. It was large and partitioned for private sleeping to one side and public meeting for the rest. In the center of the latter portion, between two posts, stood a table with a large map spread out; its curled edges were held down by weights. The king and his marshal moved around to view the map right side up, oriented northward. Hamlet had to content himself with seeing the land of Schleswig upside down. Yet he found that his mind had no trouble translating the map features understandably.

The Marcher Lord was already present in the tent. Though his glance was downward, Hamlet could see the same sensitive eyes inherited by his friend. But there was also in them a studied firmness. This was a self-assured leader whom he imagined, if wearing a Corinthian helmet, would easily have passed for an ancient archon of Greece. The man looked up from a somber study of the map to see Hamlet. His smile made him look to the young prince even more like Horatio.

"My Lord Hamlet, Horatio's mother sends her deepest gratitude for the letters which she had from him by you. She is comforted by the good care he receives there and happy to know of your close friendship with him."

"He is a true friend, my lord. We look to a strong union between our peoples in our years of authority—may they yet be some long time off though."

"That is said with princely grace. I am sure of it."

"Good sir," the king addressed the Marcher Lord. "Would you advise the Lord Marshal here of your latest reports on the German foe?"

"Aye, sire." He began pointing to locations on the very eastern edge of the map. "My 'eyes and ears' have them here in bivouac at present. They are gathering and coiling for the spring. From here there are three fords available to them as entry ways into Schleswig. Our most chief question then is the one which seeks to know by which ford they will assay our demesne. I have made a show of thinning our border garrisons as if to move against the Nordic threat. Yet our border watch remains alert. We expect their move in short order."

"Have you any thoughts on their most likely course?"

"If their aim is conquest, their likely method is to sweep. If they cross in the north and sweep down, they will cut off the larger part of our borderlands from assistance, but that would put our response at their backs, and they would yield up the fought-over land back to us as we closed on them. Contrariwise, a southern crossing with a sweep up will push our retreating border forces into the arms of our returning strength and meets us head-on with the Germans as we come up. I think we can reason out the middle crossing. Still, it is a possibility."

"So the north or the south?"

"The Germans like one swift movement, and they fear no enemy to their front. They like not to have to turn and change face unto a threat from the rear."

"Which we may yet offer them but not according to their expectations." The marshal paused but a moment. "If I hear you aright, your call is that they will cross the south ford and sweep north?"

"Aye, my lord."

"Your Majesty, consider this course for us."

Hamlet could almost see the Lord Marshal's thoughts building in his head. Like a master chess player, he mentally formed, tried, and cast aside various moves until a cogent strategy arose to be articulated with the conviction of a holy man. He watched as the marshal's hands swept in broad movement over the map to counter the Marcher Lord's equally sweeping summary of the German's intent.

The marshal continued, "Let us place a good force opposite the middle course but back and hidden. In one sense, this is our safety for it would be able to meet a force crossing from there and also be the first to stand in the way of a move from the Germans coming south should they essay a northern crossing."

"A 'safety' call you it, Lord Marshal? If I know you from of old, that portends something more audacious yet to come in your thinking," replied the king.

The marshal smiled. "Exactly, sire. I propose we position the remainder of our strength below the southern crossing also hidden, say here, in this forested area. My thought is this: The Germans cross in the south, then turn with little attention behind them and begin to sweep north according to the Marcher Lord's assessment. Good.

We move the center force from hiding to meet them head-on, as they expect but earlier and in greater numbers than they anticipate. This higher ground here likes us. As they deploy and come to battle, our second hidden force approaches from the south, and we catch them between us.

"Even should they espy us or should we move too early, they are still between us and must, at their best option, address us one or the other. If, for instance, they turn on our southern force, it holds them for the middle force to come south. Either response of their main matters not, they are between the opposing jaws!"

"It likes us well. My Lord of Schleswig, what say you to this course?"

"The plan is least desirable should they appear in the north. But our own middle and southern arms can move to affect a junction and still meet them as they move south. In that, we will be doubly strong as our forces will be then conjoined." He paused to consider a modification to the plan. "Should we post something above the northern crossing to discourage a turn that way and to harass their rear should they sweep from there south?"

"That is prudent. Can you spare the necessary men for a third force?"

"I will have my garrisons empty from that small portion of the coast and meet with some of my Grenzers. Could they appear to be the rear of my repositioning might in answer to the Nordics—as they have anticipated us to do—it might dissuade them from the adventure and turn them south as desired. If not, they will fight a hard delay until your middle force comes up to fall on their rear. All else makes a good harmony of this plan."

"Agreed. Hence, we with ours and what remains of the Marcher Lord's subtracted force will move on the morrow to the middle hiding position. Lord Marshal, if you would do us the honors, the southern jaw is yours. As we will be *ex communicato* once the Germans come between us, you must time your move out of hiding with care."

"Aye, sire. Needs we all must remember also that the German caught between the jaws will fight with Teutonic desperation. It will be a hard day however we catch him."

# Chapter 9

The Marcher Lord's assessment of the Germans' intentions was as good as prophecy, initially. The main German force crossed into Schleswig by the southern ford just as the Lord Marshal's division was closing into its hidden position. The border guards pulled back away from the German onslaught. Then things turned strange.

Thinking they would have to conduct a fighting retreat, the guard force, Grenzers, as they were styled, was surprised to find only a slight amount of pressure against it and only for a day's march from the German bridgehead. Then all stopped. The Grenzers, in their small scouting units, were able to creep back up to maintain a contact with the invaders. What they saw appeared to be a deliberate consolidation of the enemy's initial gains. The Germans flowed into the abandoned area and seemed to take their time. Certainly, they swept nowhere.

"They throw away their advantage with this delay." This was the Marcher Lord's new assessment as he stood in the king's pavilion on a cold day of overcast skies and intermittent drizzle. He pointed again to the map, but Hamlet, who was present at this meeting, had the unchanged positions memorized.

"I concur, but to what purpose is this lapse of aggression?" said the king. "They could have swept on past the middle ford in these days and still given you time to return from the coast in answer to their visible threat. Is't possible they, knowing only of your might and naught of us Danes, want to bring your force to conclusive battle?"

"Aye, sire. I was about to suggest that they mean to do just that: to defeat me in the field once for all and march across Schleswig all unhampered, perhaps with my head on some pike!"

"Were that the case, why do they not move to the same high ground where we hope to face them and cause you to have to assail the heights from the north?"

"That is what has me most in perplexity, sire. Why do they give us the good ground? Have you heard aught from the Lord Marshal? Do they trouble him instead? Is he detected and e'en now in earnest of our advance south in aid of him?"

"His couriers, though they must ride 'round wide by the west, report all quiet. The marshal waits like us." A long silence followed, and the two veteran warriors jointly studied the map as if expecting it to speak to them. The king resumed, "Well, things cannot remain thus. Do the Germans wait for you to collect and return from the north, we should oblige them. Send this day to your Grenzers up there and have them move toward us but with efforts to mask their numbers and appear to be the might of Schleswig coming on. Perhaps it will cause the enigmatical Germans to tip their hands."

"I think that will do, sire. And if the intelligence of this moves him off his strategical rump, still we will have time to take up on the high ground, so he'll arrive on the march to see Danish banners thrown into the bargain."

"That will change his day, sure. Send for your forces, my lord."

"Aye, Majesty." The Marcher Lord moved off to effect the necessary orders. In the vacancy, Hamlet stepped up to the map and stood beside his father.

"You will see, my son, that one particular habit of a thinking enemy is his lack of cooperation. But so long as we keep him in respect for such obstinacy, we are less likely to under esteem him in his courses."

"Aye, sire. 'Tis mightily bad-mannered of him. Perhaps he'll be surly in the combat as well."

His father chuckled at the joke. "Oh, that he will be. Fear it not. The German is not one to oblige us with an easy victory." In the pause that followed, the king looked at his son and remembered his own youth and young manhood. He then looked vacantly across the tent to the damp field outside.

"My first foray with a fighting command under my father was 'gainst the Polacks. There's a fearsome foe now. They are so impetuous as they come on berserker-like, one does not know where to strike first with the effect, as happened to me, that every man 'round you is a Pole, with no companions near for succor."

"What did you then, Father?"

"I considered myself blessed with foe enough that I could strike in any direction and have my man. So I walloped left and right, leaving many to bleed onto the ice, for it was a winter campaign. I must have fought to a frenzy. The Lord Marshal, who was my chief lieutenant even then, regained contact with me though I nearly took his head off for a damnable Pole. He recalled me to myself from beyond sword length and pointed out that I had laid flat the opposition."

"What, all of them, sire?"

"Well, no. There was a goodly sum of them chose discretion over an untimely welcome in Valhalla or wherever their warriors roost in the underworld. I contented myself with the round score lying, twitching at my feet, and together the marshal and I rallied our men and moved on in search of an open flank.

"Oh, I was like a young Alexander 'gainst the Polacks that day, pushing my companions through to a breach in the line to strike at the heart. I won my spurs that day, sure." He drank in the admiration in his son's eyes. "But I was some years your senior then. I watched my first war from beneath my father's standard as you will in this coming battle." He placed a warm hand on Hamlet's shoulder.

"I have learned much in these days, sire." He realized that he had almost echoed Laertes's words from back at the blocking position, and so he thought to add, "And learned something of the measure of my deficiencies in the art."

"Each battle is as different from the last as one birthing from another. Though there be similarities in the general execution, yet there are vast differences in the particulars. You will always be learning this art, as I still do. The day you hold your education complete in this is the day you begin your march to defeat and destruction at the hands of an enemy who is still learning."

"Aye, Father. And I have noted my thoughts into my tables that I not easily forget them."

"A good practice. You shall find that there's many in court will bank on the lapse of a king's memory. A king who forgets not will not easily be hoodwinked. Remember that."

"Aye, sire."

During this exchange, Hamlet's eyes shifted between meeting his father's looks and a continued study of the map. His glances kept being pulled back to the middle ford. It was slightly north and east of the high ground that the Danes hoped to hold as the major portion of the king's plan. There was something in that, but he could not form it into a complete thought. He was about to point this out to his father when the Marcher Lord returned and took up a conversation with the king on various other contingencies. By the time the discussion ended, the mental prompting that Hamlet had experienced from the map over the middle ford was buried under all the plans of his elders. Thus, he never broached the subject.

*****

The king and the Marcher Lord's premonition turned out to be correct. The Germans were indeed waiting on the return of the strength of Schleswig. It appeared that as soon as word got to them that the northern force was on its way, they began their move. Word of this reached the king in sufficient time to move the middle force from hiding up to the high ground and deploy facing south. The line stood just below the crest of a low oblong ridge with a rounded top. A few rock-strewn crags lay exposed along the summit. The rest was covered with coarse grasses.

The rank and file laughed as their approach onto the slope sent scores of rabbits fleeing in every direction. This they took to be a good omen of the Germans' response to their numbers, position, and valor.

The damp weather had cleared, and everyone was in good spirits to have some idea at last of what they were about. Hamlet stood with Bernardo, Jürgen, and Osric at the very crest of the ridge and, as his father had said, nearly under the king's banner. From this point, they could survey a full circle about them.

Bernardo had pointed out the most likely approach of the Germans. They would appear out of a distant wood line to the south. From there, they must cross a short open space before reaching the lowest ground. They would then be required to negotiate a small but gullied creek bed before they could emerge from it to the other side to form battle line. All of this effort, conducted in the face of an already deployed enemy, could be unnerving and gain the Danes further advantage.

Continuing his orientation, Bernardo turned the lads about and indicated the ground coming up from the middle ford. After following a covered route from the ford, a road emerged from a wood line, not directly behind them but to the rear of their left. Because the woods were closer on this side of the ridge, the open ground to their rear was not as vast as that on the southern slope. Bernardo remarked that had the Germans held the ridge, forcing the allies to attack them from the north, there would be little ground to deploy if they came out of the woods there.

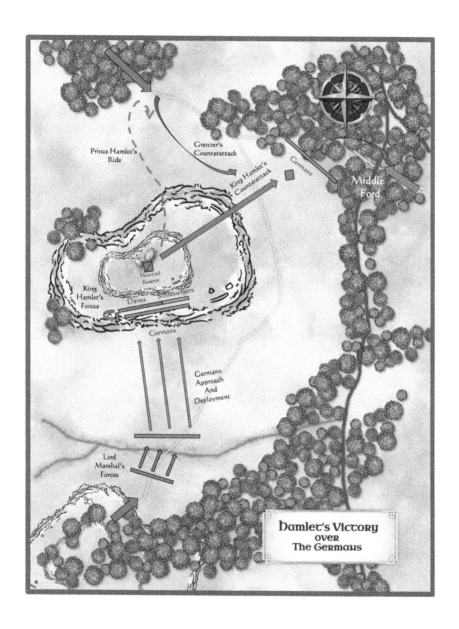

Prince Hamlet's Ride

Grenzer's Counterattack

King Hamlet's Counterattack

Germans

Middle Ford

Mounted Reserve

King Hamlet's Forces

Danes

Schleswigers

Germans

Germans Approach And Deployment

Lord Marshal's Forces

Hamlet's Victory over The Germans

"What about that more open ground on the right of our rear?" asked Hamlet, essaying analysis.

"To be sure, that is the better approach from the north. And it would hit the Germans obliquely if they followed the crest in their alignment, the which would be the natural tendency."

When the royal pages turned front again, Hamlet continued to study the road from the ford. He had asked and been told that the ford was watched and guarded by a small force.

The king's forces on the forward slope of the ridge were arrayed thus: The right and center were Danes under command of Sir Hugh on the right and the king in the center. On the left were the Schleswigers under the Marcher Lord. On the crest, the king kept a strong mounted reserve just behind the center but slightly to the right. He was counting on the timely arrival of the Lord Marshal's forces. Failing that, he planned to swing the reserves around his right and attempt to push the Germans back against the river, which was hidden by more woods in the low ground to the east.

The Danes and their allies had been in position above an hour when the Germans appeared, as predicted, out of the wood line to the south. As though watching a lesson unfold, Hamlet and the rest saw them move in column down into and back out of the creek bed. Only then did they fan out to form their battle line.

Though their movement was quick, Hamlet felt that time passed slowly as the enemy fulfilled every prophecy. When the battle lines were extended and comparison could be made, the Danes readily discerned that their line overlapped that of the Germans on both flanks. This, too, was taken as a good omen, even though the king reminded his lieutenants that the longer line was no guarantee of victory.

Almost without pause, once their line was formed, the Germans advanced up the long slope. Hamlet could hear the jingle and banging of equipment, the commands and urgings of their leaders and, as they drew closer, the trampling of the grass beneath their feet. The Danes had been instructed to receive the charge at a standstill; this was to keep their line as cohesive as possible. They were not to move forward unless given the word.

Until the start of the attack by the Germans, Hamlet's father had remained on the crest near his banner. Anyone who needed him could find him easily. Now with the gap between the armies closing, he moved forward to stand behind the center. In much the same way an individual fighter keeps himself coiled for a sudden lunge, so the Germans did not charge at a run until the last few meters. Then with a loud cheer, they crashed into the waiting Danes. The forces connected with the same clashing noise that Hamlet had heard in his first battle. There was an exhilaration in it, but one that also carried a sickening sense in his memory of the death and pain that the noise represented.

He noted the other pages' reactions. This was the first experience of battle for them. Unable to see the actual fighting at the front of the line, they were mesmerized by the noise of it. In one sense, Hamlet thought they looked like spectators at a tournament, cheering on their favorites. The thought that the life and death struggle being waged before them should be attended by onlookers in this manner left him downhearted for a moment. He brushed the thought away and continued to study the fight for its tactical lessons.

The Germans had wisely angled off in their approach to meet the defending line more on its left so that as the overlapping Danes might bend around their left, they would be attacking the protected side of their individual men, the side on which they carried their shields. Neither line moved forward after first contact, and neither gave way.

Still, Hamlet could tell that the men at the rear were slowly feeding forward either to give comrades at the front a rest or to fill in for the fallen. He could see the leaders deeply involved in directing the fight, but they were none of them physically in the struggle yet. It was still a time for the younger men to strike and parry and thrust.

As they stood watching what appeared to be an equal contest thus far, despite the differences in the numbers, Hamlet felt a sudden chill at the back of his neck. Then a voice like a trumpet call told him, "Turn!" Instinctively, he knew where to look. Pivoting, he searched the tree line where the road emerged out of the woods coming up from the middle fork. And he saw it.

A large force of Germans was debauching from the wood line and beginning to form for an assault. They would be at the rear of the Danish line shortly.

"Bernardo!" he yelled. His mentor turned and saw the same thing that Hamlet did and went nearly white. "Tell the king!"

Immediately, Bernardo mounted and rode to the rear of the center to catch the king's attention. He could see Bernardo pointing back over the crest of the hill as he explained the changing situation. Together they rode quickly back to the crest.

As his father came up, Hamlet heard him saying, "We know now why he gave us this ground." He called first to the captain of his reserve. "The reserve will come with me! Bernardo, ride to the Marcher Lord. Advise him what we do. Tell him to take command also of the center. He will need to fight with one glance over his shoulder. Pass the same to Sir Hugh on the right!"

"Aye, sire!"

Not thinking, Hamlet called out, "Father, sire! You will need Bernardo's strong arm with you. Schleswig stands at the back of his line. Let me ride to him and then return here!"

His father studied him but an instant. Hamlet feared he would decline the offer, and there was no time for argument. He would have to accept a no for an answer. Instead, with pride growing in the king's countenance, he nodded in affirmation. "Tell Sir Hugh also. On your return, keep watch for the marshal to the south. The day is not yet lost."

By now, the reserve had changed face and was ready to move. The king called out, "Forward for Denmark. This is what kings are for!"

They thundered down the hill to hit the Germans while they were still filing out of the woods. Fighting off the temptation to watch the outcome of the Danish charge, Hamlet mounted and spurred his horse toward the left rear of the battle line. There, well back of the blows but close enough for arrows to be a threat, he found the Marcher Lord fully concentrating on the fight to his front.

"My Lord of Schleswig!" Hamlet had to call out twice.

Recognition and astonishment registered together in the old warrior's face as he turned to see the prince. "My Lord Hamlet, what—"

But Hamlet cut him off. "The Germans come in force from the middle ford and are e'en now deploying in our rear. The king has taken the reserves to deal with them. He bids you take command in the center and have a care to your rear. I must ride to advise Sir Hugh. I will return to you if the outcome waxes desperate from that quarter!"

"Heaven preserve us this day! Sir Roger, do you hear?" he asked his lieutenant.

"Aye, my lord. Go you on to the center. I shall continue here."

"God's arm strike with you. Prince Hamlet, ride with me, then proceed to Sir Hugh."

"Aye, my lord."

Together they rode along the back of the line. Hamlet thought it was fortunate that the ridge itself shielded the men's view of what was unfolding behind them. Nothing takes the spirit out of a fighting man faster than knowing of a serious threat to his unprotected back.

"My lord, the king says I'm to watch for the approach of the Lord Marshal upon my return to the highest ground."

"Splendid. Let us pray he is not far behind these. I had wondered why the German's strength seemed wanting here, and our scouts could not approach close enough to them in their bridgehead to tell of their numbers. I might have suspected something had we but known."

"Aye, and as the king hath said, we also know why this ground was yielded to us so naively."

"Aye, it was to fix us between their own two jaws. Well, we shall see which jaws close first and the strongest. It has all come clear now. Here we are. Go you on to Sir Hugh. And God protect you!"

"Thank you, my lord." Hamlet rode on and found Sir Hugh right at the point where his forces bent around the flank of the Germans. Despite the advantage, the Danes were having a hard time of it. The prince met with the same response of astonishment from Sir Hugh and Laertes, who stood nearby. Hamlet delivered the same message. Sir Hugh looked to the top of the ridge as though expecting to see the Germans streaming over already. Then he shook the vision away and responded to Hamlet's message.

"This has been well-planned, to be sure. I suspect now, too, the German has placed his strength on the left of his line in anticipation of this effort of ours here. O brazen foe, to risk his might in such a throw!"

Hamlet nodded his understanding of Sir Hugh's outcry. He knew that it was more than tradition that put the strongest, more steady units on the right of the line of battle. The right was the weakest flank. But here the enemy had shifted toward the allied left, offering them his most protected flank, now manned with his best units against an attempt to turn it.

While they were talking, a ragged volley of arrows overshot the line of fighting men and impacted among them, striking one man nearby. One arrow planted itself in the grass between the legs of Hamlet's mount.

"My thanks for your brave service," said Sir Hugh. "But here is no place for royal pages. Ride you back to the crest, my lord, and keep your watch north and south."

"Aye, Sir Hugh. So have I promised my father. God guide your efforts here and grant you success."

"Thanks, good my lord."

Hamlet saluted the knight and nodded to Laertes before riding off to regain the crest. Approaching his comrades, who now stood nearly alone at the top, Hamlet called out, "Jürgen! How goes the fight to the rear?"

"The king and his reserve have for the moment despoiled the deployment of the newly arrived Germans. But if more continue to debauch as they have been, the reserve will be swallowed up and no other to throw in against them!"

"Oh, it is desperate." Hamlet dismounted to be able to turn more freely from front to back.

"My Lord Hamlet!" called Osric.

Hamlet turned to see him pointing in the distance to the south. They all saw another march column emerging from the wood line in the same way the first German force had. They were moving quickly. Hamlet recognized the armor and the mount of the man in the lead. "It is the Lord Marshal. Thanks be to God!"

"Herald!" Osric called. Hamlet understood his intent.

"Hold!"

"But the trumpet alarum, it would signal their approach to our men below and give them heart!"

"And at this early moment, it would give the Germans fore-warning and time to respond. Herald"—he called to the man who stood beneath the king's banner—"we shall wait until the marshal has cleared the creek and deployed his force mostly. Then shall we give the signal."

"Aye, my lord."

Now Hamlet felt he lived an existence in which time was out of joint. To the south, it crawled while the marshal hurried his men into position. To the north, it flew as his father fought the desperate fight to hold back disaster before the marshal's forces could come up. In either case, the minutes went by while Hamlet looked about to see if there were some portions of the main line that could be pulled out and moved to assist the king's reserve. But medieval armies were not organized for that sort of thing. All the chess pieces moved according to the plan at the outset. Once all elements were employed, there was little that could be done to change their course. In that instant, Hamlet learned the lesson of war: The victor must seek to outplan his foe.

The marshal's men were emerging from the creek bed and fan-ning out in fashion similar to the Germans earlier. 'A few moments more,' thought Hamlet. He made a quick assessment of the main line below him. It held as before, with neither side giving way. Then he looked to the rear again in those few moments to see his father's force trying to push the Germans back into the trees and prevent their further deployment, but the Germans were coming slowly out of the woods themselves on either side and about to overlap the Danes. Turning once again to the front, he gauged it time to give the signal.

"Herald! Sound the alarum!"

The man nodded to his trumpeters who, being ready, blew a clear, exultant, unified blast of notes. Hamlet spotted the Marcher Lord below and saw him look back up toward him. He and the other pages pointed emphatically to the creek bed below and beyond them. Then they shook their arms extended high with fists clenched in show of triumph. The Marcher Lord looked that way over the top of his men and saw their salvation. He must have called something to his men, but because he was turned away, Hamlet could not hear it. The effect of his words was immediate, there followed a cheer of courage that spread along the line.

Next, Hamlet looked to the right to see if Sir Hugh had heard the signal. He saw the knight raise his sword in affirmation that he had received word and understood it. From there, Hamlet shifted his gaze to study the Germans to see if they were yet aware of the peril at their backs. Then he heard Jürgen's voice pitched high, almost in a scream.

"My Lord Hamlet, they come!" His heart went nearly to his throat as he realized that if the Germans had broken through or gotten around his father's force, he and his companions were here on the crest and without arms, the first to be ridden down. But when he spun around, he saw little change where his father's men fought.

"No, my lord," said Jürgen. "To the right, away there!"

Hamlet looked and saw a group of mounted men coming from a wooded area farther back, almost due north.

"Is it a third force of Germans?" Jürgen asked in a half moan.

"A moment. Let me think, let me think." He stared at them and, at the same time, formed a mental image of the map with all the forces displayed on it. Slowly he smiled. "'Tis the Grenzers, the Marcher Lord's northern force. It must be! They were sent for to come hither. Huzzah!" He kept thinking. "But they know naught of our plight. They must be informed, else they will approach too slowly and in march column." The gears of Hamlet's mind whirred quickly, like tumblers of a lock about to fall in line and release the catch. Then he knew he had it. Once again, he turned to the herald and spoke as he remounted.

"Herald, I ride to the Grenzers there. Can I bring them on quicker and in battle form, look for my signal, then sound an alarum for the king to see the aid that comes for him?"

"Aye, my lord."

"My lord, your father, the king, his wishes—" Jürgen was trying to remind him that he was not to put himself at risk.

"This is what princes are for!" He turned his horse and galloped toward the distant column. On that ride, he kept his glance alternating between his father's situation and the Grenzer's line of march. He was happy to see that the latter was a significant mounted force. They might yet be able to respond in time and with sufficient numbers.

As the action at the rear of the allied line passed him by on the right, he saw two German horsemen who saw him. They broke away from the German line to ride toward him. They were going to try and cut him off. It was time to ride the way he did when outracing Horatio.

"Hollah, boy!" he called to his horse and whipped the reins. The horse picked up speed. Fortunately, as he was both unarmored and lighter than fully grown warriors, his horse could ride faster and be less wearied by it. Soon they passed the corner of the lower woods, putting the reserve's battle out of sight. By then, he felt sure that the horsemen would not be able to cut him off, but they would continue to give chase.

He was fast approaching the Grenzers. Four mounted men from there rode ahead of the column toward him. At first, he thought they would challenge him, but then he saw that they had come to drive off his pursuers. They rode past him on either side, and he smiled. Coming up on the lead men in the column, he called out to them.

"Who commands here?"

"Sir Ranulf," they replied and pointed him out. Hamlet saw him riding ahead of his banner. As Hamlet came up, he pulled up and turned with them to keep them all moving as he explained matters.

"Sir Ranulf, I am Hamlet, prince of Denmark. Our main is engaged 'gainst the Germans beyond the hill. They hold. But the king with our reserve is beset to the rear"—he pointed ahead and to the left through the intervening woods—"by a force come up from the ford and is in need of the most instant help you can provide. I will show you."

"Lead on, Prince Hamlet." He turned to his men. "At the trot, follow me!" The column began to move faster. Hamlet continued beside the leader.

"You will see anon, Sir Ranulf, as we breast this wood to the left, the Germans are attempting to debauch, form, and fall on our rear going over the crest. His Majesty has taken the reserve to despoil their maneuver. But his strength alone cannot hold."

In another few minutes, they rounded the corner of the woods to see the action just described. Sir Ranulf made a quick assessment, set his jaw, turned again in the saddle, and roared out his orders in a thunderous voice. "Form wedge and prepare to charge!" Then he spoke to Hamlet. "Ride clear of this, Your Highness, lest you be carried away unarmed into the fray!"

"Aye. I ride apart to catch the eye of the herald and signal the king of your approach."

"Let it be so. If God's watching, we'll meet again, my lord."

Hamlet rode away to the right of the forming group. When he was well enough clear that he could be distinguished from them by the herald, he pulled up and stood in his stirrups, waving his arms toward the crest. Seeing him, they waved back, and soon Hamlet heard the trumpets. He looked intently to his left to see if his father had heard. But he could not find his father in the melee. His line of sight lay obliquely along the Danish line, and he could not see through the press of the men.

The alarm sounded again. This time he saw his companions and the herald waving to someone in the reserve, pointing toward the Grenzer line, which was now formed and moving swiftly toward the Germans. Then he saw the king leading what was left of his force in a swift disengagement to clear the field for the Grenzer's charge. They halted just below the crest and turned to regroup and face the action again.

Other Grenzers were still coming up and forming a second wedge to follow behind the first. Hamlet walked his horse back toward the crest and watched as the Schleswigers slammed into the disordered Germans, sending them reeling. When it was clear that the threat had been nullified, Hamlet saw the king ride back over the crest and disappear down the other side.

'Of course, he wants to see how his other battle goes,' thought Hamlet with deep admiration for his father. 'Yes, live forever, my king and father!'

Coming up to the herald, Hamlet looked south as well. Below him he saw the marshal's line closed in behind the rear of the Germans, who were now fighting for their lives in two directions. The invasion was over.

# Chapter 10

"Huzzah for the Warrior Prince!" The cheer echoed through the great hall of the Marcher Lord's keep, a lusty chorus of male voices. As host to the Danish presence and as chief witness to Hamlet's actions in the battle, the Marcher Lord himself had stood to recount the young prince's quick thinking and his disregard for personal safety in bringing vital information, both to the leaders of the main battle—here he named himself and Sir Hugh—and to the commander of the relief effort that came to the aid of the king. Sir Ranulf also stood to tell his part of the story, praising Hamlet for clearly explaining the situation without a hint of panic or indecision. At the conclusion of these two testimonies, the men in the hall rose as one to raise the cheer.

Hamlet flushed crimson and tried hard to swallow back his emotions. Tears welled up in his eyes. His heart filled with a joy to see the pride in his father's face. Could he have but one wish for his life, that was it. Yet in this moment, he had no pride for himself. Indeed, the greater the praise, the smaller and less deserving of it he felt himself to be. At present, he was so overwhelmed by the praise that he found himself earnestly praying for it to stop.

'Lord of Heaven, let this cup pass' was the only way he could think of to express his desire.

A portion of this feeling was a natural humility that attended his character. Yet he was also suffering the humility of conscience. In the relative peace that followed the return to camp, a former battle had resumed in Hamlet's being. It was the battle for his thoughts. The warring camps had returned.

Thoughts of Ophelia—her eyes and her smile, chiefly, but also of her blown kiss—made up the protagonist camp. Into this peace, the images of those two camp followers bursting out of that tent continually invaded. Recognizing that the worst of these skirmishes for hegemony over his musings raged whenever his mind and hands were free of labor, he sought out extra duties and details in camp, and he performed them to the uttermost. Thus, he was able to evade the struggle for many of his daytime hours. But the nights until he could fall into the forgetfulness of sleep became a scene of torture for him.

Moreover, his reputation as one hardworking and eager to serve grew to a praise that only heightened his sense of being undeserving of it. The result was that day and night, he felt like a tightly coiled spring with wanting to be the noble youth he was trying so desperately to be. Yet never could his introspection agree with what was said of him. Ergo, he tried all the harder to live up to the righteousness credited to him. This only won him more praise that he could not measure for the depths of his sinking self-image. He wondered how long he could not only sustain this effort of work but also hide the effort and the strain of it. 'Surely it will end in madness,' he thought sadly.

Finally, in the night, one night, as his companions slept, he surrendered the struggle for his mind and allowed his thoughts to roam, speculate, project. He held one rule. These earthy thoughts would not touch Ophelia. She would remain above them, unsullied, while the lustful thoughts had their hour. Then when the scenes were played out, when the pressure was gone, he rolled onto his side to let his whimpered *mea culpas* carry him to sleep.

In a short passing of days, he fell into a pattern: fill the day with work or training, maintain a cheer through dinner, wait for the others to sleep when it grew dark, then allow his desires to fashion scenes until, with the camp followers' laughter turned derisive in his ears, the scenes left him to his remorse and weary oblivion. It was in this threadbare emotional state that Hamlet received the approbation of his fellow warriors in the great hall of Schleswig. He was grateful, oh, so grateful. But at the same time, their praise did not so much fill his heart as it expanded into the pit of his stomach, a hollow glory.

The cheering died away, and Hamlet was happy to listen to the praise accorded to other men, men who had faced their enemies and overcome them. 'How blessed they are!' he thought with a touch of envy and yet with true joy on their account. But mostly, he was relieved that the attention had finally passed him by.

To his great happiness, he listened to Sir Hugh, who rose to speak of Laertes.

"Gentles all and also men of war, I speak a praise of my young squire. At the start of this, he had much ado to attach himself to me for service. But I accepted him on good repute, and I have had no cause to regret that decision. He has performed his duties to a degree of excellence that masks his young age. By reason of his greenness at war, I held him in check throughout much of the engagement we now celebrate, not desiring that he should be too easily overmatched by foes of more experience. To this constraint, he humbly submitted though I oft perceived him straining at the start. But upon the route of the Germans that day, I let slip the reins and followed close, ready to prevent tragedy with quick aid. Yet will I tell you now, he brought down two of his men with emerging skill that I cried 'Bravo!' at the second. This campaign hath shown us the promise of the future. And in this, Denmark may rest happy in both her prince and in her young men of valor. I salute, therefore, Laertes, son of Polonius!"

"Laertes, son of Polonius!" echoed in the hall.

Hamlet was first to his feet with raised goblet while the others followed quickly with continued cheering. He would gladly have cheered himself hoarse. And he was happy to receive a smile of gratitude from his hero and the brother of the girl he loved. Laertes's smile reminded him so much of Ophelia that Hamlet's love for her was also poured out into his enthusiasm. He allowed all the tension of the previous days to drain out of him with cheering.

At the conclusion, as the next leader rose to shower praise on some junior knight, Hamlet felt purged and happily weary. He imagined the joy of relating this scene to Ophelia on his return. And in this, he opened a door.

The exultation of that portion of the evening carried him through the night immediately following. Lying on his cot, in his mind he played out a reunion scene with Ophelia in which he described Laertes's part in the battle and the unanimous praise of his comrades. It was so strong and fresh in his mind that the two camp women had no chance to intrude that night. This pleased him mightily. He decided then, against his earlier stance, that he would allow pleasant fabrications of days with Ophelia to help keep the other thoughts out.

This tactic appeared to work for the most part. The occasional reappearance of his darker fantasies, which he now referred to as his "bad dreams," had been reduced at least to some proportion of equilibrium. The threat of madness slipped back below the horizon of his concerns. Though he still felt possessed of a shriveled nobility of character and shrank from any praise offered him, he saw himself at least capable of seeing life through to adulthood. And he was able to count the days with hope until his return to Elsinore and Ophelia.

*****

The terraced garden remained cool under the shadows of late summer, where four ancient leaf-laden oaks stood sentinel, each in its corner. That is how Hamlet pictured it. That is how he found it. He knew the garden and all its seasons intimately and loved it in all its aspects. Here he had toddled. Here he had exercised his love of reading. Its walls were the first castle he defended with his first wooden sword, a present from his father on his saint's name day. Here he had sat with Ophelia to listen to the troubadour recount his sad song about the sad knight. Now here he was again, just returned home and eager to reexplore every corner of the keep.

His mother mistook his restlessness as a response to boredom following the adventure of war. He knew better. He was appreciating his home. He knew even better. There was always a chance that he might "chance" upon Ophelia. Thus, he found himself, book in hand, often relocating from room to room.

Just so, he stepped out onto the portico from the keep and peered through the deep shade of the garden below him. He knew what he would see, and he knew whom he hoped to see. Though he had no great expectation of finding Ophelia anywhere there—certainly not unchaperoned—yet he could hope. So it was that he, coming to the garden to read his book, looked for Ophelia, and he found her.

She sat at a bench toward the far end, also reading. Hamlet's pulse grew to a pounding like the surf upon the rock beneath the Sea Tower. He waited a moment for the surge to subside. In that same time, he collected his thoughts. 'Well, you who rode so boldly 'gainst the foe when it was called for, can you not take the next shaky step?' He prodded himself off the portico and down the steps into the shade.

"Mistress Ophelia! I am glad to see you well."

"My Lord Hamlet. They told me you had returned. Glad am I that you are safely home."

"My thanks. Your words complete my welcome. Is Laertes settled in?"

"Aye, my lord. And for all that he is humble, he walks tall i' the house. Father is so proud. We have had good report of him."

"That can I confirm. His service to Sir Hugh was exemplary. I saw them together at the most desperate point of our action 'gainst the Germans. He was the image of calm though Sir Hugh says he strained against the slips to be at the enemy. And later, he brought down two of the foes with admirable skill. Though that I did not witness, for I was called as messenger to other parts of the field. Glad am I that he has proved himself so well. Father—the king—also says he shows great promise."

"You are very kind to tell me. But what news of yourself?"

"Well, in fulfillment of self-prophecy, I come back saddle sore and better able to sleep on my feet at need, e'en in the rain! Oh, and my best tunic has not let go the manly odor of camp smoke." This caused a crumpled smile and a dip in her brows to appear on Ophelia's face.

"I have caught whiffs of better service from you than camp smoke, my lord. But sure, your humility, which I also heard spoke of, will not own it. Fear it not, I will sniff it out from other sources." She slid to one side of her bench and drew her skirts in to give him room.

He sat and looked about as if surveying the garden for the first time. His mind scrambled for some subject. "Eh, is Nurse hereabouts?" He glanced about with pretended purpose. "Surely, she is not asleep under some fern, else, if she be like my old nurse, the air would be thick with snoring." Ophelia laughed at this. 'Good.'

"No, my lord. She visits a sister this morning and leaves me here for safekeeping, with the injunction that I leave not the garden."

"Well, you are safe then."

"Nurse has a traditional concern for my virtue that hovers even in her absence. She took me to task for my lip-blown token of good will at your departure for the wars!"

'Was it only *good will?*' he thought. 'No, she must be shy of her words. Well, to continue the advance.' "Your token of good will gave good cheer to my mount."

"Your mount?"

"Aye, it lifted me so that he felt no weight settle on him until the border of Schleswig recalled me to thoughts of duty." Again, her laughter, oh, that he could spend eternity making her laugh so!

"Was 't potent then? Hm. Nurse had the right of it. We know not what work a smile can do, how deeply it delves or the shape of the message it imports upon the receiver. I must be more guarded then."

"Aye, with anyone but me!"

'What? Wait—wait! This won't do,' Hamlet chided himself. He opened his eyes and broke the spell of the moment. Though he had been fully awake, he roused himself as though from sleeping. Looking about, he studied Horatio's room again. He had been installed here while the Danes remained encamped about the Marcher Lord's castle. It took him a moment to come completely back to the present. He was not yet home. The army's return to Elsinore would not begin for three more days yet. But his thoughts of the garden had been so real and his mental talk with Ophelia so pleasant that even though he knew they were all made up, it was difficult to let them go. Then he recalled that his own admonishment had broken his thoughts off. 'What had I said? Oh, yes, it was something too round. Please, Lord, let me not slip into that when I truly do see Ophelia again!'

In that moment, he resolved that he must curb the conversation of his daydreams lest he get in the habit of being too forward and thereby alarming Ophelia into a repulse.

'You needn't worry about that with us, love!' spoke one of the camp followers coming out of the shadow of his mind.

"Oh, go away!" Hamlet hissed though he knew this was only his own inner voice working through his imagination.

'Now you know we won't do any such thing,' the woman spoke soothingly yet with a hint of hurt feelings. 'Why do you struggle so?' She sounded truly concerned. 'We're not leaving until you have what you want,' she added with playful seduction, her image swaying just enough to excite.

The other woman appeared with a giggle. 'Yes, sister. You know he wants us.'

"Please leave me alone. I was…busy."

'Oh, we know. It's that sweet missy of yours. Yes, she's a doll, that one. But you don't want to go to her all hot and bothered, especially now the blood's up! We won't be long. Then you can go back to her all calm-like and unafraid of any slips. See? We can help you with that. You don't want to be scaring her off with your 'urges,' do you? Now which of us is first for your fancy?'

"Oh, please!"

The second one giggled again as she moved closer. 'No, sweets, you're supposed to make us beg!'

*****

Hamlet's mind was not on his sword practice the next day. Even Osric was able to score a "palpable hit" against him. That was some new phrase the page picked up and kept testing at every opportunity. Olan stepped up to take Hamlet's place, and Osric, who should have cringed, crowed a short-lived defiance. Hamlet pondered his way back to the others at the side. Looking up, he saw Laertes standing off across the corner of the practice field. He had been watching. 'Perhaps Laertes can fathom my problem,' Hamlet thought, meaning only his poor showing at practice.

"Marcellus, might I speak with Laertes?"

"By all means, my lord. It may be his eyes can add something to my corrections."

Hamlet started for him and sensed that Laertes continued to study him on his approach. "Hola, Laertes." He tried to sound cheerful.

"Good day, my lord. How goes it with you?"

"I think you saw."

"Indeed, I saw you fighting a demon."

"Oh, Osric's not that fierce surely—"

"No, my lord. I meant a demon in the air or perhaps in your mind. Osric happened to be merely in the way and claimed the odd hit."

Hamlet nodded. "In my mind surely." He was almost ready to explain the problem of the two camp women. But second thoughts pointed out that this was the brother of that very special person. It would not do to confess to him a lust that would clearly disqualify him as a man of honor, worthy of the maid Ophelia.

"Do you still battle the Germans, my lord?" asked Laertes in the silence.

"Aye, two great, hulking Teutons, it seems." That was close enough to the truth to put an earnest tone in his voice and countenance.

Laertes fixed him a look that wondered where in the spectrum between literal and figurative these phantoms stood. "Your conviction is enigmatical, my lord. Are they that substantial in your thinking?"

"Substantial enough to win the bout for Osric, as it seems."

"That goes far."

"I think the high pitch of war bends up my spirit to this fever."

"That is apt, my lord. I think, had I not had my chance at those two Germans, who were already defeated in their minds—I'll not gainsay it—that is, had I no opportunity to strike a blow for Denmark and the proving of my manhood, I would likely be swatting at demons as well. Your day will come, my lord. And I concur that your actions in this were decisive. You may have saved us all.

If you cannot rest on these assurances, time and a goodly welcome home should restore you."

"I pray it subsides the sooner."

"Master Laertes," called a young page coming up on them from the tents. "Sir Hugh asks for you in his pavilion."

"I go. Thank you, Tip." He turned back to Hamlet. "Touching your demon, perhaps you should try to see it in your opponents and fight the flesh and blood of them."

"I shall. Thanks, good Laertes."

As Laertes strode away, Hamlet turned back toward his companions to see Olan finishing Osric off with a mean thrust. By the time he walked back to them, Marcellus was concluding the session. The others started moving off back to their tents, leaving Hamlet with his mentor.

"How fare's Master Laertes, my lord?"

"We spoke not of him, but he appears passing well."

"Had he insights for you?"

"He said I was fighting a demon of the air."

"Aye, I have seen that before in other pupils. I was about to conclude that your techniques smacked of distraction. Were we not so long in the field these weeks and so deep in the business of war and were you more idle about the camp to wander whither one should not, I'd have said 'love' hath shot his bolt to effect—what did Master Osric call it—a palpable hit! You've not encountered some fair face and shapely skirts at the castle of the Marcher Lord's these days?"

"No, Marcellus. I have eyes for no one here." Fortunately, his mentor did not press to ask the obvious question, "If not here, then where?"

"Perhaps you are simply duty-weary, my lord. I think you should give your companions a chance to excel at the menials. They have made the most of your diligence. And too much sail can strain the lines and snap the masts, if the wind picks up without warning. It may be a good ride into the outland on the morrow would prove a healthy physic for your distraction."

"I shall consider it. Thank you, Marcellus." 'Well, there are two goodly bits of advice for two problems wide of the mark,' he thought as Marcellus walked away. Yorick was correct about misdiagnosing an ailment.

Crossing the field again to head for his room at the keep, Hamlet saw the chaplain's tent pitched on one side of the practice field. He stopped for a moment. Father Frances might be one in whom he could confide. 'Certainly, morality of the mind was in his purview and confessions his chief line of work in an idle camp.' He had made the priest's acquaintance at the start of the campaign but found the man busy with pat exhortations to chastity that marked him judgmental in nature. Consideration of what sort of ashes and sackcloth the man would prescribe for absolution of his particular sins wrung Hamlet's stomach the other direction from his concerns. He simply could not move willingly into the circle of public penance, and he did not know the man well enough to expect much in the way of effective solace. With this for consideration, Hamlet resumed his walk, angling away from the chaplain's tent.

*****

The tedium of the return march was broken occasionally by small triumphs in some of the major towns through which they passed. The Danish force began to shrink somewhat as contingents dropped off to return to their homes and farms. The medieval army was not a standing force. Disintegration was in its nature.

Traveling in deep summer, the days were hotter and the road dustier. But Hamlet preferred a parched throat to sleeping in mud. With the stress of war behind them, the soldier's talk was more jovial and fuller of carnal thoughts. The excesses of camp life continued at the daily halts but with decreasing frequency and intensity as men neared their family responsibilities.

Hamlet never again saw the two women of that day—save in his own mind. He surmised them to have been local girls. He did see others quietly slipping into tents as dark descended on the camps. He heard female laughter and some snatches of discourse from some of the tents at times, but it was not the raucous glee of that first day. Still, if a woman's laughter carried to his tent at night, it set off the "bad dreams" and despoiled his slowly growing catalogue of imagined moments with Ophelia. When that occurred, he was glad that the next day's despondence in the saddle could be easily attributed to the weary miles.

*****

Came the day that Castle Elsinore appeared in the distance. A cheer went up and some of the knights sang a hymn of thanksgiving. Hamlet breathed a sigh of relief. In the compound ahead were his mother, his friend Horatio, the long neglected but not forgotten artifacts of his room, deep conversations with Yorick, and chance meetings with Ophelia. He had a notion that with himself safely ensconced within the keep, the two sisters could not assail him. The war was over. He was content.

To the question "What will you do with your first night back home?" Marcellus replied, "There are at the least two taverns in the town where my tab is not too excessive. I mean to sample the wares like a connoisseur, recount the recent wars with my old Da, and then sleep through the dawn and the next day until my back hurts."

"You've no woman to go to?" asked Olan.

"First drink, then talk, then sleep, then a woman, each in its proper time, proportion, and order. Any deviation from that will knock the orbit of the world a kilter. There's time for each, and no need to set the terms of one's life a wobble."

"By my faith, I'd take the reverse order," offered Fenris.

"You'd never make it past the woman, lad." The others laughed heartily, and the subject dropped as they entered the city by the gate. The cheers upon their return outdid those of their departure. Hamlet looked as they rode by, but no one appeared at the oriel window to Ophelia's house. 'Perhaps she is at the court,' he consoled himself. It made sense that she would be there with her father and the rest to welcome the king and her brother—and him.

Soon, the march column passed into the castle yard and different groups fanned out left and right to fill the open area with cheering voices and happy, relieved faces. The queen and her ladies stood on the broad steps leading up to the keep. Just in front of and below them stood Hamlet's uncle Claudius with Polonius beside him. Ophelia was among the ladies on the steps. Her face was radiant with joy. Her smile at recognizing Hamlet set his pulse to racing. He feared he might begin to blush at it. But then, after only a moment, he noticed her looking beyond him at the march column that followed. She cupped her hands and brought them to her face and began bouncing on her toes like a child. Though she had covered her mouth, a light sparkled in her eyes to confirm her smile. By this, Hamlet knew she had sighted Laertes coming into the yard beside Sir Hugh.

The king stopped and dismounted in front of Claudius. A groom took charge of his mount and led it away. As the royal pages rode by angling off to the right, Hamlet's father faced about and beckoned his son to dismount and join him. The prince looked at Marcellus.

"Give me the reins, my lord. I'll see to him," said his mentor, indicating Hamlet's horse.

"Thanks, good Marcellus. I will attend to him in the stables."

"You have family matters here, my lord, and there be grooms enough have had little to do here in our absence."

"Very well." Hamlet handed over the reins and dismounted. His father waited for him to join him before turning back to face Claudius.

"Your Majesty is well come," said the regent, smiling broadly. Polonius bowed in silence. Then Claudius looked over their heads to the crowd and announced, "Hail to the victor over our foes!"

The cheers rose in volume, the men in the column joining in as well.

"Our thanks, dear brother. And our gratitude for your service to the state during our absence in these wars. Our business in Schleswig being concluded, we are ready to take up once again the direct rule over the realm. We shall meet hereafter to receive your reports, but for the nonce, there are other welcomes long looked forward to."

His father looked up to meet his mother's eyes. Claudius and Polonius bowed and parted, one to each side, allowing the king to ascend to his queen. Hamlet followed a step behind and to the left of his father. At the king's mention of Schleswig, Hamlet remembered his friend Horatio and gave a quick glance about. He was not immediately visible. 'He is in the crowd,' he thought. 'I shall make my way through this and go find him.'

The king and queen stood face-to-face and embraced in that polite fashion of public accolades, brushing each other's cheeks with kisses. Then his mother looked aside to Hamlet. The prince moved forward, dropping to one knee, took his mother's proffered hand, and kissed it. Thinking quickly, he smiled mischievously as he looked up from her hand. "I have brought my father safely back from the wars, Mother!"

With a laugh, she pulled him to his feet, and together they suffered the public a warm embrace.

"He speaks more truth than he knows," said his father warmly. "But we shall hear more of that anon."

The queen studied her son's eyes with something more than love. Was there a sadness in them?

"What is't, Mother?"

There was a hesitancy, then she spoke softly. "If you have been seeking Horatio, you must find him in his chamber. He has had the fever."

The queen's words fell like a blow. "Does he get on?"

"You will see anon. Give your people here a required moment, then should you go find him." She gently turned him to face the crowd. The king also turned and raised his right arm high, almost in a benediction over the people. Hamlet endured the cheers for them all while his heart trembled for his friend.

*****

Excusing himself as soon as the king and queen and all the attendants entered the great hall, Hamlet strode at nearly a run to Horatio's room. He took two steps at a time on the stairs. The door was closed. He knocked and heard a feeble cough in response. Opening it slowly and peering around the door, he saw Horatio sitting on his cot propped with pillows. He looked pale, and his sensitive eyes were deeply shadowed, but his friend managed a weak smile upon seeing the prince.

"By Lord, forgive be for dot risink." He sat forward as if to rise.

"Be still, you ninny." Hamlet approached the cot. Horatio pointed to a chair beside the cot, and Hamlet took a seat. "How fare you, dear friend?"

"I ab on the bend, by lord." He sniffed. "Allow be but a few bore weeks, and we shall go ridink."

"Take all the time you need, good Horatio. I shall attend you myself now that I'm back. It seems the wars were safer for you had you come with us. But I am here for you daily. And I shall bring Yorick with me to help cheer you."

At this, Horatio's eyes betrayed a great sorrow. Hamlet caught it, and his blood chilled. "What is't?"

"Yorick, he is dead, by Lord. 'Twas he took the fever first and succumbed to it early in the bonth. I'b so sorry."

In the silence, Hamlet heard the flames licking up the wood in the hearth. Suddenly, one log burned through and collapsed with a clunk and a shower of sparks. The noise caused Hamlet to flinch. He saw tears starting down Horatio's face. Slowly and silently, Hamlet rose after a time and peered out the small window that illuminated the chamber. Looking out, he observed everything outside in the castle yard that there was to see, but he saw none of it.

"Yorick," he whispered, "you were supposed to live forever."

# Chapter 11

Hamlet visited his mirror image once again even though what-ever changes attended him in the last three years were not read-ily discernable to him. Why three years as a mark? It had been that long since his discovery of Ophelia's charms, since he had marched off to war and returned with his reputation in disequilibrium with himself, and since he had tasted the tragedy of Yorick's death, a triple watershed of woe, especially when one considered his use of the time.

We mentioned his woes. What were they now? Laertes's absence to Paris and school he felt surely though he had never truly cultivated a familiar friendship other than to give and receive a sort of mutual appreciation. Yorick, he missed keenly, especially when he considered the loss of the man's practical wisdom in helping him to understand the warring spirits within him.

Horatio was also gone. Two years back, he had returned to his home of Schleswig. In that time, they maintained a correspondence that spoke of tentative steps into philosophy. Horatio still had not mentioned girls in any of his missives, so the subject appeared to remain a point where their friendship could not connect.

For his thought-life and his "bad dreams," which were all one, he had settled into a pattern designed to ease the humors of the night but which by day attended him as a backdrop of guilt. This practice devolved into a confession of "impure thoughts" whenever he went to Fra Ignacio for shriving. Even this became a confusion of terms that created a dilemma in Hamlet's attempts to nail down in his soul how much was "thought." All the penance in the world did not seem to clean the stain. He began to think that though he might escape hell, yet he was destined for an eternity in purgatory and may have begun serving his time already. Life, therefore, became a series of efforts to dull the guilt and the grief.

And what of Ophelia? To be sure, she remained on her pedestal—where he had placed her—pure and sweet, a human Holy Grail, beyond Hamlet's deserts. Several factors operated here. First were the romantic notions of the *chansons*. These he had taken to heart. In them, the knight and his lady maintained their chastity throughout joint and solo adventures—at least the best of them did and those who did not had fallen. In his own mind, Hamlet hung somewhere in between, like a male demi-vierge, thinking always in the sensual realm but never acting. Though his dark thoughts still did not touch Ophelia, yet he could accuse himself of a nightly adultery of the mind with the camp women. This self-knowledge of his baser side constituted the second factor and pushed him further out of reach of her.

Third, despite Hamlet's earlier protestations that the court ladies made up no seraglio, yet they moved protectively together like a harem and, in a way, that admitted of no private audience. What chance was there for Hamlet to spend an afternoon of amiable chatter in the garden of more than his daydreams? What chance to say anything to her while in the company of the nurse that would communicate his admiration, his love, without scandalizing her? What would he say anyway, he being unworthy to possess her affections in anything but his own thoughts. If he detected at odd times a deference in her for him born of affection, she showed no frustrations over the same enforced distance between them. Either she was more patient and accepting of the situation, or he was not as centered in her existence as she was in his, another woe.

Finally, as this third year moved toward the autumn and his own departure loomed large on the horizon, the futility of forming a relationship, even of the purest love, between them could only be measured in the miles between Elsinore and Wittenberg, where he would begin his own schooling. 'We will be apart for years, and who knows what I shall return to' became his latest mournful cry.

Woe upon woe, and on top of all this was the sure realization in Hamlet's mind that Ophelia had grown in grace and beauty whereas he, by the juxtaposition of his mirrored self to his image of her, felt himself far short of anything desirable of looks.

But we spoke of changes in the mirror. Certainly, he was taller. He stood eye to eye with his mother, who assured him that there would be at least one more growth spurt to bring him to his father's stature. His arms showed more muscle, and his shoulders were broader. He was now the best of the swordsmen among the royal pages. But that was no consolation for his woes since he had assumed that position only upon the departure of Laertes.

He would not call himself comely. Indeed, he saw himself awkward in that fledgling sort of way, all fluffed and disorganized feathers (his eternally unruly hair did much for that impression) and fixing with wild-eyed stares the confusing world about him. It would be pushing it to attempt to make anything of the light down on his upper lip, and his voice was cracked like the flagstones just outside the stables. Sure, that put an end to his punning and his wordplay until such time as he could affect them without a leap or a sudden descent in the pitch. Thus stood the future king of Denmark!

"How all occasions do inform against me," he said to his dim and distorted, brass-tinted self at length. "I'd rather address my drawn and quartered innards than you, my friend." He sighed and turned from the mirror to resume his packing.

"When I was a child, I thought as a child." This he spoke to the room at large and to certain objects within it in particular. How many of these things had dropped out of his interests? How many more would fall away upon his return some years hence? He continued to study the setting with hands on hips.

Presently, taking up a short walking stick he found leaning against a chair, he struck the top of a deer skull used to prop up a few books on the table. "Speak! I charge thee, speak!"

"What should I say but ouch?"

Had the familiar voice not come from behind him, Hamlet might have started. As it was, the unexpectedness of it still made him pivot sharply. "Marcellus, what make you here?"

"A disposition to a concern, my lord."

"Concern?"

"You have lost your mirth of late. You have not the manner of a young man about to be turned loose into the larger world."

"To me, the larger world looks a yawning maw."

"Is't an object of fear to you then?"

"Dread rather. I meant 'yawning' in the sense of 'tiresome.' 'Tis the dark void and not the teeth swallows my mirth."

"Think then but that the dark void is all a lack of familiarity. Once you have settled and can remember your way to the tavern and back from your student's quarters, the large world will shrink again to daily usage. You might find companionship of a more suitable nature than has presented itself here. I know you have sorely lacked for kindred kind among the other pages these last two years." He read Hamlet's wonder in his slightly raised brows and continued.

"Well, Olan and Fenris have moved on to bigger and better one, supposes. I taught them at least enough to get them into trouble. I pray it was also enough to get them back out of it. Jürgen stagnates under his self-sufficiency, and Osric remains a lusty infant. There is no other promise among the rest. It is time for a prodigy to appear— but I digress. Will you be seeing Master Horatio on your way?"

"I have been invited to visit him on my journey up. And I shall that kind offer take."

"Splendid, my lord. Please pass to him my regards. For one so empowered by thought, he did show some promise at arms. Oh, you must also remember to seek out a good sword master at Wittenberg and thus keep your form and your strength. I will expect improvement upon your return."

"I shall, thank you." All through this exchange, Hamlet found himself surprised at Marcellus's insights into his character and at the man's concern for his mood. He began to wonder if he had missed an opportunity for solid spiritual mentoring from his trainer. The thought almost depressed him the more as he realized that there was now no time to make amends for that miscall. Yet he was cheered that this rugged man of war had thought to come by and ask after him. Perhaps there was time for one important question. His mind spun to formulate one, something whose answer would sustain him for the journey at least. 'Think, think,' he thought, and a silence grew.

"Well, I shall not take any more of your time, my lord. Know that my best wishes and good prayers, such as they are, go with you." He started to turn for the door.

"Marcellus?"

"Yes, my lord?"

"You mentioned prayer. Do you trust your prayers?" He could see the man considering a thoughtful response.

"There has always been an answer to them, my lord, though not always the answer I desired. A generous few were a definite 'nay' while other answers came better than I could have—or would have—affected for myself, even were I God himself. Your psalmist says, 'Some trust in chariots and some in horses, but we will remember the name of the Lord, our God,' or some such words. Though I am read, I am not entirely versed in the Holy Writings."

"Just enough to get you out of trouble?"

"Exactly, my lord."

"Thank you, Marcellus. Could I trust my prayers, I might have more cause for mirth."

"Where is your trust then, my lord?"

"I have yet to find my trust. Perhaps it will come to me in Wittenberg. For I go there to learn."

"But if your trust be not in God, then in whom?"

"I trust God *is* God. It is my prayers I doubt. To me, they linger like damp smoke to swirl and eddy and never rise. And as such, they leave my eyes red and stinging."

"Think you he would not consider the earnest prayers of a future king of Denmark? The young Solomon was able to post his prayers before the Lord and received wisdom and wealth for his troubles. So says my Da. Be of good cheer. Your prayers will fly up, my lord."

"'Tis my hope at any hazard. Again, I thank you, Marcellus. Always you do good service to Denmark."

"My service is my joy, my lord." With a bow, he turned and went out the doorway.

"But for what should I pray that the Lord would honor it?" he spoke to the incorporeal air. "I have prayed for deliverance but to no avail. I am told God will deliver me from my enemies, but he will leave me to the meager mercies of my friends. 'My friends.' How can I unmake these two phantasmal sisters as friends, them who nightly attend me, being both wanted and unwanted at the same time? Even in the act of renouncing them, within me stands the desire not to send them entirely off. No, not yet. But when?"

*****

On the afternoon before he was to leave, Hamlet's restlessness grew to a stress as taut as a drawn bowstring. He was leaving Ophelia without anything having passed between them but the shallowest, if well-intentioned, pleasantries. His desperation fought with his practical side. In struggling to fashion a declaration of his feelings, the argument turned from "*What* can I say?" to "What *can* I say?"

What could demonstrate the depth without the desperation? What could elicit a favorable response from her that was not an unfair call to a commitment that should have to stretch across distance and time? How could he explain love in the purest sense in which he felt it that touched the height of the *chansons* but remained as simple as the word *love* itself? What could fill the gap of his three-year silence and turn one afternoon's confession into a lasting love?

In this frame of mind, he found himself, as was his habit, walking up and down in the great hall, staring vacantly at an open book. Almost exactly as on that day just over three years before, he heard a rustle of skirts and some snatches of feminine chatter. He looked up to see the queen leading her ladies once again across the hall up to her apartments. Without thinking but with desperate resolve, he strode the length of the dais on a path to intercept them. All the way, he kept his eyes on Ophelia.

She had grown in height and possessed a slender, willowy build and a graceful manner. This he saw when she looked back at him. As before, she had been listening to the talk of a woman walking beside her. The woman caught her locked gaze at Hamlet and let her discourse fade away in midsentence. This dropped thought caught the attention of the queen and made her look about in curiosity. She saw her son approaching like an oared galley at ramming speed. Everyone went silent and stopped. Hamlet kept his gaze fixed on Ophelia lest the now blatant stares of everyone else dissuade him from his purpose. Ophelia's look turned helpless. Two paces from the group, Hamlet stopped. Time froze.

"Mistress Ophelia," he finally croaked out. "A word with you?"

Ophelia shot a quick glance to the queen, who nodded and then addressed the rest of her entourage. "Ladies?" She turned forward to continue on to her rooms. The others followed, leaving Ophelia and Hamlet to continue their study of each other's faces.

Behind Ophelia stood the open doorway to the terraced garden, the scene of so many of Hamlet's daydreams of her, of them. With an unintended brusqueness, he closed the distance and took her by the wrist, pulling her out into the daylight.

They continued across the portico with broad strides, and he got down the steps. She halted at the top. His grasp of her wrist, not being a tight one, broke. At the bottom, he turned to look up at her.

"My lord, your manly stride does not suit a lady's skirts." Her words started out as an apology. But then, a virtuous indignation took possession of her. She pouted as she looked beyond him toward the far end of the garden, whither it appeared he was leading her. "Speak. I'll go no farther!"

For Hamlet, though the setting and the girl were the same, the mood, different from anything he had ever imagined, called him to improvise. He could remember none of his opening lines to her in all those daydreams.

"Ophelia." His tone was everywhere and nowhere in the range of his emotions, unanchored. Yet it had some effect for she softened.

"Aye, my lord?"

"May we sit?" He indicated the middle step below her and brushed away a few fallen leaves. She warmed to a smile at the oddity of his choice for this, stepped down to his level, and offered him her hand in courtly fashion for him to take and help seat her. On second thoughts, Hamlet decided he could not sit, not yet, but began to pace in front of her. Her look turned quizzical.

After two complete oscillations before her in silence, he stopped and stared at the side wall of the garden, at its top. But his gaze followed his thoughts beyond that and back into time.

"I have wasted three years," he said almost to himself.

"Wasted, my lord?"

"Oh, thrown them away entirely!"

"Your reputation gives the lie to any charge of indolence against you, my lord."

He turned to face her, her whose eyes now bore into his soul. "My reputation is one thing. It is the outward me. And it is some time at odds with the inner me."

"'Tis clear now, you are troubled, my lord. I pray I am not the cause."

"The cause, the source, and the essence." This made her nearly as unsettled as he. He saw what his words had done, far from his intent. "Peace. It is not a displeasure you evoke."

"What then, my lord?"

He studied the confusion in her countenance and recalled Yorick's words like an echo. 'I would counsel a slow simmering of this pot. Be like the cook who seasons sparingly and tastes often.' He was right. Here was no place for ardor. Perhaps he should take her back to the last known point.

"I spoke of three years back. Recall you what that brings us to?"

"Aye, my lord. 'Twas the first day we spoke together." She looked downward at this for a moment, then back up to his gaze, a genuflection of her eyes that affirmed in his heart all his love for her.

"Do you remember it well?"

"Passing well, my lord, such a pleasant day as that."

"Pleasant? That's odd. You were thoroughly wetted!"

"'Twas an adventure fitting the dreams of my age: to be rescued by a prince."

"Truly, as I spoke then, you were in no peril."

"You rescued me from tedium, my lord."

"Tedium?"

"Nurse's devotionals were growing worn. I could mouth them like a poor player. Thereafter, in her droning, I returned to your gallantry quite often in my mind."

"That moment only?"

"And the few more we passed: our afternoon here with Master Guilliame and our walk after, and your passing out with the great company to the wars."

"Did Nurse take you to task for your blown…good will?"

She laughed at this. "She threatened to drag me to the stocks"—here she whispered—"for harlotry!"

At this, he finally relaxed, smiled even. What is more, he could see that her eyes invited him to declare himself.

"I, too, have returned to those scenes. For me, they have comprised the only joy of these three years. I must confess that I had sorely wished to add to them by your further company. And in all that time, I have done nothing but wish."

"Be that the waste you decry, my lord?"

"Aye—and now—I go. But what could I have done? When could we have spoken? And what could we have said?"

"Peace, my lord. I think we have spoken together after a fashion and much in our separate fancies. Three years is a long time for dreams not to grow in the telling."

"You too?"

She nodded happily in response. "I even invited Yorick's dragon into a few. We tamed him once and flew together a-dragon-back to visit Laertes in Paris. 'Twas a longtime favorite of mine."

"Well then, my fancies pale in comparison. No, truly, they are merely a collection of discourses here in the garden."

"Back at the far bench?" She pointed that way with her eyes.

"Aye, and never on these unworthy steps!"

"I am content here. And—look not upward, my lord, but trust me—we are in view from the queen's window above. It is best here to be seen but not o'erheard. At least we may talk freely."

"Agreed. Hence, I should remain standing or familiarity will summon a pair of ears. And besides, talking only was my intent, always."

"Truly?"

"Without a 'may I' or 'buy your leave,' I dare not fashion else. I can command that much restraint though your proposed flight to Paris calls to my imagination. Still, we shall but talk."

"We shall have our day a-dragon-back, my lord. And if it be not today, yet it will come. We must wait."

"Are you steeled for such a wait? I cannot ask you to—"

"To wait while you go?"

"Aye, go—and for years. That's the manner of my desperation. It is not born of passion thwarted but of opportunities lost. Yet you have given me a hope, one to which I'll not hold you. Fear it not."

"I thank you, my lord, but I am not assailed by suitors as yet."

"They must be blind!"

"Or too considering of their advantage in marriage for a minister's daughter."

"Sure, they are blind. You are a treasure beyond all earthly advantage." Her blush deepened at this.

"You wax poetic, my lord."

"It is a flaw in my character, especially where beauty is concerned."

"That's too polished." She laughed. "Do you quote now from your inventions?"

"Discovered. There will be no wooing you from out of my 'fancy,' as you call it."

"Still, it is a sweet sentiment. I thank you." A moment of silence from them both was filled with the song of a bird up in the branches. "My lord?"

"Hm?"

"Dare we call this love?"

"It is very like, from all I have read. So will I call it and swear by it! Thus, by your leave and before I take leave, I will say I love you. There, that's done."

"Go you now in peace to Wittenberg?"

"I am satisfied but not happy. And you?"

"Sure, my lord. I am in love."

*****

Hamlet remained on deck through most of the daylight hours of his voyage. As the islands of his homeland slipped by him, he reflected on his meeting with Ophelia. At first, it seemed to him enough to sustain him through the duration of his years away. Then he doubted. Then he resolved it would have to be. They spoke together for another hour. At one point, he stole a quick glance upward toward the keep and saw a face at the queen's window. 'Well,' he thought, 'that gives them some meaningful task and a taste of rotating the watch, sentry-like.'

Ophelia was gracious enough to recount some of her daydreams of them together. They impressed him with an inventiveness and a lightness that left the *chansons* sinking in the mire of form while they rose like autumn leaves born on the sea breeze. In comparison, his own fancies were truly all discourses, witty at times, but in the main, they were attempts to define or establish their relationship. They were more philosophy than romance.

Now as he stood at the ship's rail and measured the increasing distance between them in the rolling of the deck, he wondered why his own daydreams had been so heavy. 'She never could have suffered such long discourses,' he thought. Why had he not thought to concoct for them a daring rescue or the overthrow of a rival at love?

'Sure, my thoughts are weighted,' he concluded. 'They are heavy with guilt, for one, and not just over the two sisters (as he now referred to the camp women).' There had been a certain guilt attached to the notion that in his fabricated thoughts of her, he was borrowing her life, appropriating her eyes and her smile for his own use, the which he had no right to do. That at least had been set to rights by common agreement between them to dream of each other to their heart's content. It was the only pledge between them. Still, the heaviness in his thoughts troubled him. Why could he not simply think of her without the mass of doubts and the fear of overspeculating?

He formed an idea that her purer feelings served to lift her thoughts upward, give them freedom to please and to take wing, to move playfully through her mind, like the swifts that swooped and rose in the cool evenings about the castle yard. To be sure, his feelings for her were pure. She stood in his musings like an angel of light, not by reason of her beauty alone but for her absolute lack of guile or pretense. He longed to reach out to her spirit as to one capable of his salvation.

He, on the other hand, found himself to be too calculating. Even the purity he maintained toward her had his deserts of her as its aim. It was enforced and encased in a hard shell he was building within himself to keep away the baser desires that would break into it to destroy it and consummate his damnation.

"Love should be easier than this," he spoke to the foaming wake that rushed by. His life, to him, was becoming a *chanson*, one with a limping form and a litany of mischances. He wondered if, in the telling of it, it would produce damp kerchiefs or if the pathos were too strained. This heaviness affected every part of his being and how he received life itself.

In his dinner discourses with the ship's captain, he listened as the man spoke of the seaworthiness of various craft in his experience. Some, like the one on which they now rode the waves, were truly wedded to the sea. There was in her spirit no struggle to push through the waters. There was only the joy of dancing upon them. That was Ophelia.

"She handles easily," said the captain in reference to his ship. "And yet her sister craft hath not her grace. She bucks the waves and defies the wind's prodding's. Like a jade, straining against the leads. And there's no accounting for the difference. Sure, there must be some defect in her lines, but it must be in her very heart. And for the one defect, her life upon the sea is a sore trial. Oh, she'll sail well enough i' the fair, but in squalls, all we must pray that her contrariness and her tortured ways lead her not upon some rocks."

'Am I like that sister ship?' he thought. 'Too ill-made to dance upon the waves? Would I be dashed upon the rocks in the first squall to come upon me? The captain said that all we must pray. We are back again at prayers. Do I mistrust my prayers? That's what I have told Marcellus, and he asked me where my trust resided. I must begin to answer that question e'en now and not wait upon the wisdom of Wittenberg.

'I trust God is God. I said that as well. He possesses all the attributes of divinity that we mortals have the capability to comprehend.

Yet God seems too far off there in his heaven. Sure, it must be that he has more important matters to attend to than the whimpering of a lovestruck prince. Must I find my trust nearer to earth? It is not in myself for I know myself too well. There are so many ideals that I come not near. I think of my father, my mother, Ophelia, Horatio, Yorick who was, and even Marcellus. There's a grace in them, a beauty of the soul. Sure, I feel it, and it warms me to them.

'Is that where my trust is? In them? Certainly, everything about them is to be trusted. They have not turned down the path that my thoughts have taken. They sleep the sleep of the guiltless while I, that am not made for easy repose, must twist the bedding up as I turn the eternal circuit of the night back to side, to front, round and round. Did I lie in the earth, I'd bore my way a yard a night with turning. Will I lie peaceful when I lie in the earth? That remains.

'Perhaps, there is something in the nearness of them that can be for my salvation. Some grace that from them I can glean by proximity and by study, some virtue to be learned of each of them. My tables, 'tis to be set down. I'll study them—well, my memory of them—now that distance makes them memories only. I'll sketch them in words and learn their graces that I might accomplish something good in myself by it.

'The scripture is right that says *put not your trust in princes*. Nay, trust none of us, not princes nor even demigods. Let Hercules himself, and such another, do what he may, yet this prince will trust in those who tread the ideal way!'

# Act 3

# Chapter 12

The rain had stopped at midday, and the sun shone golden upon towering clouds as they parted above the city of Wittenberg, reflecting golden light into the street. Seen from Hamlet's upper floor window, the puddles that formed in uneven parts of the cobblestone below gave the impression of pools of liquid gold. A warm breeze blew through his open window, promising a glorious afternoon and an evening for taking the air.

Yet Hamlet remained inside for the present. His studies called him to apply his careful thoughts to them for at least the next hour. But the passing minutes kept turning him from his duties. He reasoned that the weather, which had something of the sea in it, was too much like Elsinore's. It transported him, will-he-or-nil-he, not only across distance but also back in time to every day in his home that was like this one. He had but to close his eyes, and Wittenberg dissolved into its constituent atoms to drift cloudlike and resolve itself into images of Elsinore, Elsinore with Ophelia. And that thought held him there.

Conceding the futility of further concentration, Hamlet set his text down, leaving it open to the window light by which he studied, and reached over to take up the latest letter from her. It had arrived the day before, and he already had it nearly memorized. Early in his sojourn here, he had arranged for the courier to slip his letters to Ophelia in the castle whenever he sent correspondence for his mother and father. Likewise, Ophelia sent her responses on the sly by this same loyal retainer. Thus, neither the royal parents nor Polonius knew of this exchange. Truly, there was little, if anything, in them to take them to task over, as the letters were innocent enough.

There was nothing profound in Ophelia's missive, certainly nothing speaking directly of love, mostly the less pernicious bits of court gossip—she knew his dislike of slander. She described her latest "dream," which he understood without her mentioning it, to include him in a leading role. Indeed, Hamlet was able to read "love between the lines," as he termed it. She also mentioned a return visit to court from Master Guilliame, in which he presented a more uplifting conclusion to the *Chevalier mal fet* and was accorded a special monetary largesse for his pains.

Finally, she provided good word of Laertes's doings. It appeared that the Danish ambassador to Paris had taken him under his wing and was grooming him for duty at the French court. She owned an appreciation for her brother's care in describing "things French" for her to relate to the "slavering, culture-hungry" ladies of the queen's circle. This, she suggested, made her popular among them for she offered the information freely (Hamlet knew better and credited her popularity to her sweetness).

In short, her letters, though they lacked romantic ardor, satisfied him. Needless to say, his return letters were much the same, mostly anecdotes of his learning and points that he thought might interest her yet which were not too deep in import.

Paging quickly through her letter now, as though assuring himself that it was entirely present, no part being lost or mislaid, he turned back to his favorite section near the center and began to reread.

> I shall tell you of my latest dream, which I pray will be for your entertainment.
>
> In it, Nurse and I, while gone Maying in the woods without the city, were waylaid by fierce brigands who cared not that we were of the queen's court. Indeed, that intelligence, provided indignantly by Nurse with lack of forethought, only served to encourage them in the outrage in hopes of a larger, more royal ransom in exchange for our return.

I'll not horrify you with the threats to our persons uttered so menacingly by these louts. Suffice it to say, Nurse was kept from a long swoon only by a rough-handled prodding from a paunchy villain who seemed to fancy her. His repeated suggestions of a life of lawless bliss together with her in some woodland fastness kept her aquiver with terror. Whether this was ill-considered mischief or if he truly had set his cap for her, I could in no wise tell. But I think you might laugh with me now to reflect on the scene.

There were Nurse and he in a cycle of threat—swoon—prod—a yelp—romantic entreaty—refusal—another threat—swoon—prod and so on, as we were transported deeper into the woods. We made an uneasy camp for the night and were provided meager fare, sufficient to keep our strength up for further walking on the morrow.

To shorten matters to essentials, an errant knight of royal stature [by this he knew she meant Hamlet] came upon us by stealth and spoke to me in whispers from behind the tree to which Nurse and I were tethered. He assured me that matters were well in hand and that I had but to persevere through a short time and all would be set to rights.

The gallantry in his words and the tone—if tone could be got from whispering—are still in my ears as I write these. [She could still hear Hamlet's voice in his letters as he could hear hers in this reading.] His last words were "Be ready." Then his voice disappeared into the dark, and I was left to imagine him. I saw him with bright blue eyes, and something of his vibrato bespoke a tousled shock of blond hair that caused an unaccounted for shiver of glee in my being. A firm chin, well-defined jawline, and a pensive brooding brow surmounting a noble proboscis completed the countenance [Hamlet warmed to her description of him].

How I longed to stand with him vis-à-vis and confirm my mental image [read that: 'I long to see your face again and to know that your feelings have not changed,' he thought]. Indeed, his visage remained with me until I slipped into the realm of sleep ['I dreamed that I dreamt of you']. So in this way, I know not how much time passed.

However long my uneasy and upright repose was, I awoke to a sense of impending action. Sure enough, in an instant, the "zip and thunk" of arrows flying to their mark preceded by half seconds the grunt of surprise and the sudden felling of our two guards simultaneously. Starting with a flinch, I brought my arms around and thus discovered that my bonds had been cut. I was free, therefore, to essay an escape. I remembered that Nurse was with me and, as she had slept on sitting up beside me, was still oblivious to the situation.

The demise of our immediate captors roused no one else of the camp. I took a chance and shook my companion. She moaned, and I shushed her as she came to consciousness. I quickly clamped my hand over her mouth to prevent her from crying out. Our eyes met, and I communicated that we were on the verge of freedom and that to complete the caper, we must observe strict silence. I asked her to determine if her bonds were likewise severed. Almost instantly, she brought her hands around, and when I asked if she was ready—my hand still covering her mouth against an involuntary squeak—she nodded affirmatively.

Thinking that our best chance lay in embracing the most immediate darkness, I indicated that we slowly, and with determined silence, slip around to the back side of our tree, as regard the campfire, and follow its shadow into the deep of night.

We had about brought this plan to successful fruition when Nurse stumbled heavily on a fallen branch and went to ground with a great *oof!* This woke the captain of the band, who gave the alarum, pulling his sword from its scabbard where it lay beside him, and made for us as we crossed the last bit of the distance into the dark. I had helped Nurse up and urged her to make haste, pushing her ahead of me.

Just short of the trees, I felt a hand grab my arm and spin me around to face the silhouette of the chief brigand. I could not tell you which was more repulsive, his oath or the odor of his breath that carried it. In either case, I was retaken and had little recourse though I struggled mightily. He dragged me back into the light and kept close so that no arrow could be loosed at him without chancing to strike me instead. My assertions that this bespoke unmanly cowardice fell on deaf ears.

The brigand's crew was now roused and stood in a loose knot facing outward from the fire. "Sir Paunch" inspected the two guards who had been dispatched by the mysterious arrows and confirmed their demise. On the instant of his report to the captain, two more arrows struck out of the night, each claiming its man. The brigands were now down by four, yet that was but a third of their number. With surprising swiftness, the chief dropped his sword, drew his dagger, and pulled me over nearer the light of the fire. Then he set the weapon to my throat. Presently, he addressed the darkness in the direction whence came the arrows.

"Oi! In the wood line! Any more o' my men fall to your arrows, an' the wench gets 'er throat a parted!" He gave me a rough yank and pressed the blade closer.

I could not refrain from a yelp myself though it came out garbled under the blade's pressure. Emboldened by the lack of any additional arrow, he called out again. "Now, the two o' you come into the light and throw down yer weapons, all on 'em!"

A tense moment followed, forcing him to squeeze my arm and press again with the dagger to elicit another cry from me. Shortly thereafter, two figures emerged from the darkness with un-nocked bows. Both were hooded, and I could not make out any facial features, even at the modest distance at which they stood

"Drop 'em!" commanded the captain, referring to the bows. The two let fall the bows and unslung their quivers. "Everything!" again the captain. At this, they loosened their belts and let fall their scabbards and any daggers they possessed. "Step off!" ordered the chief brigand, nodding to his right. The two men stepped away from their weapons in that direction and stopped.

"Ere, Slouch, bind 'em. Check for any hidden weapons. Trick, pick up what they dropped."

When all this was accomplished, I was taken over and retethered to my tree. My two would-be rescuers were securely bound and made to sit near the fire. As it was near day, another meager repast was doled out before they began to break down their camp.

In all this time, I wondered what had become of Nurse. I thought sure she might turn herself back in, trusting to a rough clemency rather than wander the dark of night on her own. But she never showed herself. Despite my concern, I dozed again but with no clear recollection of any dream.

I woke to a gray dawn and the prodding of Sir Paunch's booted foot. He bid me to rise the which I did. I saw that all were on their feet and ready to move on. We had followed no discernable track through the last part of the previous day, and so we appeared to make our way again without benefit of trail or markings. Yet we seemed to follow a course and direction with a certainty. There were now eight of them and three of us. I had begun to accept the notion that poor Nurse had been snatched in the night by some ravenous beast and carried off in a swoon to some lair where she might prove variable service to a family of carnivores. 'It would have been the same with me had I been there,' I thought.

We proceeded in file in this order: the one called 'Trick' led, followed at an interval by two others. After another interval, I was urged along by the leader, whom they singly addressed as 'Boss.' Behind us were two who attended to the other prisoners, and again at another interval, two more brought up the rear. We continued in this fashion, again following no discernable track for upward of an hour. Much of the time, we remained in deep woods, only passing through an occasional glade or clearing.

As we approached one particularly bright clearing, the man in the lead stopped, then waved us all forward.

"Mind yer manners, missy, while we investigate," said my captor with a shove at my shoulder. The next two closed with the lead and also stood. When we came up, having left the rest of our party back, I could more readily see the reason for their halt.

In the center of the clearing stood a young warrior in the armor of a knight. He had drawn his sword, and his stance conveyed the message "None shall pass." When I could make out his features, I realized that this was my blond-haired, blue-eyed champion from the previous night. I had incorrectly assumed he was the taller of the two captives who remained bound at some distance behind us. Apparently, the boss had made the same erroneous assumption.

At the sight of this unforeseen impediment to our progress, he growled with an oath. Then he turned and called the two rearmost guards forward. When they came up, his orders were curt and clear. "All o' yers 'ave at 'im!"

"Our pleasure, Boss," said one as they moved to join the forward three. It would be five against one. My heart beat loudly within me.

"You could make this easier and release the lady and the rest!" announced the knight in the most pleasant of terms.

"Not on your life," responded Trick.

As they advanced together, I noticed that none of them possessed the brains to circle around behind their challenger. I suspect the young knight anticipated this deficiency in their tactical bent. He spread his stance as they closed and prepared to meet metal with metal.

"My life is not the one in question here, my friend," replied the young gallant. Soon, the forest rang with the sound of swords clashing accompanied by grunting and enough oaths for an unholy lexicon. The five were truly having a difficult time of it.

"I believe you need reinforcement!" called the knight brightly over their heads to the boss.

"Hmph!' responded Boss. Then he called over his shoulder. "Slouch, give 'em a hand!"

Shortly, the sixth man came past us and entered into the fray. I will own, the fight appeared more balanced after that. I could not fathom the brave knight's purpose in this and began to ascribe to him some measure of bravado, even hubris.

But what I did not know was that this was the signal to our dear Nurse to go into action. As it happens, she had been taken up in the night, not by a wild creature but by our rescuer. The departure of the second guard to assist his companions left only one to stand for the two captives behind us.

Now all of us were intent upon the battle to the front, which was also increasing in the clamor of oaths and the din of weapon play. Ergo, what we could none of us see or hear was the approach of Nurse from behind, wielding a goodly length of hard tree bough.

As the last guard stood behind the two men, he was thus in Nurse's direct path to them. Originally, I'm told, she was to approach the captives with stealth and cut their bonds, leaving the guard to them. Here, I must credit her with courage at least born of vengeance. As my attention was also with the struggle to our front, I must report from the witness of the two captives.

I am told that Nurse was heard to say a soft and sweet "Sir Paunch?" And at his turning to respond, she clouted him, felling him with one blow of the branch. The captives heard the exchange, being closest to it. They also turned and, perceiving, allowed themselves to be set at liberty.

Commandeering the dagger from Nurse, the taller man approached the leader from the rear and did him in with one quick thrust. Sensing the muffled altercation behind me, I turned to see Laertes leading the man to the ground. Straightening back up, he looked at me with a smile of victory. The other young man approached, helping Nurse, who was now quaking from her valiant effort realized. He had an oval face, deep eyes, all coherently effecting a most sublime expression of a duty well-performed. ['Hm. Horatio. It must be,' Hamlet thought.]

My joyful reunion with my brother was curtailed as I recalled the peril of the gallant knight in the clearing. "Laertes, the knight!" I exclaimed. When we both turned to determine what could be done in his aid, we saw that he had accomplished three of the six.

Laertes took up Boss's sword, and I saw that his companion had acquired the now defunct Sir Paunch's. Leaving Nurse with me, together they put a quick end to the scene and thus were we rescued and returned to our dear home of Elsinore—and a good, hot scrubbing wash.

And that, dear Hamlet, is my dream. I
will not relate to you the details of my gratitude
toward the brave knight. Yet will I say, it was
commensurate with his efforts toward my succor.

Hamlet set the pages down and reflected with a smile. 'Here
was love between the lines, to be sure,' he thought. 'I must compose
some similar epic in dream form that I may convey my love back.'
Retrieving his book, he returned to his studies but saw in them nothing relevant to the fanciful world where he longed to reside with
Ophelia. He had been away for nearly four years.

*****

Horatio had also come to Wittenberg some two years back. He
and Hamlet resumed their companionship on the same footing as
before and with no effort. His friend was now cozily ensconced in
apartments adjoining Hamlet's. They took their meals together at a
tavern near their student quarters. On this same evening, they sat at
table, facing each other and reciting snatches of their lessons by way
of confirming their learning for the day. With the meal completed,
the conversation turned casual but remained academic for the most
part.

"So the *logos* of St. John is a Greek concept?"

"Aye, my lord," replied Horatio with contained enthusiasm.
"And it is one that predates our Savior by some four hundred years.
So says the good doctor of divinity with whom I am studying."

"Hm. So the *Gospel of John* opens with a familiar to his Greek-
speaking audience."

"Greek-speaking and Greek-thinking."

"And what thought they of this *logos*?"

"'Tis remarkable, really. Allow me a dissection of the scheme.
The *logos* is first the 'creative idea' for the cosmos, as well as the power
to bring the material into existence. To my thinking, this is something like the wisdom personified in *Proverbs* who attended the creation of all things. Second, the *logos* is also the power that sustains

the creation, that keeps the stars from colliding, and that establishes and upholds the laws that keep creation functioning without mishap. And last, the *logos* is the connection between man and, as the pagan Greek would have it, the gods. That is, it is through the *logos* that man has the capacity to perceive that there is a realm of the divine, that allows us to approach God himself, generally through a priesthood, but also through an understanding of him and is, therefore, the intermediary between man and God—or 'the gods,' if we retain the pagan concept."

"And you see in this…the Trinity?"

"No, my lord, not the Trinity itself but a pattern of it in its functions: creator, maintainer, and intermediary or to rearrange the whole, creator [Father], intermediary [Son], and maintainer [Holy Spirit]. I recognize it to be not a perfect analogy if, as John has it, Jesus as the *logos* is but one person of the Trinity. But as you see, if we assign to him the third function of the original concept, the intermediary, it falls right.

"But this most wonderful, my lord, that follows. Imagine the import to the Greeks to learn that their *logos*—to them a power and a philosophical concept—'became flesh and dwelt among us,' as the Gospel maintains directly! Imagine the stuff of a waking dream materializing into your real world!"

This last set Hamlet into a whirlwind of the fanciful as he instantly thought both of Ophelia and the two phantasmal sisters. These antithetical worlds collided in his quiet mind like the chance meeting of a wife and a mistress so that his thoughts had to duck. The expression on his face as he shook off the notion communicated to Horatio that his point was well-taken but not in the way understood by his friend.

"For my part," continued Horatio, enthusiasm waxing full in his still slight frame, "it is the marriage of reason and theology!"

"Sure, that were a tottery marriage at best!" said Hamlet skeptically.

"But can you not see it?" Horatio's excitement caused him to fail of the honorific. Hamlet smiled at his friend's uncommon ardor. "Men of faith and men of reason in accord with each other? The

Scriptures confirm the philosophy, and the philosophy renders the Scriptures comprehensible!"

"*Your* philosophy renders it comprehensible for you are an optimist. But there are more things in creation as yet unaccounted for in your philosophy, Horatio."

"But, my lord—"

"Thus runs the world away!" Horatio's reply was clipped short by the entrance of two students into the tavern, arm in arm and singing loudly.

"Angels and ministers of grace! It is 'Sir Left-Foot' and 'Sir Right-Foot'!" groaned Horatio. "Sure, there's two who stand outside of philosophy!"

"Rather, their philosophy is of a more pragmatical bent," said Hamlet in defense of the two merry interlopers, as he waved them over.

"Since when is hedonism pragmatical, my lord?" Horatio could now barely contain his indignation.

"'There is a purpose to everything under heaven,' my friend."

"You misquote, my lord. It is 'a time to every purpose.'"

"Well, 'tis a time to this purpose. And all we must bow to the merry heart, lest the too unremitting pressure of academics infect us to an unhealthy fever of thought. Let us put the *logos* aside from our deep considerations—it will keep—and take light amusement for our, how do the Germans call it, *nochspeisen*—our dessert."

Seeing disappointment in Horatio's resignation, Hamlet added in undertone, "Suffer it now. We will discourse on the *logos* to all your heart's content but on the morrow." His friend nodded a defeated assent. In the meantime, the two revelers spied Hamlet's salute and made their way to the table.

"My Lord Hamlet," said the leaner, broadly, and with an overdone sweep of the hand. "Good e'en to you and you, Master Horatio. It is good to see you rise from your books. Are you here from them on a short visit?"

"Sure, Ros," joined in his friend. "He is the special legate from the realm of Academia, here to make pronouncement from the latest"—here he whispered behind the back of his hand—"Papal Bull!"

"Some form of bull, to be sure, Guilders!" added the other.

"Master Rosencrantz, Master Guildenstern," returned Horatio dryly with forced politeness and a modest bow.

"I would have you three be friends, for you each among you play a part," said Hamlet, rushing to make peace. "You two are the wind that fills my sails and propels me through the tedious sargassum of rote learning while Horatio here is my good compass and the rudder by which I steer a course non-perilous. 'Tis he who keeps me from the rocks of your ragged coastline of pleasurable schemes."

"Huh," said Rosencrantz, "spoken like a Dane, all wedded to the sea."

"Have you twain dined?" asked Hamlet, trying to get matters to settle.

"Dined but only half drunk, my lord," said Guildenstern with an affected bow from which he almost did not recover for the drink that was already in him. His friend pulled him back upright.

"I see. And now are you in search of sobriety or adventure?"

The two looked at each other with mild incredulity and swayed slightly as they chorused, "Sobriety?"

"Never, my lord," Rosencrantz said thickly. "The world's too harsh a place to navigate it soberly."

"You are something of a misplaced Dane yourself if you speak of navigating upon dryland."

"'*Dry* is another word not in our lexicon," spoke Guildenstern. "Is it, brother?"

"Lest it be a—how those French *pardoné mois* style it—a dry wine."

"I think you two should sit, lest the wake of a passing serving wench knock you to the floor!"

"Sit in the Royal Presence?" Guildenstern was clearly starting to have some focusing problems.

"It is my wish. Or need I make it a royal imperative? You'll not stand much more on your feet in any case. Better a seat with grace than an untimely and indecorous pratfall."

"Then shall we grace your grace with an—oh, confound it," said Guildenstern, plopping onto the bench beside Horatio. "I'm too much in the cups for wordplay. Ros, tell you His Highness our plans for his evening." With that, Guildenstern put his head down upon his folded arms on the table.

Hamlet turned to Rosencrantz as the latter took seat beside him. "You have charted out my evening, good sirs?"

"Sure, my lord. It will be unforgettable, could we keep sober enough to remember it."

"That speaks volumes. What is your proposal?"

"Our proposal, my lord, is this." Rosencrantz paused to think. "It is—Guilders, what was our proposal?"

Without raising his head, Guildenstern spoke into the table; hence, his reply came up muffled to the others. "The players, you ninny!"

"Ah, the players! Now I remember me! The players have returned from their tour and have, as we are told, some new presentment." At this, Horatio rolled his eyes. Rosencrantz fixed him with a dignified, if glassy-eyed, stare. "Pre-sent-ment. 'Tis a Christian word, to be sure."

"It is a term at law. I believe you meant *presentation*!"

"Touché." Guildenstern chuckled from his folded arms.

"Well, *presentation* then, legalist!" He knit his brows at Horatio. "Howbeit, we boarded them in the street on the way to the *Scholar's Cap*, where they plan to pre-sent their pre-sent-ta-tion."

"Which players?"

"There is only one 'players' for us, my lord. Sure, and they are friends of yours."

"The Tragedians of the City!"

"The very animals!"

"This would be scanned. What do they enact?"

Rosencrantz spoke slowly. "At present—they are presenting—a presentation to enact—Guilders, what do they enact?"

Guildenstern raised his head, his eyes half lidded so that he looked like a sleepy cat. He took a moment to focus them on Hamlet.

"They do enact *Julius Caesar* or one of those Romans. Who cares, there's a play afoot! 'Tis all the provocation we need. Sure, someone will fall on his sword before the evening is out, some capital fellow in the capitol, or some brut of a Brutus."

"Agreed. Horatio, do you come with us?"

"I don't know, my lord."

"Oh, come. I will vouch surety for these two." Turning to his other friends, he said, "You will behave yourselves in the royal presence, will you not, gentlemen?"

"We are sadly out of funds for any but the players. Therefore, by the middle of the second act, will we be more sober for lack of… reinforcement."

"And besides, I cry at tragedies."

"Oh, hush, Ros!"

"Well, you see then, Horatio. They are hobbled, and afterward, will we meet with the players, and then can you direct your finer questions of the art to them. It is a classical subject. You must take your first step away from this rigid scholasticism and into the liberal arts, else your education be not rounded out." He changed to a pleading tone. "And I do desire your company in this."

"Very well, my lord. I shall attend."

"Excellent. The play's the thing! And therefore, let our fancies, if not our consciences, take wing!"

# Chapter 13

Shall I speak thus boldly of mighty kings,
Th' anointed of the Lord, their thrones to hold
In trust, as shepherds of the promise?
Israel, God's chosen to bear the law,
And walk in righteousness before all nations,
With faithful circumcision of the heart.
O double-minded Israel, stiff-necked
And obstinate, troubled in your history,
Who struggles ever with the Lord and yet,
Prevailing, presumes on hopes of mercy.
One King, in death, whose headless body
Hung in shame from Beth Shan's ancient walls,
Whose bloodstained armor graced in great disgrace
The temple halls of Philistia's gods,
Leaving Jacob's sheeplike children lost,
All scattered o'er Gilboa's gullied hills,
A Benjamite king of failed trust: Saul,
O rejected king of shreds and tatters.
Yet comes another, born of humbler seed,
Youngest in the line of Jesse's sons,
A man whom God's own heart doth seek to please.
No donkey wrangler he, to buck like Saul
Against the goads and strut before the eyes
Of wanton Israel with stature great,
And, with pride of might, to claim the power of God,
And stand against the armies God hath sent

As trial against the pride of Israel.
O lowly shepherd, knowing well the patience
Of a careful watch and humble heart,
Who stood against the fearsome lion
And the bear, this shepherd whom the prophet,
By command of God, anoints to kingship,
Who championed Israel 'gainst Goliath,
Philistine of Gath, and for his feat
Won jealousy of the king he served;
This David to the vacant throne now comes
To serve the God of Abraham aright,
And dance before the Lord with might of joy—

"I thought you said it was a Roman subject," Hamlet whispered to Guildenstern.

"Sure, my lord."

"David and Bathsheba?"

"Are they not Roman?"

"As Roman as Ben Josef at the moneylenders' quarter!"

"What? Are they Hebrew then?"

"Shh!" hissed Rosencrantz, already caught up in the orator's recitation.

Hamlet rolled his eyes and continued to listen.

Now i' the budding springtime of the year,
When all the kings go forth to war well-served,
And leave behind the pillowed couches
Of the palace, where dalliance holds court,
To share in common perils with his host
And sleep upon vigilance's stony ground.
Now marched the numbered and assembled ranks
Of Israel's tribes to war in far off strands.
Not for vain conquest did that host go forth,
But rightly to humble the proudest
Of the host of haughty Ammonites,

Faithless scions of Lot's wanton youngest girl,
Whose name is lost to us in dusty time,
Wayward children of a drunken incest,
Begotten in the wake of Sodom's fall,
God's armies march in answer to Hanun,
Rash son of Nahash, for ill-considered
Insult to David's envoys royal.
The king sent on the levied tribal hosts,
Yet forebear himself to quit his palace hall,
Leaving the tainted "right arm" of Joab
To order the direction of the siege.
Oh, that he did but heed the trumpet's call,
And marched to waiting glory, led the host,
And stood against the enemies of the Lord.
For in the obedient heeding of that call,
Would he have spared his troubled household
Such a curse of fourfold retribution paid,
For sins which lost him sons to shameful lust,
And unto rebellion's ruinous maw.

Thus intoned the actor, a man of stature himself. The shadows of the fluttering torchlight playing across his face. He stood forth in costume of the Eastern people—as understood in the minds of his audience. His booming voice filled the courtyard of the tavern where the troupe had set up its properties. As his narration unfolded the story of the most famous king of Israel, his fellow players mimed the action.

In the beginning, the story takes place in two locations. Hence, the playing area was split in half with the left side as the audience viewed it, making up David's palace in Jerusalem. Representations of columns were draped in silk and stood as backdrop to the referenced "pillowed couch" upon which lay an actor-king in repose. On the right stood the entrance to a camp tent. Behind that, a sheet of canvas stretched on a frame was painted to imitate the stonework of a city wall, the besieged Rabbah.

Hamlet looked to his friend Horatio to see if he was enjoying the performance. Satisfied that this was so, he again returned his attention to the orator and the action.

> But now, how does the conscience of the king,
> As Israel's arm encamped 'round Rabbah's walls;
> Her yeomen and her mighty men doth sleep,
> And fill the night with homeward thoughts and dreams,
> That wafting softly on the westward breeze,
> Cross Jordan's muddied flow and then ascend
> The arid heights and highland hills of Zion,
> To touch the brow and burn the heart of him
> Who marched not off—the sleepless David hears.
> Mark him now, shepherd of an empty fold.
> He rises restless in the night and moves
> On slippered feet to tread with heavy heart,
> Down halls that cosset comfort in numbered
> Foreign wives and countless concubines.
> But finding naught in these to ease his heart,
> To open rooftops and to freedom's air,
> His wanderings lead, and paces he beneath
> The star-strewn sky that someday will a new
> Anointed One proclaim to other shepherds,
> And sing in fields beside his place of birth.
> But now he looks not up to godly praise,
> Nor utters heavenward the humble prayer,
> But down to earth he looks to comfort him
> In self-assurance of his mortared walls,
> That 'round the peaceful city stand this night.
> And thus, a proud and guilty heart leads on
> From there to godless sights and godless deeds
> Against the which a God-tuned conscience pleads.

The tempo of the chorus's words as he advanced the story, describing the alluring sight of Bathsheba accomplishing her bath, carried Hamlet with it like a heightened pulse. He filled in the ora-

170

tor's artful inferences of sensual sights with detailed images of the sisters, a double Bathsheba. And David's rooftop struggle became his own.

"Oh, quit the roof!" he whispered to himself and to the actor-king, closing his eyes and wishing for the light of day. Night and dark meant struggle. His soul craved the safety of light.

"My lord?" asked Guildenstern with some concern.

"'Tis nothing." He shook his head in an unsuccessful attempt to break free of his own thoughts. He knew well that he was afraid of the night, this night, the time alone in his bed when he would have to battle again. He watched, wishing he could intervene to stop the action of the play, as David dispatched a servant to fetch the woman of his desire, and he thought of his own surrender to fleshly thoughts. Then Bathsheba herself appeared and allowed herself to be wooed into sin by her king.

'A king cannot do this!' he moaned inwardly. 'If a king cannot command his own conscience, how doth he expect to command a nation to any good purpose? Sure, they must follow him into iniquity.' A new doubt began to form in his mind. He remembered his father's words to his mother on the morning of their departure for the war against the Germans. 'Even should some untimely death take me, which the Lord forbid, this crown shall pass to the next Hamlet, saving some unforeseen undermining of his character as to render him unfit and undeserving.'

His brooding on this thought carried him through the rest of the performance. The chorus's words turned at times to a soft blurring of sound as though Hamlet were listening underwater. Only the action held his attention through the murder of Bathsheba's husband, Uriah the Hittite. The Prophet Nathan's visit and David's repentance were lost on him for the noise of his thinking, as he pondered through the implications of his lack of self-control.

'Denmark. Denmark is my flock,' he thought, mixing aspects of the story into a hopeless muddle of symbolism. 'Can I allow her to be ruled, shepherded by such as I? Without correction, I, too, would be a king of shreds and tatters.' In that moment, he saw his troubles as more than simply a private sin. They had national ramifications, perhaps even historical significance. 'I must make correction of this fault,' thought he as the play moved on to its conclusion.

*****

"My lord, you grace us with your attendance here," said the lead player, the man who stood as the chorus in the play. Following *David and Bathsheba*, the troupe performed a few shorter and much lighter pieces so as not to leave the audience in a glum. Hamlet was able to bring his spirits up with the enjoyment of these, at least outwardly, so that he would not throw the others off their fun. He made good his promise to sit with the players afterward and introduce them and Horatio to each other.

Now they all sat about a pair of tables in the nearly vacant tavern. Most of the patrons had headed home or wherever they planned to complete the night. Some of the younger members of the troupe were putting away the last of the props, and the four companions had joined the players for ale, compliments of Hamlet. He suspended his usual frugality to treat his friends and show his appreciation to the players. Despite the ominous portent of his thoughts, he was grateful that they had given him much to think about. At present, he was reluctant to call it a night and return to his solitude. He craved companionship that did not stand on ceremony, knowing his friends and the players would not disappoint. Only Horatio was still ever careful of his court manners, but Hamlet knew this was out of his nobleness of heart and not from any fawning habit. On reflection, he was not sure that Horatio knew how to be completely at his ease with anyone.

Finally, in the actors collectively, he felt a closeness that he had missed since his loss of Yorick. They were of the same stamp—honest and open in all their weaknesses to the point that he counted it a strength—and envied them their simple joy of life.

"Sure, I would not have missed it," he answered the player, who sat on his portion of the bench faced away from the table and lounging back against it. His fellow players had taken places about the two of them. He looked so much in command of himself, his companions, and his own humor that Hamlet felt himself a visitor to the king of a roguish court. "Though we must instruct 'Messour Guildenstern' in the true catalogue of Roman legends and in the difference between a Roman and a Jew."

"Why? 'Tis easy enough. To borrow your Danish nautical: 'tis most readily seen of the latter in the 'cut of his jib'!"

Hamlet and the rest laughed at this offhanded reference to circumcision. Even Horatio managed a smile.

"Well, his changes to the play since the last performance of it threw me off my reckoning," said Guildenstern in his own defense.

"Changes, Master Guildenstern?"

"Aye, I missed the famous line about the 'mobled queen.' 'Tis an ill phrase, a vile phrase, but still, it makes its point. Why had you circumcised it from the drama?"

At this, the player's jaw dropped and his companions went glassy-eyed with mirth. "Your memory, good master, is in the cups."

"Nay, I've not drunk since dinner and time enough to fetch His Highness from his meal. How can you thus accuse me of a drink-muddled memory?"

"On two counts, Sirrah. The first is, we have not this work enacted before this night. 'Twas a virgin performance."

"But—"

"And the second, the 'mobled queen' is from *Priam and Hecuba*!"

"Well, there you are, my lord"—Guildenstern turned to Hamlet—"my confusion that they were Romans."

"Uhm. Priam and Hecuba are Trojans and not even proper Greeks and of a time when Rome was not but two mud huts on Tiber's grass-grown banks!"

"*Ack!*" Guildenstern threw up his hands in defeat.

"Concede, dear Guilders, thou art not a scholar of the ancient world."

"Tush, Ros. None of your classics for me. I endorse the newer disciplines."

"Heh, a man of science." Rosencrantz chuckled.

"Tell us," interjected Hamlet to bring the subject back into focus. "Did you pen the lines for *David and Bathsheba* yourself, or is't the work of some other genius of the art?"

"I own it is the work of my poor brain aided by a mendicant monk with time on his hands and a knowledge of the Scriptures as my accomplice. And much was borrowed from the Word itself. 'The budding springtime of the year' is more the work of Samuel's scribe than yours truly."

"Samuel's scribe?"

"Aye, that is, one presumes. The prophet himself expires before the conclusion of his first book. Though his ghost returns to curse Saul for disturbance of his repose, I think it not likely he stayed to pen the rest of the opus that bears his name nor the second book neither. You see, my lord, I have become a Bible scholar myself!"

"Like enough. May your Bible learning gain you immortality beyond your art then." Hamlet thought wistfully of Yorick. "Immortality of the sort that matters."

"We are all bound for immortality, my lord, as I read it. The question is where to spend it."

"In the tap room of a celestial ale house for me," said Guildenstern.

"Cosseted in a courtesan's cozy—"

"Indeed! But one question more." Hamlet rushed to cut Rosencrantz off. "You have it that David's passion for Bathsheba never flags, as say Amnon's did for Tamar once he had his knowledge of her. Can you, with scriptural authority, back that surmise? I ask this because it would seem to me that a passion inciting to murder would not hold well through the troubles that came."

"Well, my lord, the succession of Israel passed from David to Solomon, who was also of Bathsheba gotten, and this crown passed o'er the heads of older sons by other wives. It would seem his favor held. And I have it by the monk, who carefully traced the descent, that our Savior came of Bathsheba's other progeny by David, one Nathan, in the Virgin's line. So it would seem that passion's ill-begun budding, fully flowered into proper love in this king."

"You're as good as a priest from the pulpit, Master Player!" exclaimed Guildenstern.

"Not so. I haven't the wit to reckon indulgences in doling out penance past the shriving."

"No matter," piped in Rosencrantz. "We shall merely follow our own indulgences!" He nudged Guildenstern with a wink.

"Have a care, Master Ros, lest indulgence before make the penance more!"

"Ha! Rather, make the transgression worth the penance. So say I!" Rosencrantz looked triumphant as he held up a small purse and shook it to the sound of jingling coins.

"What!" exclaimed Guildenstern, sitting upright from a slouch. "We were broken when we came into the play. Have you been cutting purses?"

"No, my friend." Rosencrantz effected a wounded look. "I encountered young Heston standing among the groundlings and shrived him out of what he owed me for a last month's indulgence the which he had appealed to me for finance. Whatever other penance he had of the matter, he could keep."

"You never had such funds as these to 'finance' one of Heston's follies!"

"I am a man of unknown and untapped resources." He shook the purse again.

"Verily, by these 'signs and wonders,' but to what use shall we put this restored resource of yours?" Guildenstern's eyes brightened.

"Your talk of where to spend eternity, Master Player, and my curtailed alliteration"—he looked pointedly at Hamlet—"puts me in mind to pay a visit to our dear 'Esperanza.'"

Mention of this famous name brought laughter and backslapping from members of the troupe though Hamlet caught a mildly reproachful look from the lead player. Guildenstern clapped down his tankard on the table and wiped his mouth on his sleeve. "My friend, I am for you. Shall we four approach the fair wench in company, like sworn brothers off to the combat?"

"Not for me, thank you," said Horatio quietly but firmly.

"Of course." There was some derision in that, but everyone chose to ignore it.

Guildenstern looked to Hamlet. "My lord?"

"I have more words for the players, touching upon some verses of my own composition wherein I desire their advice."

"Sure, 'La Esperanza' might be of some aid to you there. Saving the present company, she could coax the highest poetry from the most unversed bumpkin. I have heard dullards wax poetical in her praise, who learned from her a '*goot* German phrase'!"

"Rather, a good Danish expression from one for whom the play of words engulfs his whole profession."

*****

"It troubles me that so great a king as David should chance the fate of Israel at one throw of the dice in love." Hamlet had confessed that his earlier excuse about some lines of verse was mere pretext to decline a chance at "La Esperanza." Even in this noble decision, he felt himself a coward in the face of Horatio's simple "Not for me, thank you."

After his two carefree friends departed and some of the sleepier members of the troupe dispersed, Hamlet and Horatio remained to discuss in greater detail the drama they had witnessed. He apologized for keeping the lead player up, but the man, who was the figure of robust health, owned that he was not a whit sleepy. Indeed, artist that he was, he enjoyed the opportunity to explore his new work in the minds of two earnest listeners. Having allowed Horatio to unfold his own mind and gain satisfaction on some fine points first, Hamlet broached the subject as it affected his thinking. The player pondered Hamlet's comment while studying the inside of his half-empty stein.

"There is a vein of mercy runs through the life of David, my lord. Wherefore, I know not. For all his faults, he was accorded a goodly king—and a godly, the greatest in Israel. There was none like him to follow."

"There was Solomon in all his splendor."

"Aye, my lord. But for all that he was wise, he had not the wit to stand against the idolatry of his many wives."

"Sure, they turned him this way and that to honor the pagan pantheon of Canaan and her neighbors," added Horatio.

"So father to son goes the lustful habit," said Hamlet. "And so it should to the third and fourth generation, as the Scripture hath it. That were a heavy burden for a king to bear, to know that in his sons and sons of sons would creep and root the sinful heart and all its cravings. And led they then their people, too, to venerate the Baals and Ashtoreths, the Molechs, and the like.

"But how now to a deeper thought? If each son passes on the sin from father down, does not he, being a father also, become the first of another four generations and, therefore, shall the transgression continue in the inheritance in perpetuity?"

"Your words are too heady for me, my lord." He chuckled at a thought. "And makes me glad I'm not divine that I should have to parse it out. I'd recommend the counsel of a priest, but such as they are these days, a priest would only muddle it into indulgences and throw in a relic at cut rates. But sure, there must be mercy operating somewhere. And Judah knew a few good kings in its unbroken line of succession. That is until the might of Babylon came to put an end to that line and carry off captives to broad Euphrates's grassless banks. Whereas the northern half of Israel's lopsided tribes was truly the worse for kings. There were never more than two or three successions could keep the throne before the dagger forced a change of crown. Beyond that knowledge, I am all out of my depth and cannot fathom it. Any wisdom you see in me is but the painted-on presentment of some actor's role left residual when the playing out is done."

"Not so. You actors have great wisdom. For you can see into a soul and make your own a mirror to it to show the image of a type of man. You command the body to an expression of face or manner commensurate to that man. And you bend up your spirit to the height that carries us all along to heaven's glory or to perdition's flame. You paint your canvas with men's lives and make us see where we fall short of God's *poema* by reason of our sins." He sighed heavily, then added a new thought. "I would you could see into my soul with your actor's empathetic eyes and paint me a portrait true, that I could the necessary corrections make in my heart—where lies the heart of the matter. What would you see?"

"I would see a king-to-be who would, for the souls' sake of his people, walk barefoot and in sackcloth the length of Denmark's lands."

177

"Aye, that I would for Denmark's sins. But what of my own?"

"A good shriving, my lord, and that were the end of the matter, save the odd thousand or so days in purgatory. Yet up against eternity, a thousand days is but a gnat's bite. Do you take theology, my lord, to make your thoughts so heavy with overspeculation?"

"What, at the university? An apprentice course only to introduce me. Horatio here is the theologian-philosopher. But you have spoken aright. I speculate, and I would not that I should lead my people all desperate-like into the arms of idols."

"Idols, my lord? Is there danger of worshipping wood in Denmark?"

"'Tis more than wood and stone or gold or gilt makes an idol, a sort of god in whom we put our trust and to whom we turn for comfort and succor. So I have heard it preached. Would I, as king, lead my people astray after their own lusts?"

"A king with such a care as yours to turn the flock aside to other trusts? I think not, my lord. The lambkins of Denmark should be blessed in the heart of such a king."

"Think you? Yet 'tis so precarious a theme, the fate of nations contained within the conscience of a king."

\*\*\*\*\*

Hamlet lit a taper from the embers of his fire and carried it to his bedside candle. He was still not ready for sleep, or the attempt at sleep rather. His anticipation imagined the flood of thoughts that would fill his mind as soon as he laid his head to the pillow. So for a few minutes, he sat and studied the candle's flame. He fought an impulse to place his hand directly above the flame, hold it there against the pain, and let this tiny taste of perdition coax him away from thoughts he knew he had no strength to resist.

Reflecting on the day, he found himself in envy of everyone who was not him: the servants who had but their menial duties to perform under his undemanding charge; Horatio who truly felt no pull to carnal thoughts; and Rosencrantz and Guildenstern who yielded so easily, sleeping the guilt away until midafternoon and rising to the next indulgence—he wondered if he could only pull himself away from guilt and become callous to the shame, would it somehow break the evil power of it?

He thought of the lead player who seemed to have his temptations all in perspective, of Laertes who frosted over his passion with the fortitude of excellence, of his father—well, he had a wife to help him with any such cravings—and of his mother who somehow kept everything in simple balance and gauged her life by how well she kept the peace among her ladies. He thought, too, of Marcellus, thoroughly professional and above desires. He envied all these and asked himself why he had been cast with such a sharp edge to his conscience.

Finally, he thought of Ophelia, of how her letters showed her to be so sweetly human in her feelings, possessed of the nobler romantic notions that allowed her to love in a plane where the physical was all affection without the burning flame of passion. "The burning flame of passion," the candle spoke to him of that. If he could know that he was capable of containing it to a single flame, but what if it should burst into a conflagration beyond control and would devour even all those whom he loved, even a state?

Would his private yielding to this flame result in nothing of consequence—nothing save an eternity of private pain hereafter—or would it, like his experiment with the hearth fire so many years back, grow with what it fed on? This was the fear, that like a captive, feral beast, it would attack the master who attempted to bring it to discipline with too stringent measures. And yet, the master dare not loose it to roam free within the home or yard.

"Who then is master?" Hamlet asked in a soft sighed whisper to the candle. The flame, perhaps responding to his breath, fluttered once in reply.

# Chapter 14

Hamlet stepped softly along the northern aisle of the cathedral at Wittenberg. He desired that not even his careful tread should make the merest sound. He had a place in mind to visit, and he wished to hold all his conflicting thoughts at bay until he could arrive there. Vespers had come and gone, and while most of the believers had filed out to their evening plans, Hamlet walked instead deeper into the arms of the church and deeper into the shadows.

Normally, he craved light and viewed each day from twilight on with dread. But here was a different dark, a dark that seemed to offer the comfort of the womb and that somehow helped him to focus. Used only to the private chapel at Elsinore, the vast height and depth of the cathedral as it rose all around him held him in awe.

Unlike to modern visitors, this marvel in stone, so gargantuan and at the same time so intricate, spoke to him not only of the faith of those generations who built it with their hands but also of the very nature of the creation itself. Looked at in this way, the cathedral reflected both God's blessing on the work of faithful man and his love for the colossal yet very complex world he himself had fashioned.

At the moment, Hamlet was in need of the full assurance of that love. In the face of his struggles of conscience, he deemed himself among the most unlovely of God's works. So he walked slowly, humbly, and with head cast down, from shadow to shadow down the aisle. Yet he felt warm among all that surrounded him. Even the very flagstones beneath his feet, worn almost to a polish, were a comfort. The columns rose with a stately assurance to support the unseen vaulting well above him. On either side, he passed expressions of faith in the form of artifact, contribution, or artwork meant to highlight the life of Christ so that even the unread could be instructed and know the truth. Racks of votive candles provided subtle lighting beneath placid statues of the saints.

It was the statues that first caught his attention during a Sunday Mass shortly after he first arrived in the city that put in him the idea of visiting them and that brought him back to study them. 'Holy lives' was the thought that kept sounding in both his head and his heart. Here were representations of people who had overcome the trials of life. He did not pray to them as others did when they stood beneath these figures frozen in ageless benediction. To him, that smacked of idolatry. But study them, he did, especially their faces. He found there, in every one of them, an expression of peace that seemed to invite the viewer to lay his or her troubles at the feet of the blessed. Here, where no voices could be heard from stone, the statues spoke with tenderness, a kind of absolution missing in the prayers and pronouncements of his confessor. Here he could remain to study their faces and glean from them some comfort.

But these were not yet the object of his visit. So he moved on. Padding eastward toward the transept, he passed recessed niches on his left that formed small chaplets. In later years, these would be partitioned with wrought iron grillwork to become the private chapels of prominent families of the city. Now they contained small side altars flanked by more statues of the saints. Some held figures of the Virgin as their centerpiece.

The statue he sought was one he had noted before and knew that he would come back to. Upon its altar stood a crucifix, a wooden cross upon which was fixed a figure of the Christ sculptured in stone to show him in his passion. Counting the niches showed Hamlet that he was nearing the one in question. He knew there should not be any changes or anything amiss, yet his heart beat faster as he approached. He was in eager anticipation of a few moments alone with God. The figure in stone was not God, but it would help him to visualize the one to whom he spoke.

As with the other chaplets, votive candles illuminated the figure on the cross and made it real to Hamlet. Our modern eyes, more attuned to the smoother, rounder molding of Renaissance and Baroque forms, might consider the elongated and almost stylized form of this suffering Christ, a figure devoid of pathos. But to Hamlet, who would never know these future forms, here was artistry at its best in the service of God. He approached and knelt.

Humility and custom bade him keep his head lowered. But the need to study the figure and make a personal connection pulled his glance upward. He sensed he would be forgiven any impropriety in that. He had come to look up. It was the focus he needed for his thoughts.

At first, he let his gaze and the attendant thoughts rest on the wounds of the Christ: the feet and hands and side. 'What part had I to do in that?' he asked silently. No definite answer came to him, only the sure conviction that his "wanted/unwanted" thoughts helped drive the nails and press the spear home. His thoughts bent to sincere contrition.

'Oh, my offense is great! Against thee only have I sinned. That Word is true. 'Tis not seemly in a king that is to be that I should with one eye seek the purity of a chaste love yet, with the other, cast my vision low to thoughts of baser matter. 'Tis not in nature that the pure shall have discourse with things profane. They cannot continue in company and hope the good shall outweigh the bad.

'Why cannot my ripe contrition move me to the turning away of repentance? These wounds are for my dark desires effected. This I know. And yet even knowledge of the painful cost to thee turns my fleshly thoughts not away. 'Tis an insult to divine love that I continue in those thoughts. But something else pulls me, and I, in weakness, yield and yield and yield again. And so, weak contrition makes a mockery of resolve. And so, my soul, like the cycle of the seasons, moves from summer's warmth through the autumn of growing dark desires to the chill of winter's sin wherein I turn a cold heart to restraint and blast resolve to icy shards until the winter being spent, contrition buds beneath the returning sun of grace. But what's to stop this cycle? A stronger sense of guilt? What can guilt, and what can it not? Why doth not guilt move before to check desire at temptation's door? No, instead, the guilt of impure thoughts comes after and bows the spirit's knees to hear temptation's laughter.'

In the long silence following this, somehow it seemed to him that even in the presence of this visual accusation of the wounds of the Crucified, he could feel the guilt draining out of him. That feeling came mostly from his study of the face of Christ.

The artist, out of his talents and his personal devotion, had managed to convey Jesus at the moment of his prayer. "Father, forgive them."

Hamlet had felt this the first time he encountered the image. He realized that his quickened pulse at each subsequent visit, on his approach to the chaplet, was born of the fear that the feeling would not return, that God had had enough of his wavering resolve. But by the grace of God, here it was again, as it had been in times before. And it remained fresh in his heart so that his next response was gratitude.

'O Lord, that you would forgive me even until the next time I weaken and even after that. Oh, after that! If plucking my lustful eye could but be the curative, but the lust is in my mind's eye to continue even when the vision is cut off. It grows sharper in the dark.

'What is there to pluck the thoughts, to pluck the heart? I am by thy boundless mercy forgiven and will of thy mercy ever avail my sinful self. But, Lord, if you will pluck my heart, I cannot go on, yet must I and to a kingdom! Your saddened eyes of love, deep set in stony face, bespeaks a prayer o'erheard and answered with true grace.'

*****

"I once saw you perform a Passion. 'Twas in Holy Week upon the market square," said Hamlet as he sat once again with the lead player over a midday repast at the *Scholar's Cap*.

"Aye. Well, that's the business of the Lenten season for players. 'Tis sin to stand forth at that time on any theme save the Gospels and a stiff fine, if not a 'special performance' at the stocks."

"But was that all? Was there no conviction in it?"

"Oh, aye, conviction, to be sure. Our hearts are in the right despite the hell-bound baseness of our ill-repute. The passions and the weaknesses of our masks in playing are oft attributed to ourselves, and unjustly so. Oh, there be players have earned these lowborn epi-

thets. The general clepe us drunkards and seducers on the strength
of these noisome and weak-willed witnesses and on the strength of
our best imitations of villainy. Sure, 'tis odd how we pour such a
heart into the portraying of evil to the entertainment of our righ-
teous patrons, who think they see beyond the mask and the player.
And all we suffer for it. One would think it grounds to lay down the
profession and take up…knitting! But playing! You hit the mark in
your assessment of the other night, my lord. We plumb the depth
of souls to stir them to their correction or to damnation and thus
become a lesson contained within the tableau. How did you say it?
'We paint our canvasses with the lives of men!'"

"Those were my words exact!"

"And good words. Be not surprised, my lord, if your words find
their way into some soliloquy or other hereafter."

"Sure, you are welcome to them, especially could you fashion
them into a couplet. But to the Passion, played you the Christ in that
instance, as I recall."

"Aye, and 'twas a sobering role to play: to see with the eyes of
God and to hold the rapt attention of e'en the groundlings on the
authority of the holy words."

"And upon the cross you hung. I remember it."

"Aye, my lord. They had me roped. 'Twas agony enough without the beatings and the nails." Then he chuckled lightly to remember. "At one performance, our new man, a youth really, performed
the office of the soldier who jabbed with the spear. His enthusiasm
o'erstepped his temperance somewhat. The simple knave ran the
spear nearly home betwixt the second and the third ribs of me!"

"No!"

"Aye. That he did. I'd have cried out but that I was already two
minutes dead i' the part, and 't would have argued a premature and
painful resurrection and ushered in an early Easter with an oath and
not an angel! In short, it hurt!"

"Heavens!"

"Well, we suffer for our art. And the lad's contrition was real
and proper. It also added something to the drama for, knowing on
the instant what he had done, he let fall the spear and dropped to

his knees, hands to face, just as the centurion bespoke his confession of the Son of God. 'Twas well received. Sure, there were tears among the groundlings."

"All things work to the good, eh?"

"Like enough, but in the parlance of the theater, 't would be 'all's well that ends well.' I have meant that for a title, but the story escapes me."

"But tell me. On the cross, saw you with 'the eyes of God' from up there?"

The man nodded profoundly. "Aye. 'Twas an odd feeling too, to look down on all else looking up. The heart of the audience matched in their faces the woeful masks of the players immediately below. And there was a kind of forgiveness touched me toward the viewers. My own heart realized as well the cost of my sins. I thought, too, how 'he, who knew no sin, became sin for us,' as the Scripture has it. To play such a part is not to glory in power or fame but to be immersed in humility."

"But…what if the viewers had a calloused eye turned to you? What then?"

"There were at times, one or two within the somber mob, who by reason of drink, offered up a smirk in prayer, as though they knew better or so believed. Whatever anger I had at these, drained away, leaving a kind of pity for the weakness that caused it. For I think none are truly calloused who look upon the cross and give it honest thought."

"But think you that such a weakness, as say to drink, in the repetition—conceding the sin of it, even in the practice—is an insult to divine mercy and therefore worthy of the condemnation that attends it? Is not witting sin that which the Scripture calls unforgivable?"

"That's a puzzle for a theologian, my lord. To a player, 'tis a Gordian knot."

"Methinks theologians and confessors too oft look down from an unforgiving cross. They do not plumb the heart so much as they dredge across the jot and tittle of the law. Their call to righteousness would strain the quality of mercy 'til it was dry pulp."

The man cocked his head and raised a brow to study Hamlet for a moment. "Come you to me for absolution, my lord? I am not equipped. In that, I am but one poor beggar advising a fellow beggar where to find bread."

Hamlet thought he had better back off, lest the give and take of the conversation lead to an unready confession. "Not absolution, my friend. For I know 't would beg the advantage of your good heart. I simply find, in my speculation on these matters, that I know not where the guilt of sinful habit lies. It would seem to presume too much upon mercy. Yet if it be a matter of a weakness indulged in—a sort of bondage unbreakable—wherein is the culpability assigned, when our arms are found lacking in the struggle?"

"There you have me, my lord. If I scan the catalogue of the characters I have played, I can prophesy only tragic ends for such as those—saving the advent of angelic grace. But drama is the realm of fate, and the furies jealously guard its bounds wherein the hero must play his part and move inexorably to a conclusion that is writ for him. He cannot escape this ending—however strong the will or epic the struggle—and it remain the same play. The player hath not the license to effect *ex tempore* a change unto his fate. In this, the theater is unlike the life of a man. For in life, a man may fiddle as he may, but woe betide the hero who fiddles with the play!"

"Hm."

"Sorry am I that I can be of no help to you in this, my lord."

"Not so. Not so. You have given me a surer view from off the cross, that in weakness, mercy acts to mitigate the loss."

*****

"Whilst this machine is to him, Hamlet."

Hamlet concluded this strange appendix to his letter in a wave of melancholia. He debated with himself whether even to send it on with the body. Sure, it began with a bold, if awkwardly metered, declaration of his love. Should it fall into Polonius's hands, "'t would drink the cup and all," as the saying goes. He felt that his contrived dreams in response to hers fell woefully flat and that he needed to explain his lack of art. If she could see that a certain lovesickness tied his creative hands, she would at least not attribute such a stale letter to a fading love. No, his love for her and his desire to return to her was stronger than ever.

Only Horatio's constant attention to academic questions infused him to any effort at study. Unlike his younger friend, he had lost the purpose of possessing great knowledge and strained to be at practical matters. He had written his father to express an earnest desire to become involved in some small part of the machinery of state upon his return and thereby begin preparing himself for the responsibility of good rulership. Ophelia's letter would accompany this to his parents and be spirited to her as usual.

Lowering his pen, he stared out his window to the predawn dark. It was becoming a frequent habit that punctuated and thereby prolonged his studies. As he peered into the street scene below, looking for nothing in particular, there was a knock at his door. That should have been Horatio—also an early riser—who usually followed up by poking his head in after a short interval. Instead, when the knock was repeated, he realized it was not his friend.

"Enter!" he called over his shoulder.

The door opened tentatively to show a boy of about ten who looked the sort who ran errands for a tavern. Behind him stood Odain, who would have let the lad in downstairs. As the conversation progressed, Odain, anxious to recover lost sleep, withdrew.

"Yes?" Hamlet turned toward the door.

"Pardon, sire, I seek the prince of Denmark."

"You have found him, lad. Come in." Hamlet spoke amiably to put him at his ease. "What is thy errand?"

"I am sent by two gentlemen, *Master Rosenkatz* and *Master Guildenstar*, to fetch you to their immediate aid." The boy did not really enter but remained at the door with his hands behind his back, no doubt afraid to touch anything in the room. He rubbed a bare foot against his left calf, which appeared to Hamlet to further express his nervousness.

"Immediate aid?"

"Aye, sire. I am to guide you to them and to implore you to come with funds."

"Funds?"

"It appears they are 'beset with creditors.' 'Twas their words, sire. I am to say by way of watchword that 'La Esperanza' beckons and that would stand as proof that I come from them and not some false brigands who would accost you with your funds i' the street. I am also to say, as additional surety, that David and Bathsheba are still Hebrew. But…if they bespeak King David of old, I thought him a Jew."

"Hebrew and Jew are one these days though in their history, Jew came later as an epithet. Funds? Let me see, let me see. Give me but a moment's privacy. I will meet you in the street, and we shall proceed in company." He approached the boy with a plate of assorted fruits and held it out to him. "Avail yourself by way of compensation for your troubles. I recommend the pear. It is in season."

The boy studied the plate uncertainly. "If you please, sire, which is the pear?" He went wide-eyed.

"It is the bulbous one." Hamlet picked it up by the stem and set it upright. "Or rather, it is in form much like Doctor Hexenmeister. He teaches at the university. Go ahead, boy, no doubt you have come far and you have delivered your message with good celerity." He remembered his experience reporting battlefield events to various leaders back in his only war. The boy took the pear with an awkward curtsy, almost like a girl.

"Thank you, sire!"

"It is a blessing to give. I shall meet you downstairs anon."

*****

"Thus runs the world away!"

Hamlet could hear his friends singing jovially even from the street as he and the boy approached the salon belonging to "La Esperanza."

At the door, the boy stopped short and explained. "I must attend to my duties, sire. It is not meet for me to enter the house of 'La Esperanza.'"

Hamlet fished two small coins out of his purse and pressed them into the boy's hand. "Here's for thy pains." Then leaning forward a little, he spoke in a hushed, almost conspiratorial tone. "The one is for your 'benefactor,' who is sure to take it from you. The other—unreported—is for yourself."

"Thank you, sire!" The boy bowed again and ran off to turn down the next alley.

Hamlet knocked and was let in by a liveried servant. He found himself in what would be a lavishly ornate sitting room, except that it was something in disarray though some of it—what furnishings had not been broken—was already set to rights. Off to one side, following the noise of singing, he saw his two friends seated back-to-back in two straight-backed chairs and tied together with a length of drapery cords. They did not seem to be any worse for wear and, as their singing and lurching attested, were still under the influence of strong drink. Certainly, they were making the best of a dire situation. Guildenstern sat in a position to spot Hamlet first.

"My lord!" Then he spoke over his shoulder, "Observe, Ros, did I not attest him to be a true prince?"

For his part, Rosencrantz merely smiled and nodded in greater lurches which, pulling against the chord, caused his bound companion some consternation at his end. Hamlet wiped his face as if to dispel the image of his two friends.

"I would ask what has happened, but I can see a battlefield by daylight."

"Indeed!" He heard a woman's voice with a measure of annoyance in it.

Hamlet turned his gaze to see a richly dressed woman standing where a hall opened out to the sitting room from deeper within the house. She kept her hands on her hips as she looked at her two bound patrons. Her look reminded him of a taverner's wife he knew. She was the true impetus behind her husband's business and its success.

When the present lady glanced over to assess Hamlet, her look softened. Hamlet did not pride himself on any effect of charm. He knew she was sizing up prospective business. Still, once she completed the transformation from outraged entrepreneur to a lady with much to offer, he had to admit she was beautiful.

Her gown kept up with the fashion of the city—from what he could tell—to an extent that would probably have set many of the wealthier matrons of Wittenberg to murderous envy. Her light brunette tresses were swept back and then let to fall in waves, one side behind her shoulder and down her back, the other side falling forward to swirl and gather above her bosom. Though her dress covered her modestly, yet somehow, she filled it in a way that could not help but please.

Her face was pleasantly rounded but with a dainty pointed chin. Her eyes were dark and large and luminous, on either side of a delicate nose that turned up ever so slightly at the tip. Finally, her lips were not full but small and pouty, like a child's—he had seen this before she graced him with her smile.

"I am Esperanza, Your Highness," she said pleasantly.

Hamlet nodded politely. His rank and her station required a certain courtesy but nothing more. "Madame."

"Your friends have sent for you. I think their needs are evident." Glancing back at the two men, who sported silly grins, her countenance darkened again slightly.

"A man of unknown and untapped resources," Hamlet reflected *soto voce* as he recalled Rosencrantz's words. He returned his gaze to the woman. "Aye, madame. But there are two sides to every skirmish, and one cannot dance alone. Have the opposing quit the field, or is manslaughter among the charges?"

"Hee!" Rosencrantz emitted a high-pitched guffaw, and Guildenstern snorted.

"The other party has made amends for their part and gone to nurse their wounds."

"Nurse their wounds!" Rosencrantz quipped in imitation.

"Hush, you two!" Hamlet chided, yet his thoughts began to churn over the recent topic of mercy.

"On your assurance that they will do their part to make reparations, they will once again be in my good graces. For I believe they were not truly the offending party. Still, there is some measure of responsibility."

"I understand. I will do as I can. I ask you to believe that I do not allow myself much in the way of lavish expenditure. I do not command such a princely sum as might be imagined."

"Nor am I a woman to avail herself liberally of a princely purse. I am plain dealing. We can speak more to the point in my office." She turned to indicate a room off to the side. Seeing hesitation in Hamlet's eyes, she added, "'Tis a smaller sitting room only from which I conduct my business. It has been a long ordeal. The dawn is upon us, and I should like to sit."

"By all means, lead on. I'll follow thee."

"Shall I enlarge your friends?"

"Let us leave them to consider further of their deeds."

*****

Hamlet agreed to the tally of the damages and had word sent to loose Rosencrantz and Guildenstern to wait upon his reappearance. Meanwhile, the conversation moved to pleasantries for conclusion.

"How is it you are not come hither with your friends, my lord? They speak of you warmly. We have other royal guests. Surely you would find something here to suit your taste."

"My tastes are my own." He tried to sound pleasant. He noted that she had read him well enough not to attempt to entice him with sensuality. Nor did she seem to feel repulsed by his guardedness. Indeed, she kept her talk matter-of-factly and her manner demure. That in itself became a subtle attraction against which he knew he must guard.

"You speak like a man with a distant sweetheart."

"Aye, madame, you have found me out. There is someone waiting for me in Elsinore." He felt surprise that her demeanor invited him to speak to her of things he had never mentioned to anyone. In the back of his mind was the thought that she might understand, might be of help. He almost read an affirmation of this idea in her eyes.

"Are you promised?"

"No, but then we were young at our parting for this." He indicated the city. "It is my intent to draw closer to her upon my return."

"But do you manage in the meantime? You are a man after all." Her tone bespoke an empathetic curiosity. In his silence, her eyes bore into his, and she instantly knew all.

"I have no answer for you. I simply wait upon our reunion." He caught the epiphany within her and wondered what she thought of his secret as he tried to read either laughter or pity in her eyes. He saw neither. In all this, he began to feel his young age before her years of experience. He suddenly realized he could not tell her age, except to note that she was still in her best years. Yorick's words came to him from a deep past. 'There be some lads whose eye first falls upon a mature woman.' He could begin to understand how that might occur.

"Still would you find friends here. We are not your common bawdy house but a place to gather for talk and good company. And 'tis sure, you would grace us with your presence, my lord."

"For your kind invitation, I thank you." He rose to go to his friends. In rising, he had to struggle with an urge to talk with her more, even about Ophelia—to name her, describe her, and voice his desires of her love.

Esperanza rose as well and followed him to the door. "We will be here ever, my lord. And we can prove good friendship."

In his mind, Hamlet heard the same call of the sisters from his fancy, the call he had never been able to refuse. But here and from "La Esperanza," it piqued him into the thought that there could be no half-way use of this place that would not eventually lead him to one of the back rooms. He knew he must decline and turn his back—on this call, at least—forever. But could he? He shook his head gently but firmly.

"I must take my leave of you now. And I must say farewell."

# Chapter 15

Hamlet's return to Elsinore was, by nature, a subdued triumph. The daily traffic of the castle yard doffed caps or curtsied at his unannounced arrival and took up a good-natured and heartfelt cheer as he rode up to the steps of the keep. He greeted servants at the door as genially as he did the knights and noblemen who stood in the great hall waiting on business with the king. The council was in session—indicating that little or nothing had changed in his absence—so Hamlet handed the few things he carried to Odain and took the stairs two steps at a time up to the queen's apartments.

One of the serving girls saw him as she was exiting the queen's chamber with a tray on which were the remains of lunch. She gasped and then remembered to curtsy. Coming up to her, he took a cut of meat from the tray and popped it into his mouth—only then realizing how hungry he was. He smiled warmly at the girl and then pointed with his glance at the door behind her.

"Would you announce me, girl?" he said pleasantly.

"Aye, my lord!" She turned about, nearly dropping the tray, and darted back in. Hamlet heard the muffled declaration followed by "oohs" and "aahs," and judged it time to enter.

As the girl passed him again on her way out, he took another morsel and smiled at her. Everyone's face, even those with whom he was not familiar, filled him with the joy of a homecoming.

On entering the queen's sitting room, he saw the half-dozen ladies in attendance rise first, all beaming. His mother rose as he approached, and they fell into a warm embrace. There were murmurs of approval all around. Drawing back, the queen studied her son. She now had to look up into his eyes.

"How now, my son. Thou art a man." Admiration and wonder and a little sadness shown in her eyes. It was not the sadness of tragedy, as that which had met him at his last homecoming when he found his one friend ill and the other in his grave. He could tell that her sadness was at the passing of the years and the fact that the "boy" was no more.

"Aye, madame, and returned am I to fill a man's niche, one hopes."

"Thou'lt fill any niche to thy credit. Come, sit next to me. I have kept a chair for you since word came that your studies were concluded and that you purposed a quick return to us."

The lady nearest the queen stepped aside to allow Hamlet that chair, and the women on that side all shifted one. The pecking order would not be thrown out of kilter by his interposition among them.

"Your Highness, we should withdraw and afford you the privacy of this reunion," said the current favorite.

"Nonsense," Hamlet declared. "I would for a time hear the chatter of women. Too long have I sat among the counsels of the wizened wise. And I must practice my good graces for the society of court ladies. Besides, this is but a preliminary to a lengthy tenure of my return. There will be time."

The truth was, he was struggling hard not to fix his gaze on Ophelia, who sat one chair removed from the favorite on the other side of the queen. He noted from the moment he stepped in that she was easily the most beautiful among the ladies. He was loathe to let her go from his presence and would gladly suffer the company of the others to keep her in his sight.

At his words, everyone regained their seats and settled in, returning to their pursuits from before. A few took up interrupted stitchery. There was only a short moment of awkward silence. Ophelia looked about and saw that no one was first to speak, so in a moment of boldness, she addressed him.

"Tell us of Wittenberg, my lord." That won some approval of those who were lost for a good topic.

"Shall I discourse on the university or tell of the fashions there?" he teased with a smile meant for her but accepted by all.

There was a tittering of expectation.

"The fashions, to be sure," the queen picked up the conversation.

"Well, as the city is greatly attended from many lands, the fashions flux with the times. Though I must confess there be ladies whose sole employment is chasing fashion's tail, much to the exercise of a husband's purse. They be not as"—he searched for a good word—"steadfast as our Danish ladies, who follow the trend more soberly." This earned him a slightly wicked gleam from Ophelia, who understood his hidden indictment of the fashion-followers among them, of whom she was not.

"The cut of the bodices, if I have the term correct, rises and falls as the price of wool in Flanders's markets. And all we pray there be no serious slippage there. Eh—for the nonce, the skirts are broader abeam. Some say from a surplus of cloth. But I have heard it whispered across the back of the hand that thicker skirts are mere disguise where schnitzel graces thicker thighs!"

There were whoops from all the ladies, an especially gay bout of laughter from Ophelia—hands covering mouth in that charming way of hers—and a mildly reproving look from the queen.

"Shall I go on?" he asked innocently.

"By all means," said the queen with some heightened dignity. "But tread more genteelly, my son, if you would learn good society." She was still smiling as at his boyish pranks.

"Well, to the coiffure then…uhm." He swirled his hands around in an ascending spiral above his head as he improvised a description of the most outlandish style he could recall. "They like to pile their tresses like a topping to a fruit tart, meaning no disparagement of their character." His hands seemed to become entangled with each other at the apex. "But to my thinking, 'twas a poor imitation of a hurrah's nest."

"Mean you a *heron*, my lord?" asked Ophelia. It appeared to be accepted that the young could address the young. Yet some matronly eyes exchanged speculative glances.

"Oh, what you will. But to the sea-born Dane, 'twas too much topsail for a high wind and was like to come toppling down at the first squall!"

"You have a man's sense of the fineries of fashion, my son."

"And that is, dear Mother?"

"It is governed by the purse and too easily bewildered by innovation. We ladies seek ever to improve upon that which nature hath bestowed, both individually and collectively."

"Granted. We men—and I speak as a new initiate among them—prefer pragmatic principle in the practice of personal plumery. Sure, we have no patience for all the layers that disguise fair nature. We are to the point, madame." This last produced a confusion of reflection as the women scrambled to understand if an impropriety had been uttered.

Hamlet, who meant every possible meaning to all he said, lounged back, satisfied with his scattered broadside. He did manage an affirmative nod to Ophelia in confirmation of his intended verbal mischief among the covey. She returned him a smile of superiority over the muddle he had created. But the smile also renewed for him her vow: 'We shall have our time a-dragon-back!'

*****

"You are well come, my Lord Hamlet," said Polonius, who was the only one who seemed to have aged in all his time away. He encountered Hamlet just outside the council chamber, carrying his usual armload of papers in semi-disarray. Hamlet had a mental picture of him shuffling them at the conclusion of the council meeting and giving them a quick tamping on the table before starting for his office, where he could resort them into the premeeting order.

"I would ask some accounting of your studies, my lord, but that I know your father, the king, stands within and would feign greet you ere much more time passes. For there is an old proverb—well, it is not so old that it be found among the Scriptures nor that it was ever lost and should be found—but such is the usage of the time—eh—where was I?"

"An old proverb?"

"Aye, an old proverb that runs thus: 'When time is running, he who walks ahead must still fall behind.' A curious phrase, yet there is truth in it."

"Aye, my Lord Chancellor. I see your wisdom continues to grace the court unchanged. But as you say, to my father. Good day to you, and greetings to your family."

"Thanks, my good lord." Polonius bowed and turned to shuffle off. Hamlet watched him go for a moment, shaking his head. Then a thought struck him. Could this man become his father-in-law? The thought of passing holiday meals in his company was a dark cloud quickly dispelled by the freshly renewed image of Ophelia's eyes and laughter. He turned and continued into the chamber.

His father sat at his place at the head of the table. To the king's left, in the place opposite Polonius's chair, sat his Uncle Claudius. He and the king were discussing some matter as the latter scanned a document held loosely in his hand. His father looked up from what appeared to be earnest conversation. Instantly, his whole being transformed to gladness. He rose. Had there been room, he might have run, like the prodigal's father, to an embrace.

"Hamlet! And son! Here's good tidings indeed!"

Hamlet stepped quickly around the table and into the embrace; this one was just as warm as his mother's but somehow more manly. Perhaps it was a certain curtness that eschewed any thought of clinginess. Again, as with his mother, father and son stood regarding each other. "Hast seen thy mother?"

"Aye, Father, and run gently amok through the bevy of her stitchery circle, a fox cub, to swat in play at loose feathers merely. No harm done among them."

This brought him a pat on the upper arm and a chuckle from Claudius, who only belatedly dispensed with his urgent demeanor.

"Good! 'Tis good the mothers and maidens among them receive notice early on in your return that Denmark's future king is not parlor-bred. Oh, if only we had a good war to wage. A month or two under canvas with the lean meat of the camp were just the curative."

"Have you an illness, Father?" Hamlet grew concerned.

"The illness of us all, my son, a steady compilation of the years. But your return has breathed new life into me. I have considered of your desire to 'learn the ropes' that serve for rigging to this ship of state. We shall have duties for you anon. I have thought it good to appoint you deputy to your Uncle Claudius in dealing with all our embassies. In this wide world, 'tis best to take a good measure of your neighbors. From there will we proceed to the purse strings of government and thence on to jurisprudence and royal prerogative. Kept you up in your military art?"

"Caesar and Xenophon have been my constant mentors, and my sword master of Wittenberg reports me passing competent. I have brought with me, by way of a homecoming remembrance, a few techniques of the blade for Master Marcellus. Hath he still charge over the royal pages?"

"I would not deprive him of so apt a calling, especially in the good service of the state. Claudius, have you any initial instruction unto the prince?"

"None, my lord, save that he meet with me on the morrow and prepare for a litany of alliances, embassies, and other scantily held promises. The other matter"—he indicated the papers they had been discussing—"is not urgent. I shall leave you to your reunion." With a bow to both the father and son, Claudius departed the chamber. Hamlet's father nodded to the door leading to the king's sitting room, indicating they remove to more private quarters. They moved together, his father leading.

*****

"Come you 'educated' now from Wittenberg, my son?" The king handed his robe of state to a waiting servant.

"I return steeped in knowledge, Father, but the measure of it that can be put to useful purpose remains to be seen."

"A fair reply. You have snatched the words from off my tongue. I had meant to follow up my inquiry with a fatherly admonition to be wary of scholarly hubris. But I see in your answer that you have acquired wise perception in your character. 'Tis a good sign. Sit. We shall share out a lunch, like that day so many years back."

They took seat, and another servant brought a tray with the same selection of meats, fruit, cheeses, and bread as before. His father lounged back and looked beyond Hamlet, even past the far wall.

"Those were good days. Matters were simpler, and trust easier to come by. The world's grown dishonest. 'The love of most will grow cold,' goes the saying."

"Aye, Father. You have quoted from Matthew's gospel."

"The Scriptures, eh? Truly? I did not think it to be in me. Well, 'tis only half true—the saying. There is still love in the world though I think it be found under rocks, generally."

"You are troubled, Father?"

His father started at the question, only then realizing how negative he had sounded. He shifted in his seat to help break the spell of gloom he had been projecting. Then he smiled a fond smile at Hamlet. "No, my son. I am but weary. Remember you the council meeting of those years back? They have grown markedly more tedious."

"Angels and ministers of grace! Is't possible? Nay, I will answer my own question. Master Polonius hath found his stride, no doubt. Why, just outside the chamber, he mangled an 'old' proverb with which I had no familiarity. And then evoked he the Holy Writ in employment of some exposition over it though I rather think it be of Aesop's mold. Sure, 'twas lost on me. I quake to consider the effect of his defective witticisms upon the already shriveled-up matters of state. It must be dry service indeed for an out-purposed law to stick i' the throat." The king chuckled sleepily. "But forgive me, Father. I stretch out my venom against the man in like manner to him. I have learned more words in these years—that much is true—and must therefore rein them in."

"Yet will you find cause to give them good exercise in your new office to learn the art of talking around the embassies. Diplomacy is among the most evasive of man's endeavors, next only to the art of the advocate at law, I think. Claudius will teach you well. He hath harnessed a deceptive nature in service to the state. Have you learned to read character as well as *Caesar*?"

"Well enough, I think, to know where my trust should lie, Father. I kept good company at Wittenberg and was passable good influence to two roguish mates, at least. They may swing ere the story is done but not by my hand!"

"So had your deportment been rightly reported. 'Tis good to know. To read a man correctly is essential in a king. In such a world of self-interested men, especially when right and wrong have been muddled into their opposites, 'tis almost wisest to keep counsel with oneself."

Thinking back to the morning of his departure for the war and to his father's parting words to the queen, Hamlet entertained a cautious line of thought toward his uncle but then brushed it aside. "I heard you once say that a king must learn to be alone."

"That is two profundities in as many minutes that you have accorded me. I shall wax wise ere long in your return. It is good to have you home!"

*****

"Lord Hamlet, it is good to have you home." Marcellus stood in the middle of the armory flanked by the racks upon which were stored superfluous weapons as well as the training gear that he used in his instruction.

"So have I been told and do, in all sincerity, believe. It is good to be back." He studied the familiar practice swords, "baited" as they were called by reason of their blunt edges. "Has your prodigy yet risen from the ashes?"

"I continue to expect him daily, my lord. But in the main and in the meantime, my pupils exercise their art with care, passible diligence, and some clarity i' their form."

"Hm. Clear pupils is good to keep as we grow older, I hear."

"Now do I know you are home, my lord, and in good spirits with such mirth as I recall of old. The 'yawning maw' of Wittenberg was not so equal to your worried anticipation, it seems."

"Unless, like the lukewarm believer, it has spewed me out again."

"There was never lukewarm in your humor, my lord. But to the point, have you kept at practice, or are you now all book-heavy?"

"I would answer you in more than words, and shortly too, but that I know your pupils await you. If the times and the chimes continue to remain unchanged for you as well. Therefore, will I boast only that I acquitted myself well among the sword-pupils of Wittenberg—I have been in continual practice—and I have brought for you some half-dozen uses of the blade to add to your lexicon the which I believe you will seize upon like a glutton at his lunch."

"You have me slavering already, my lord. Ah, Helmuth." Marcellus shifted his gaze to a point behind Hamlet where one of the pages had entered. "You are come, but where is Sten?"

"He comes anon, Master Marcellus. He has been waylaid by Master Osric and set at some task too menial for the latter." The boy spoke breathlessly as he came in at a run and had to pull up short to keep from colliding with Hamlet.

"Osric? Is he still pupil to you?" asked Hamlet in surprise.

"Nay, my lord. But as son of the Seneschal, he makes himself important at the most inconvenient times. Go ahead, lad, take up the usual number, minus one. It seems Alan is down with the sniffles." This last he directed at the page who slipped around Hamlet at Marcellus's beckoning. Then it occurred to him that the boy may not be familiar with Hamlet by reason of his age and short time at Elsinore.

"Helmuth, this is Prince Hamlet, who is to be your king some-day i' the future."

The boy spun around wide-eyed and barely remembered to bow. In his blond hair and blue eyes and especially in his eagerness, Hamlet almost saw the ghost of himself at that age. "Your Highness!" the boy said.

"Peace, lad. The crown is a long way off for me yet. You may be past your training and into service ere it come to me. Where stand you in the form?" Hamlet pursued his natural interest in others.

The boy looked uncertainly at Marcellus. "Go ahead, boy. 'Tis meet for you to speak when bidden."

"I am still in my parries, my lord. I have trouble on the off side and high, so says Master Marcellus." The trainer nodded his head in mild agreement.

Hamlet remembered his late discovery that Marcellus was perceptive in more than the swordsmanship of his students. He wondered again if here was a confidant to his thought problems. But he would consider that more freely later.

"Marry, well bespoke. You obviously attend well to your master's corrections to have such a ready and studied answer. Shows he promise, Marcellus?"

"Aye, my lord. Around him the ashes are warming to a stir. If he continues to apply himself, I may yet see that prodigy take wing."

"Go on with your chores, lad. I can see you are eager to work out your corrections." As the boy fumbled a bit at taking up the swords and then went carefully back around Hamlet, the latter told him, "I'll give you time to work up into your stride, then will I come to see you at your practice, all right?"

"Aye, Your Highness!" Helmuth nearly fumbled again his hold on the double armful of swords he carried as he turned to go out, leaving the two men to chuckle.

"Was I so haphazard at that age?"

"I'm afraid in the comparison he comes out the more graceful, my lord. But 'tis the sort of enthusiasm that rewards me in the undertaking of this charge. I see them come, and I see them go—and hopefully better than they came."

"Without doubt, Marcellus. 'Tis your careful instruction has helped Denmark maintain her sovereignty in the world, e'en more than her stout embattled walls and her yeomen's stubborn and unyielding host. Was 't your father who taught my father the sword? I remember he was before you the sword master of Denmark."

"Aye, my lord. And I was junior to your father but in the same class. As it was, your father followed his father's profession—as who would not—and so I followed my father to this."

"Well, here at last, is blessings from father to son for a thousand generations."

"My lord?"

"Nothing. 'Tis nothing, the full-round completion of a thought begun in Wittenberg. Have I your leave to witness the latter portion of your instruction this day?"

"You needn't ask my leave, my lord."

"'Tis an earned professional courtesy. The interruption of a class at swords is a delicate matter, like to the spilling of a bag of glass beads in the midst of a lesson at dancing."

"I will make it a request then, my lord, that you attend to see the mettle of your younger subjects. And afterward will we dine upon these sword techniques you have imported—or are they smuggled?"

"Imported for I have made no promise to secrecy in learning them. I shall come."

"Good, my lord. News of that will add zeal to the flagging attendance of a few who think they have learned all."

"Hm, a dangerous place to linger in a student's journey of notions."

"Aye, my lord, but 'tis easily corrected with one of Osric's 'palpable hits.'"

"To be sure. My bruised knuckles and gouged ribs of old helped me to remember my lessons. Too bad for human nature that pain is oft the surest deterrent. Yet even it, or threat of it, hath not the power to keep us to the narrow way for pain's not sweet and won't defeat the will's design to set the mind and let the will dispose the day!"

"Hah! Were I not so sure of your quick wit, my lord, I would say you had been brewing that triple couplet some time."

"It is the natural effulgence of a joyous homecoming, I am sure."

*****

Hamlet's first night back in his old room was a combination of comfort in the present among the things of his past and speculation over the future. He marveled at his boyish collection of artifacts that he had carefully packed away before his departure. That such dried, pressed, rusty, fragmentary bits of creation should have not only held his interest but inspired him to sort and preserve them filled him with an amused patience for his younger self. And yet to toss all on the morrow into the trash heap would take an act of the will. It would be a streak of his mother within him to hold that he would be throwing much of the "boy" away. Yet to persist in their retention would be a form of unmanly grief. He must simply do it with no thought and then rejoice in the new space available to him in his room. But space for what?

Certainly, he must give thought to his growing library. It already outclassed his father's. But his father was of an earlier age, he mused. He could readily understand the subordinated place given to books in a world dominated by warrior spirit. In this present age, diplomacy appeared to be the thing. Sure, he would attend his uncle's instructions and then look for a type of Horatio to help pilot him through the shoals and guide him between the Scylla and Charybdis of international waters. For all this, he knew he had time.

That thought brought him back to Helmuth, his comment to him that the lad would be grown and in service by the time he came to the throne. The boy did show promise in his sparring practice. He would be sure to follow the lad's progress. Then his thoughts made another short jump.

Marcellus was thrilled over the techniques Hamlet had showed him. The two had agreed to collaborate on a written description of them that Marcellus could keep for a reference to a time when his students were ready for them. His old master also owned himself favorably impressed, and greatly so, at the demonstration of Hamlet's skills. This and a dinner of his favorite dishes—carefully ordered by his mother—capped his day.

In this last part of the day, he spent reviewing every minute, every look, every message passed silently between him and Ophelia in his mother's sitting room. In his memory, all else was mere background noises, almost ghostly images of no substance. He could not remember anyone else's questions to him. They were all blurred. How he managed not to give over and simply stare at her the whole time, he could not say. He prayed that he had not given himself away with overlong study of her.

But now, the question of how to see her again and speak privately the myriad of things he wanted to say to her moved to the center of his thoughts. Perhaps he should simply approach the queen, state his intentions, and ask her to arrange matters. That would be the easy and certainly the most honorable way. He truly had no desire to be clandestine about their relationship. But—and this was the big question that had begun to trouble him—what if his wedded fate had already been determined as a matter of state policy? He was of royal blood. Though her father was first minister of the realm, Hamlet was not sure if that were a high enough station from which to draw forth a queen.

Hamlet remembered an offhand discussion of this issue with Horatio some months back at Wittenberg. Without indicating that he had anyone in mind, he and his friend explored the implications. Horatio owned that his father possessed the requisite wisdom to choose a spouse for him who would both add to the family name of Schleswig and who would be a helpmeet in all his duties.

"What about affection?" he had asked Horatio.

"Sure, I would accord her all the affection of my husbandly office. She will not go wanting on that account."

"But how if she feels not affection in equal measure for you?"

Horatio's raised eyebrows—which made his face go almost completely oval—and his look of innocent shock truly gave Hamlet his answer. How could anyone not feel affection for such an honest countenance as that? He also could not see Horatio's father handing him a Jezebel or an Athaliah for reason of state. No, his consort would be carefully and lovingly chosen, and she would be compelled by gentle affection to return affection in kind.

"But what of myself?" he asked the darkened room. "How should I thus carefully proceed if expectation is thwarted to fill a politic need?"

# Act 4

# Chapter 16

How to proceed? Hamlet feared the hand of politics reaching into the stuff of his dreams with an arresting purpose. This fear stayed him from approaching the queen with even the most vague questions about future marriage plans for him. Neither of his parents broached the subject to him even though he had been two years back from Wittenberg and was now approaching twenty-two.

At times, his mother seemed to have considered Ophelia favorably. She would mention her by name specifically from among her ladies and discuss some of her merits before him. But he was not sure how to understand this, and he was not willing to chance an open rejection of his hope should he voice it.

Though she, too, had advanced in age and, by the standards of the day, was nearing the horizon of spinsterhood, there had been no talk of marriage plans for her from Polonius. This situation was the occasion of one close call. One day at a private lunch with Hamlet, the queen mentioned in passing that she thought either the chief minister was too busy to notice the promise of his lovely daughter or was unwilling to empty his house of the feminine touch. She added that she did not think him holding out for an advantageous marriage. Hamlet wondered if this was a possible invitation to advance his own dream. But with no informed or ready response from her vastly interested son, the subject changed quickly.

After a final sigh from the queen, she wistfully added, "Well, we may have to do something."

No pointed look from his mother had accompanied this, so he let it pass into silence.

But again, how to proceed? Hamlet was fortunate in being able to enlist the aid of the same courier who had delivered his letters to Ophelia from Wittenberg as a messenger between them. In this way, he was able to maintain a contact for the making of plans. But plans there were none. His first letter expressed this new dilemma. Even as he penned it, he owned himself a moral coward, devoid of honor, unable to stand in what would be most assuredly a lost battle for his druthers. She should rightly recoil at his doleful and plodding reasoning. But she responded that she, too, feared to lose the little bit of what they shared by reason of the stronger argument of the needs of state.

For some months, they continued at correspondences with no clue from either of them for how to have their day "a-dragon-back." As an unattached maiden, she was still kept close, either in company with her nurse or with one of the matrons of the queen's entourage. Neither of them was willing to chance a clandestine meeting of any sort, and Hamlet made it clear that he had no intention of leading her down that path. He thanked the Lord that she at least remained patient even while he burned.

Then one day, chance favored them.

*****

The soft washing of the sea waves upon the shore had about lulled Ophelia to sleep as she sat upon a cloth with her book of romantic poetry. Nurse was already far gone beside her—snoring happily—and would likely remain so for hours. The strand just beyond the sea gate bent around to a cove made semiprivate by large boulders that had been carved away from the bluff above them by wind and waves. To this place, she and Nurse had started coming since the willow beside the brook was getting beyond the range of Nurse's rheumatic hobble. It was peaceful, secluded, and yet near enough to fortified succor for two ladies to take their ease. In short, it was perfect for what followed.

Unwitting of their presence, Hamlet had made his way out to this same spot some three months after his return from Wittenberg.

There he found them. He had known of the place for years. Every so often in his younger days, he and Horatio would venture out to mount an offensive against a pirate lair. They would leap and dodge among the boulders and then rest and discourse with boyish solemnity all to the same lapping of the waves.

On that first day of his return to the spot as a man, he had come out to ponder his dilemma and let the sea speak to him. Chancing upon Ophelia at that time and noticing Nurse benignly supine, his heart rejoiced. She rose to his proffered hand and continued to hold it beyond courtesies. Wordlessly, they had studied each other's eyes in a way they never could have before.

On this day, now with over a year and a half of these meetings between them, Ophelia could almost sense Hamlet's approach. Certainly, she could picture it as it had occurred at least two score times before. He would appear from around the large boulder, book in hand—a pretext usually—though sometimes there was something for him to read to her. Then she would rise and go to him where they sat together upon the rocks, always in Nurse's sight should she awaken but well out of her hearing by reason of the waves. Here they would speak of pleasant thoughts.

As she conjured this happy image, it occurred exactly. Hamlet appeared. Neither of them had grown tired of what could nearly be classified as a ritual. The next two hours would be wonderful, with little chance of Nurse waking—Ophelia had always had to rouse her from deep slumber. So now, coming to him again, they held a long embrace and let the warmth of affection eddy about them as substantial as the sea breeze that played with Ophelia's hair. After a time, they took seat side by side and gazed out to sea, their hands clasped together. Silence at these times was as wonderful to them as talking.

But this day, Ophelia gauged a heavy brooding in Hamlet's being. His gaze reached farther out to sea than usual, and his silence was pregnant with sighs. His thumb massaged the back of her hand with a demi-peevishness. Though reading most people did not come easily to Ophelia, yet Hamlet was her book, and she often noted his moods; though of her own, she knew not their causes. She did know that she could broach the subject of his moods and receive a fair report of them, if he had had time to think them out.

"You are restless and unhappy, my lord." This seemed to her enough to get him started toward an explanation.

"Aye, that I am. Approaching circumstances divide my mind and constrict my heart."

"A divided mind is your common ground, my lord." She meant to sound playful. "Saving those times when circumstances usher you to one half of your mind or the other." She smiled meekly in hopes that he would see her teasing as an attempt to cheer him.

He looked into her eyes and accepted the offer to step back from his mood. "Well, you know me then. Shall I speak of my constricted heart?"

"What you will, my lord. And I pray I may possess the power to loose the hold of that which binds it."

"You bind my heart but not to a constriction though the circumstance touches you. Oh, lest I continue in riddles, let me say bluntly that I must leave you for a time. That is the manner of my sadness."

"Leave me?"

"Aye. I am to go on embassy, one of some time and distance. It is necessary for my training and to effect some additional measure of earnest to the proceedings by reason of my royal standing."

"Time and distance. How long and how far, my lord?"

"Months, if not a full year."

"Oh, no!"

"But there is some good to it. The distance is as far as here to Paris for that is the destination of our embassy."

"Paris? Laertes!"

"Aye, it will be good to see him and to bring to him from you any special affection you may desire to send. It will be good also to remake his acquaintance and to work jointly to a successful conclusion of our business."

"I would I could journey with you." She gasped at a sudden idea. "Could I go, do you think, as a visitor to my brother?"

"I have thought of that. But our business, it seems, though not covert, is not for general consumption. We take no entourage, travel not in state, and must be seen to have been nearly spirited away to a summary arrival there."

"Oh." Her own disappointment was clear.

"I am reminded by this to tell you that you know naught of it should you be pressed. And you must guard against offhanded reference to it."

"I will be careful of my words." They paused for more thought. "I should consider of my tokens to Laertes. They must be small then."

"Aye. But as he is a good brother, as I trust he is, e'en the smallest token will be a treasure to him."

"A good brother, sure. He still writes dutifully. Did I tell you?"

"Nay, but that's good to hear. Perhaps he'll be moved to mention me in his missives back to you for I see no way to affect a correspondence betwixt us by courier to Paris as in our former days apart. Thus, in the midst of the largest city of all the world, will I be secluded!"

"There is life in Paris, I hear. Even Laertes writes of amiable diversions. You must not tuck yourself away. No, not on my account...my love." That last form of address, coming at the end of a slight pause, made her comment more tender, even as it highlighted the woe he felt.

"To be sure, I can't. Once there, I shall have princely social obligations. And I will mask my true spirit with one of attendant interest. But by the Mass, my heart remains here, as it did in all my years at Wittenberg."

"Then take my heart with you in fair exchange. Locked therein were all my love, and you will keep the key of it."

"Unless should your father come calling to make withdrawal of your love upon some other note of promise."

"Say not so, my sweet! That's a bitter thought. And with you away!"

"Peace. We'll think on that no more."

"And I must contrive some token of mine for you as well, one to keep your heart from straying. I jest, my love," she added this at his look of surprise. Then she paused as if uncertain whether or not to go on. "I…had a dream. We kissed and woke so warm with remembrance of it that I thought it had been true. If ever there was a sweet dream, that is it surely."

They locked eyes again. Hamlet smiled to think that at this close distance, he could in truth only focus on one eye or the other—for they were nearly nose to nose—but not on both eyes. At her mention of a kiss, his pulse quickened, especially when he sensed a corresponding quickness in hers as well. Over all these years, fear of falling into his darker desires with dreams of her had kept him from even imagining a kiss with her. At the same time, kisses were too sweet a thing for his dreams of the sisters. These fears became thoughts. 'Would a kiss with Ophelia be the prelude to a torrent of passion, to be a later cause for remorse? Was there sin in it? Would it make of her a Bathsheba to his David?' These thoughts gave a tentative look to his gaze, a look that she read as shyness. Yet they drew closer.

"I heard it was good counsel to essay our dreams. 'Tis the occupation of the young." He found himself close enough to her that he could whisper this last and be heard above the waves.

"I…we…" She tilted her head, and he found himself tilting his head the other way.

Their lips touched as their arms wrapped around each other. Their first kiss was but a moment. At its conclusion, Ophelia dipped her head, and Hamlet kissed her forehead. They both drew back as if to study its effects. Ophelia smiled nervously. Hamlet looked past her for an instant, and she snapped her head around. Nurse was still sleeping peacefully. When Ophelia looked back, she was smiling fully. For some reason, she sniffed. They whispered a laugh and then kissed again and again.

After a while, Hamlet began to worry. He knew the source of his concern. The darker thoughts stood poised. He knew it would be the easiest thing to cross the threshold from light into dark, if only in his thoughts. To act was unthinkable, and he had already purposed in his heart that he would steer Ophelia away from any such fall from grace. Soon, he found himself praying that she would be satisfied with their present kissing to leave off. After one particularly long kiss, where a pause for breath was required, he dipped his head to touch foreheads with her. They remained for a time nose to nose.

"I have now my token though is it not a token but an earnest of our love." She seemed to understand for she nodded her head in little affirmative nods in a quiet acceptance that, for now, kissing was done. With one quick peck on his cheek, she concluded the matter. They returned to their usual habit of talking. At the end of their time, they made arrangements for one more meeting just prior to his planned departure.

"I will save my kisses 'til then," she said softly before returning to the nurse.

His hand remained extended out as hers slipped away from it.

"It was as saving every breath to be absent from your kisses is living in the midst of death."

*****

"Here are the introductions to the minister of France and to our own ambassador thereof," said Claudius, handing Hamlet his portfolio. "Without these seals, you are no different from John-a-dreams."

"I comprehend the import of them and will keep them close. Yet should mischance befall them, in desperation, Laertes could of a need vouchsafe my verity to the one and the one to the other." Receiving no indication of amusement from Claudius, Hamlet added, "Fear not, good uncle, I am careful in my office. Have I not shown that these two years in thy service?"

"Indeed, you are careful to a fault. But a confirmed countenance is always best policy in the dispatch of embassies. Your mission, when concluded successfully, will be to Denmark's advantage through more kingly reins than the present. Think of it as one less worry to your father."

"And so I shall. I will convey these to Sir Hugh ere we quit Elsinore and be like a doubled watch o'er him and these his effects."

"It likes us well. Also, here are the dispatches to our embassy and the odd personal briefs to our ranking Danskers in residence abroad in Paris. In this, you fill the office of our courier, who e'en now should be on his return from there."

Hamlet idly thumbed through the sealed letters. "Here's two for Laertes."

"His father, Polonius, and from his sister, I believe."

"Aye, that would be it." He recognized Ophelia's hand on one. "I have good cause to bring him tidings of his family."

"Oh?"

"Well, though we are not fast friends, we oft faced each other under master Marcellus's tutelage, and we had served in the war together, he under Sir Hugh. He is a worthy servant of the state."

"I see. I have good report of him from our ambassador there. Perhaps he would outshine his father in the future."

"Easily, save in the volume of words employed to a trifle. He is of few words, but his mind is keen and his swordsmanship eloquent. If our embassy allows us some time at leisure, I have hopes of a gentlemanly *pas de deux* at swords with him."

"That would be a difficult wager for all reports of you both. Would I could be there to witness it."

"Fate may bring the bout closer to home, Uncle."

"We make our own fate had we the wit and the daring." Claudius seemed to speak this last more under his breath and to himself, as if pushing himself to a decision. In the short silence that followed, the king entered Claudius's office.

"Hamlet, sorry am I that I was indisposed at your call. I presume it was to take your leave of us?"

"Aye, sire."

"And your mother, is she well visited?"

"I have left her most recently. She is 'satisfied but not happy,'" he replied with a smile at one of her well-used phrases.

"I have known her thus." His father also seemed to speak to himself. Then the king marshaled what appeared to be almost a brave smile from a previous gloom. "You have, in this embassage, been keenly briefed and know of our great hopes for its success. Therefore, shine like the prince of Denmark but with a deference to the skill of Sir Hugh. You will learn a thing or two in his service."

"Aye, Father. 'Tis listed in my expectations."

"I shall not stay thee with fatherly advice. My own expectations on your account do not flag for doubt. At one time, you departed here a boy and returned a youth of renown, then once again you departed a youth with promise and returned a man without question. Now you depart a man. What you shall return only fate knows, but with wit and daring you may bend fate to an end of your choosing. My only inclination is that you not return a king—for all that would mean!"

This turn of the conversation, though it was meant as casual banter, sent a prophetic chill up Hamlet's spine. His father's near echoing of Claudius's words on fate and the suggestion of his own death struck a nerve. Hamlet quickly cast the mood aside as an unlucky thought.

"We are in common accord there, Father. As I once spoke unto Yorick, I would gladly be prince eternal to an everlasting king." Yorick...why did he have to mention his deceased friend?

"Yorick. I had all but forgot him. And what said he to that?"

"He accounted it blasphemy for purloined titles of the divine and, at the same time, employed his wit in polemic against my offer to him of the regency. For owned he the wit, yet dared he not attempt the fate of it."

"Regent?"

"'Twas the morning we rode off together for war, a time for speaking of regents."

"Hm. Yorick as regent. There was a wisdom in that, to a point, meaning no disrespect to you, brother Claudius. Your service as regent in that time was exemplary."

"No offense taken, Your Highness." But Claudius's humorless formality as he bowed to his older brother—king by accident of birth—seemed to Hamlet to bespeak an offense taken at some degree.

"Your pardon, Your Highness." Polonius's voice broke into the modest tension as he entered the chamber. Looking past the king, he spied Hamlet. "Ah! Yet here, my Lord Hamlet? Sir Hugh has sent to inform you that he and his are embarked and that however much they might exercise the virtue of long-suffering, yet the time and the tide will not, as the saying goes, attend upon you. You are wanted aboard. There was a seaman's way of putting the wind into the sail as a turn of phrase to hurry one who is stayed for, but I cannot now recall it. Ergo, farewell it for a forgotten figure unless it should return to me at next need."

"My thanks, Lord Polonius. My effects are also embarked, and it is only for me to bring this commission on board to Sir Hugh. Father, Uncle, I take my leave. And of that, there is nothing I am more loathe to part withal."

"Except it be your life for that would be the hardest leave-taking," spoke Polonius in an attempt at blithe philosophy.

'Even my life were not so hard a thing to let slip as your daughter, old man!' Hamlet thought and had to check to make sure he had not thought it out loud.

"Then since I have a choice in the matter, I choose—this once—the easier way and depart merely with my presence, leaving my life to ride the waves of fate. So depart I now, lest I be…tardy! Goodbye, Father, my lords."

"You could have rhymed!" his father called to his departing son. "Godspeed and success to your mission."

"Aye, thank you, Father." Turning about to wave a parting salute, the sight of his father and uncle standing together left him again with an uncomfortable premonition. He held his smile until he turned back and walked again toward his future.

*****

Paris. It was bigger than all his imagination unleashed. There was more humanity encompassed by its walls than he had ever seen. All other cities paled. Yet lest anyone think it the eternal city of Revelation, the "New Jerusalem" come to earth, let us say that Hamlet saw in it merely the most vast collection of stone, mortar, and half-timbered plaster. If he let himself, he could even have viewed it an opulent and well-stocked prison for all that its walls held him in and that his tenure there kept him from his true desires. Almost, its promises mocked his predilections for there was nothing of Ophelia in it.

Well, almost nothing. Laertes's countenance could be said to be a comely masculine rendering of hers. The family resemblance teased him for though there was none of her softness in it, yet there was the light of a noble soul in the eyes that matched hers. He feared his admiration might be misread. On the one occasion so far that Hamlet had witnessed of Laertes's full and unrestrained laughter, there was a gaiety in it that also mirrored hers.

Her brother had greeted Hamlet affably and took him in hand, so to speak, in introducing him to the ambassador's working staff. Hamlet could readily see where the labor lay. Laertes and a half score of other bright young men, culled by reason of their promise at the university, operated efficiently to gather and sort the information that fed the appetite of state. It gave him a vision of how he could help his uncle organize the same at Elsinore into the beginnings of a bureau. A half-formed idea from out of the past—his father's assessment of Claudius's desire to wield the machinery of state—led Hamlet to consider that such an agency might satisfy and yet limit his uncle's need for power.

But all that was business, a business to which he had kept himself in order to sustain himself throughout his separation from Ophelia. Others, less kindhearted in their thinking, as generally lazy people are wont to be, might attribute his tireless efforts to a rivalry with Laertes for renown in the profession. His ardent supporters merely claimed that his diligence had been no different in all his life, only more easily channeled into the efficiencies of the bureau. Odain simply shrugged his shoulders if asked about it and thanked his Maker that Hamlet's industry did not bend itself toward any extra demands on his service.

Only Hamlet knew the truth. Idle time was still his battlefield. The sisters had followed him like baggage, even patiently waiting his needs, knowing he would turn to them in time. They owned the night, not every night, but he came to them with enough regularity to account themselves victors in the field.

For his part, Hamlet had ceased struggling, guilt only attended him in the rearmost of his busy thoughts and surged when he let his thoughts turn again to the sisters—another reason he kept his mind busy with work—work and social obligation.

As prince of Denmark, he stood colossus-like astride the two banks of his world. On the one bank was the work of the proto-civil servant—which we have said he relished for its activity—and for the other, there were the social and diplomatic demands of his station. These latter were, at best, a duty to be performed, at worst, a test of his impatience to be elsewhere.

Meeting with other princes and high ministers with whom he could discuss diplomatic matters was a clear relief at such events. But at these occasions there was little of that. Mostly, he dreaded the parade of marriageable royalty before him. Here his disdain was not due to any comparison of royal flesh to his beloved Ophelia. To be sure, there were eyes that surpassed hers, forms that filled skirts in ways that excited desire—had he let them—and even a round number who spoke and moved with a grace that left Ophelia in the country.

The sore point for Hamlet was that he saw in all their motivations, no matter how cannily contrived or subtly exerted, merely a genteel version of the sisters' invitations to the flesh. Could he have taken to his bed these polished beauties? Undoubtedly. Would they have stepped down from their pedigreed pedestals and into his heated embraces? Sure, and with their nurses' contrivance and blessings. Could he achieve a life of wedded bliss with any of them? Perhaps, but along with them came the strings of diplomacy, such that to wed one was to wed one's nation. To wed the nation was to embrace its aspirations, its assets, and its liabilities. It would be to wed Denmark to the woes of Europe, to the one side or the other of what he saw was merely the dynastic feuding of an overlarge and power-ravenous family called the nobility.

In the end, he knew it would be all these considerations first with personal feelings following in the wake. Yes, in the wake, not even inside the vessel itself but struggling along in the after-wash. Hamlet's conscience had too keen an edge to suffer this blithely. He could begin to understand why kings took mistresses. But that path was not for him.

Throughout the cycle of these social cattle shows, he was amazed and gratified that he could refuse the invitations of the two sisters in the material waking world—as he had done when facing "La Esperanza"—even though he knew himself powerless to resist in the world of his fancy. He supposed it to be a fair enough irony but, at the same time, agonized over what he felt was a decidedly double life.

Though some matrons and their protégé daughters may have sniffed at his proud chastity—proud in their eyes because they could not fathom any sane reason for his rejection of the flesh—yet he had grown to understand the truth behind his reading of the proverb: "The heart knows its own bitterness."

With all this to cheer him, Hamlet settled into his quarters and his routines. In truth, he looked forward to the present moment of solitude in his rooms, had looked forward to it since his departure from Elsinore. At their last meeting by the sea, Ophelia presented to him a packet of a half-dozen "letters" that she had begun following his announcement of their impending separation. They were for him to open one at a time, each a month apart, as though they had come to him by post.

She teased him unmercifully that he would, like a treasure of sweets, open and read them all on the first day of his voyage out. Yet she knew he would maintain his discipline, and so he did.

Here at the conclusion of his first month, he held her prime letter to him. Its exterior he knew by heart. Its message within he would soon have committed to memory as well. With almost solemn ceremony, he ran his dagger under the flap to break the wax seal. Seated with his back to the windowlight of his sitting room, he unfolded the letter and began to read.

> My dearest love,
> Knowing that you have not forgotten me yet, I take pen to remind you further of the love you will find on your return—

# Chapter 17

Hamlet carefully tested each of the baited swords from the rack before him. He sought the balance and the grip that best suited him. Returning to the third one from the left, he took it up and confirmed with a circular swipe in the air that this was the weapon of his choice. Across the yard, Laertes did the same. When he, too, had determined upon his weapon, he turned to face the center and saw that Hamlet was ready.

Both men had looked forward to this match from the moment Hamlet suggested it. But their business and Sir Hugh's mission had kept them so busy that only now, in the middle of his second month in Paris, was there found a convenient time to try their skills.

Much as they tried to keep this essay at arms informal, word soon got around and a flurry of wagers ensued. The odds heavily favored Laertes as the contender more familiar to the ambassador's staff. But Hamlet also had his loyal defenders, and Sir Hugh was able to give good report of his prince even though he had also been witness to Laertes's prowess from their service together in the war. He owned them equally matched, and the wagers came down to counting the odd hits.

The yard now ringed with all the young men of the staff and a few guests from other legations. It was known that the two were friends; therefore, the interest in the event was far from sanguinary. At a nod, both young men stepped up to the sword master and stood at the acceptable distance.

"Good day to you, Laertes," Hamlet spoke first according to his rank, but his tone showed him eager to dispense with rank for the moment.

"Good day to you, Your Highness."

"I hope you will find here no German in retreat but a Dansker of able mettle."

"Let us say that whoever is victor, the glory goes to the one man who trained us both."

"Indeed. To Marcellus then!"

"To Master Marcellus."

"Your Highness, Master Laertes, you each know the rules. Have you any questions in your mind concerning them?"

"None, sir," they both responded in turn.

"Then touch swords and you may begin." The master backed away.

Each of the opponents turned, took a half step away from each other to be in the proper fighting distance, and brought their weapons to *en garde*. A brisk and cheery tap rang out, like the stroke of a tuning fork, and both men smiled.

Hamlet anticipated Laertes's initially defensive strategy—the one that had worked so well so many years back. He thought he would oblige him by pressing forward first. But he would not wear himself out as at that time for he put only moderate strength into each beat and thrust of the sword. He would test Laertes's guard. Gauging each parry—high, low, left, and right—to determine if any particular one was slower or weaker than the rest, he found that they were nearly equally all covered.

"Your Highness fights to a caution," said Laertes with barely any effort of breath.

"I have learned, 'quick to the plunder, quick into blunder!'"

"Indeed. A good truth. Where learned you that, my lord?"

"At your hand, Laertes!" He smiled at Laertes's laugh. "O'er the years, I have digested your helpful corrections. Do you feel that you fight yourself today?"

"'T would be a tiresome turn of events to do so. Nay, my prince, I am well occupied with this."

"Good i' faith. I would that I should not bring on a drowsiness for you with my efforts."

Through all this banter, Hamlet continued to test randomly for openings. He began to think that he detected a slightly slower response when Laertes parried low to his left. A strategy formed in his mind in which, after random beats, he would move to cause his opponent to parry left and low but always follow that with an approach that was left and high. He repeated this short pattern often enough until he saw that Laertes's reaction had become automatic. At that point, he advanced low to the inside and was met with the expected parry. Then he feinted a move to the high inside, and when Laertes responded, almost in advance, Hamlet switched directions coming under his opponent's blade, beat it farther to the left and lunged.

"A hit! The first hit goes to the prince!" announced the master.

There were cheers, but Hamlet also gauged a thin undercurrent of disappointment over the first wagers lost. He smiled modestly on the outside. Inwardly, he beamed to think that he had finally scored a hit against his hero. Should he lose the entire match, this accomplishment was a joy enough.

Laertes bowed and bestowed an appreciative smile. "Well done, Your Highness." But there was something in the smile that also said, "I have discovered your strategy and will guard against it."

Hamlet returned a smile that he hoped conveyed the message, "I have others."

Reengaging for the second bout, Hamlet found his efforts a little harder going. Laertes claimed an early hit with a feint, beat, and lunge that came quick as lightning. Interest on the sidelines perked back up, and there were confident looks in Hamlet's peripheral view, looks that warned him against thinking he had completely sounded his opponent out. He reminded himself that Laertes was a mature fighter who would not begin with all his skill displayed at once nor would he exhaust all his strategies early.

During the third bout, when caution swelled on both sides, a page came hurriedly up to the master and spoke in his ear.

"Gentlemen!" the master announced. Both heeded the call and turned to him, lowering their weapons. The master deferred to the page, who spoke breathlessly to Hamlet.

"Forgive me, Your Highness, but the ambassador requests you attend him in his chamber without delay." Hamlet and Laertes exchanged blank glances. The page continued, "The ambassador hath said were you e'en at the bath, you should come in your towel. It is that urgent."

*****

Hamlet sat in a plain chair across from the ambassador. He was still dressed for his match with Laertes. His breathing came quickly but not from any exertion. He looked up from the paper he held, a letter from Elsinore under his uncle's signature. In his expression, unbelief mixed with a loss for what to do next. The ambassador fixed a concerned gaze at him. Yet he, too, was uncertain of how to proceed. So he waited.

"Dead? My father is…dead?" He glanced up from the paper as if, in looking away, somehow the wording would change to something less dire. Still, he had to speak his astonishment. "But he was hale at our parting. Looked he weary, aye, but not unto—oh, heavens!"

"The letter states further that His Majesty was discovered thus upon his couch at the portico above the terraced garden. He had retired there to nap for the afternoon."

"Aye, 'twas his custom, always."

"Forgive me, my lord, for informing you in advance of the letter, which you shall read, but it says also therein that it is believed he succumbed to the sting of a venomous serpent. His…appearance had the look of one so assailed. The queen requests your immediate return. For reasons I am sure you understand, I cannot spare Sir Hugh in this current business, so I have a mind to send Laertes as your travel companion and attendant. He has been some time away from Elsinore and his family. I also understand that you are friends."

"Aye, Lord Vanardt. It will be a comfort to journey with him. I thank you."

"Word will now go out from this, and our embassy will observe a heartfelt mourning. But I have also ordered the arrangements for your return journey on the morrow. In the meantime, think of me as one to whom you can unburden your grief. I loved your father and have ever striven to serve him well. I would I could be like an uncle to you in your time of need."

At his use of the word *uncle*, Hamlet flinched as though from an electric shock. "I am grateful." After a moment, all he could think of to say was "I shall pack." He rose stiffly. "I should like to read this over in my chambers."

"Of course. It was addressed to me only that I might be the one to advise you of its contents with some preparation. Consider it yours."

"All my thanks are but somber fare; yet are they genuine. My apologies, my lord, if I fail of ardor in their expression. I am benumbed in my brain at present."

"No apologies are needed, Your Highness—pardon, Your Majesty."

Hamlet bit his lower lip at that. He closed his eyes and inhaled deeply. Before his mind could go spinning off with the contemplation of such an unfortunate blessing, he wiped his face with his hand and cast a tear-rimmed look at the ambassador. With a nod, he withdrew to his room.

*****

Odain met Hamlet at his door also with tear-reddened eyes and an expression of personal sorrow. Hamlet studied his face as if seeing it for the first time. His servant's passion surprised him.

"Odain? Loved you your king so much?"

"Aye…Your Majesty, and the current one as well." He nearly sobbed. "I have been blessed in my service to them both. This has put me in mind of my own Da, who served your father as steward. Certain am I he is likewise in heavy grief and all Denmark with him. Your father—you should hear often enough, even on the commonest lips—was a goodly king."

"Aye, a goodly king and an uncommonly good husband and father. We will not see his like again."

"Except it be i' the son. But excuse me, my lord. 'Tis not my place. I go to have your bags brought down."

"Thank you, Odain." They passed a moment in silent regard. Then the latter moved to his task.

"Odain?" The steward turned from where he stood after entering the hall. "It is the place of every man to speak his heart. I thank you for your words."

"Your Majesty," he said, backing away a few paces before turning again.

Hamlet watched his servant go, then entered his room, and sat at a chair near the window. It was the place where he had read Ophelia's letter. Now he reread this from his home. Its news still seemed incredible to him. How could his father be dead? Yes, a serpent's sting. Such things happened usually to babes in the cradle or to the unwary in wood or field. But to attack a sleeping man upon a couch above the ground, how likely was that?

That the terraced garden, completely encompassed, should harbor a deadly serpent also struck him as unfathomable. How often had he played there, read there, and on one satisfying afternoon, spoken with Ophelia there? It must have come from without. Perhaps it was winged. 'Is the serpent still loose in Elsinore?' he thought almost out loud. 'Or did it, beelike, deliver of its venom and fly off again to perish?'

"Oh, we linger in futility to speculate the manner of his death." This he addressed to the empty room. "The thing is done, and now my father walks Elysium's fields that range beyond mortality. *Mortality*, 'twas once a word to conjure up the soft goodbye of blissful years, whispered at the peaceful bedside of some beloved ancient's halting drift toward his desire for repose while we go on, less one, into the remnant of our own tomorrows. Tomorrows that all must end in like mortality. 'Tis sure, no man can journey past its bounds and then return and in reporting, make us wiser with our lives. What's done is done, no matter what we would. Therefore, must I now consider of the future, nor mine alone, but intertwined with mine lies Denmark's fate, fated as she is to couple with a king the likes of me. For Denmark, having lost a king is not without a king. I am he, and I like me not.

"Likewise, it is profitless to speculate upon what manner of king I shall become. Nay, 'tis a question held against the day mortality comes again to call whose woeful answer follows me into the grave and thus it falls beyond correction. I must simply be a king and bend my all unto that most best manner of ruling I can with grace effect. But e'en that peers too far ahead to pave my way with misty 'what-ifs.' And like the future, I have no leisure to consider of my sorrow only. What of my mother and her grief at this? What could my swift-est return remedy of her deep sorrow? They were so longtime happily in love. Why, he was so gentle of her needs and form that he would not have the blast of winter visit her too harshly. Oh, go not that way with my thoughts. The thought's too bitter, and comfort have I none in it. And it may be that I must be a king to her as well and tap her fervor for the state, that she takes comfort in a son who answers well the call to rule. Thus, my course is clear, and pray I now God's grace to be a goodly king and rightly rule those hearts I hold most dear.

*****

"Does nature now contend against me and seek to keep me from my throne?" Hamlet asked the turbulent waves against which strove the ship on which he had embarked. Rain, though in sea-son, had slowed his progress all across northern France and the Low Countries with muddy quagmire roads and washed-out bridges and ferries broken loose from their moorings.

Though eager to serve his monarch and like-minded that they should at least make the attempt, it was still with some misgivings that the captain agreed to sail out for Elsinore in the heady weather to complete the last leg of Hamlet's journey. The wind, already against them at their start, turned vicious and beat them twice back in their attempt to round the surf-dashed headland.

This same wind carried Hamlet's question unheard across the deck and out to windward. It mattered not for he spoke now to no one, if not to God. Each delay along his route had struck his spirit in the same way the roiling swells slammed against the vessel's bow, leaving him with a growing anguish. He fought against the mental image of his grief-laden mother, anxious for her son's return, and wondered for her strength to weather such a loss as hers, with only questionable comfort tardily on the way.

The search for simple happiness had been her faith and the goal of her constant endeavor in presiding over a court emasculated of any intrigue. But now he questioned if this soft faith was strong enough for the heartbreak of such a sorrow. It was a sorrow that could not be patched over with kindly words and trifling gifts and consolations designed to divert the injured ego of a court lady. Death was too immediate a question for such baubles and, like this ship upon this storm, could only be faced head-on against the battering of all its unkind swells. Like the captain, he knew that to turn before the wind without care would leave the craft broadside to the waves and at the mercy of a sudden broaching.

"Mother, I come!" he yelled into the wind, willing the message to reach her lest she be swamped in failed effort to face the personal storm.

*****

Finally, the wind abated, but still it blew against them, causing them added time in tacking. Also, they must be careful of the shore to windward lest they be blown to a grounding or a smashing against the rocks. The low clouds of a broken sky scudded from horizon-east to horizon-west as the ship took the waves more easily. Hamlet stood again at the rail, staring out at nothing, his emotions nearly dulled with overuse.

At the height of the storm, his emotions had likewise peaked and assailed his weakened self-control. He had felt like a wounded beast at bay, confused by the apparent contrivance of a creation turned against him and for sport. Had not Laertes kept a close watch, desperation might have shortened Hamlet's story and left us with a lesser legend to consider. The loyal subject had nearly to wrestle him from the rail and down to his berth, all the while fearing for the sanity of his king.

But that was in the yestereve. Hamlet, coming to his senses, owned himself enfevered of his thoughts. With his calm assurance that he was better armed against despair, Laertes and Odain suffered him to mount again to the deck. In truth, the seas were still unsettled enough to make life a physical misery down in the hold and to compound the spiritual one that was his constant travel companion above deck.

"It should not be long now, Your Majesty," spoke Laertes, joining his king at the rail. "Though I have not made the crossing often, yet the distant landforms speak familiarly to me, like the doors and windows and shop signs of my street at homecoming."

"Aye, Laertes. I, too, have felt the air of home hearth's warm welcoming. Almost I scent the moldy corners of the keep under the stairs as you go by the lobby, where in my boyhood life I scratched for secret hidden treasures. Once in sport, I hid from your father, Polonius, to assail him suddenly from my darkened ambuscade. I think he has been something skittish of me ever since."

"He told me of your prank and claimed it set his hair to graying. Whereat my sister, Ophelia, commenced to counting upon his locks and found there not but a dozen strands of gray. Yet it seemed to me that that was as far advanced in her numbers as her very young years had brought her to. I believe she is but a little shy of your own age, Your Majesty."

"Like enough. Have I told you she sits a beauty among the queen's ladies and is well favored in all the graces, yet of such a gentle and unforced accord in her nature that no vicious envy of her attends her person?"

"You had good report of her when you delivered to me the letters from her and my father on your advent in Paris. But in this you have added in the kinder details to make a brother proud. I thank you. I do wonder that she has not yet been married off. Not that I am keen that she should ascend to irrevocable womanhood, as is the station of a wife. We were affable playmates in our childhood, and the thought of her in that frame is dear to me. Would we could turn back the years. Oh, forgive me, Your Majesty." He realized that his last comment may have constituted a painful reminder. "You have greater cause to desire the return of former years than mere sibling sentiment."

"No need, Laertes. 'Tis a sweet and commendable sentiment from a brother. And sure, could we all profit by such a wish granted. Looking back upon the years, even without death to sorrow over, is bittersweet in the happiest of families. 'Tis good to hear of tender feelings. All my rage of yesternight was concern for my mother and her weathering of this our joint storm. I confess that unashamedly. Perhaps it speaks a lack of faith in woman's character or of a pride of place that I alone could be a comfort to her. The truth is, I have no compass to guide me through the first hours of my return. There will be my mother. But most assuredly, there will be Denmark and decisions pressing for the continued functioning of the state. Which is the most immediate, I know not. I tell you here that I shall indeed look to your father and his like for good counsel."

"There is your uncle."

"My uncle. Can you a confidence keep?"

"I have the ambassador's trust for my credentials in the keeping of confidences. You must not forget my profession. It is an edifice of sworn secrets." Laertes spoke lightly in this, so Hamlet knew that he had taken no insult at the question.

"Forgive me, Laertes. I spoke without thinking, a thing against which I now must most carefully guard. The question came to me like a parry, on instinct rather than by design. I meant no doubt of your character. But to my point, I must say, but wherefore I know not, that I attend mine uncle with something short of wariness. Let us say a guardedness—perhaps against his own self-interest. Brother to a king is as close to the throne as son, if election runs that way."

"I see. Then shall I also carefully regard him, as do you, and if it be understood as loyalty, I shall report to you aught I hear or see that should your guardedness justify."

"My thanks, Laertes. My second confession is this: that I have, since my youth, anticipated your good talents in service to me as king though I had no notion that those times would come upon us so soon. There is a king and a country needs your good counsel."

"I am honored, Your Majesty."

"Nay, but you will be if my vision of the future has its way."

"Your Majesty!" called the ship's captain from beside the helmsman. "Forgive the interruption, sire, but I recognize the headland of our home and thought you would desire to know the soonest. Elsinore lies beyond that bluff!" He extended his arm out to port a few points off the bow.

Both Hamlet and Laertes looked to see the topmost tower rising behind the indicated bluff.

"Thank God!" Hamlet exhaled this short prayer.

"And pray we on that home will be as much as we recall, as little changed as time and circumstance can effect and as ready for her king as loyal hearts can be."

"Truly. Hold we fast to lessons learned along the way. Our yester-times are past, and all our future starts today."

*****

"The prince returns! Huzzah for the prince of Denmark!" The cry was taken up everywhere as Hamlet rode up from the port to the castle. He smiled wanly at those who cheered for him. There seemed to be in their cheers an element of relief. He felt perhaps that he and they were sharing a loss. His thoughts focused on nothing else but that he was finally home. Yet as they passed under the portcullis and through the gate complex, where the walls could carry his voice forward and there was some measure of privacy for low-key speech, Odain, who rode behind, could not help voicing their common thought.

"Wherefore do they still hail you as 'prince of Denmark,' my lord? Are you not their king by succession even though there is yet no coronation? The simplest among them should know you are their king!"

"I know not, Odain, what this betokens. Sure, 'tis a mystery. But I am too weary to sound it out."

"Is't possible, my lord"—offered Laertes cautiously, who rode beside him—"that the king, your father, hath not died, but upon their summons to you was thought near death by the serpent's sting, and yet in the interim hath recovered of his life?"

Hamlet snapped an incredulous look to Laertes and nearly went white. "Oh, 't would be a joy past all hope as well as an answer to this mystery. Pray, Laertes. Pray indeed that it may be so!"

They passed out into the light of the street and were met again with salutes to "the prince of Denmark who has returned!" Coming up on Ophelia's house, they saw that it was still and appeared closed up. The windows were shuttered though the day was fair and well advanced. Both men studied the house. Hamlet suddenly remembered that it was Laertes's house as well. He turned to him.

"Laertes, you may take your leave here to find your family, as I will shortly find what's left of mine. I thank you for your services on this journey. Remember what we have spoken about the future. But for now, a happy reunion to you. I shall be well with the help of Odain here. Take thy fair hour and greet thy family with love from me as well as you."

"An it please you, Your Majesty—I shall call you that still—I will ride on with you. I expect my family is in service to yours and therefore shall be at the keep. My father is a man wedded to his duty, and my sister may yet be in attendance upon the queen's dearer needs."

"As you will. Your company continues to bring me comfort."

As they approached the steps to the keep, grooms came out at a rush from around by the stable to take the horses. Odain acknowledged that he would take charge of Hamlet's effects. Dismounting, both Hamlet and Laertes bounded up the steps. The old door keeper greeted Hamlet with sobs welcoming "the prince" back. Hamlet took the man's trembling hands and blessed him for his service and his love.

The doorkeeper called to them as they continued inside. "They are in the council chamber, my lord."

Together, they strode into and through the great hall toward the chamber. Servants moved about the hall in their usual numbers and with their usual dispatch, but they were all something more quiet as if there was more for each of them to contemplate while going about their chores.

Almost as if on cue, Polonius came out of the chamber and turned to close the door. Hamlet and Laertes came to an abrupt halt as they heard him speak back into the room before bringing the door to.

"I shall look into it personally, Your Majesty." Turning, he saw his prince and his son. Something, some emotion, drained from his face. But with the quickness of it and in the dim light of the great hall, Hamlet could not make out what emotion it had been, perhaps a relief from the days of stress.

"My lord, you are returned at last. Our hopes were waxing frantic. And Laertes, welcome home, my son. You'll find there is much to do. I shall enlist you presently as my aide. The time is out of kilter, and 't will require more than a kick in the slats to set the springes and the cogs of it to rights."

Laertes waited for Hamlet to respond first, but his prince only stared at the closed door, dumbfounded. "Aye, Father," he addressed his father, but his sidelong glance remained with Hamlet. "I am yours to command, saving the needs of my prince," he finally said softly.

Polonius addressed Hamlet. "Your Highness, the king is within and would meet with you on the instant of your return. That is his expressed desire. Laertes, to draw aside with you a moment?"

"My lord?" Laertes returned to the old form of address on the strength of Polonius's words about "the king."

"Yes, by all means. We shall meet again hereafter. My thanks to you again for your good service." Hamlet continued to stare at the door as he said this almost absently. Then he spoke more slowly. "And now, go I within…to see the king."

Laertes stepped off and joined Polonius, who took his arm by the elbow and immediately began speaking lowly, some instructions as they drew off. Hamlet came up to the door and knocked tentatively.

"Enter." He heard a mature male voice.

Opening the door, Hamlet stepped in. Seated at the head of the council table—in the king's place—he saw the king, his uncle.

# Chapter 18

"Sit you down, Hamlet." His uncle said so much in so little. First things, he had glanced up briefly to see that it was his nephew but spoke only after he returned his gaze to the papers he had in hand. It was all very matter-of-fact. Hamlet also noted the simple use of his Christian name without appellatives. This was not meant to be an exchange of equals nor was it frankness in respect of his adult years.

Then, there was not a word of welcome in it. Hamlet was familiar with his uncle's effusive "court manner" when such was called for before a public audience. He had also been the recipient of his inner "curt manner" when dealing with him over matters of his office and those under him. The greeting was spoken in that second tone. True, the tone was gentle and inviting, if officious—a concession to his bereavement, but only just so. Yet, at the same time, it demanded a response, a decision to compliance.

Therein Hamlet recognized this as a test. He would rather have remained standing for the coming explanation. But was it wise to decline the king's bidding and appear to the man with the upper hand as a young hothead or perhaps even a tantrum-driven child? That was it then. In this one short simple, emotionless "invitation," his uncle had set before him the decision that was to establish the tenor of their relationship.

His uncle was king. That much was clear. Hamlet reflected that he had no sense of the basis by which he could claim his own right of kingship, except that it was his right. He fought the urge to seethe and consoled himself with the thought that no matter how it appeared in this interview—that he was submitting to his uncle—he could still inwardly bide his time. He thought of Laertes's sword tactics and moved down the length of the council table toward the king.

Short of the end, he pulled out the chair heretofore occupied by his uncle while his father was king, the place across from Polonius. At this starting off, at least, he would claim a high place on the council. Pulling it well clear of the table, he sat and waited, not taking his eyes off his uncle.

Claudius did not keep him waiting though he could have. The point had been made. Apparently, he knew better than to push matters beyond reason—a point in his favor. He, too, pulled his chair away from the table and turned it to face his nephew. Then he brought his hands together, fingers intertwined, and rested them in his lap. He studied them for a moment—or was it the king's signet ring he studied? At length, he looked up to speak.

"I am king by default of necessity. Your father died with such swiftness and your return so long delayed that the council was of one accord in passing the crown on to me. What's done is done. Before I ask, let me remind you that I have no heir and, being unmarried, am not likely to produce one. You are young and have not yet completed your schooling in kingship. If you accept this circumstance now and live out the tenure of my reign, it is you who will rule after me. In that time, you will have learned all that you need for a good reign in your own right. And to persevere in your claim now might raise the banner of war and bring a heavy and lengthy disquiet upon our state. Do you accept what God hath placed before us, or do you dispute the succession? Make your decision well bethought ere you answer. There is time."

Time. Perhaps that was the answer. He should bide his time in this. But how long to delay a counterclaim? He considered his uncle's words: 'To persevere in your claim might raise the banner of war.' There was no "might" about it. If he wanted the crown now, they would have to fight. He quickly considered the assets on both sides. No doubt the machinery of government was firmly in his uncle's hands. The council would not have been easily swayed. He, the young prince, was unknown to them. His uncle and his skill at government was thoroughly known to them. They had laid aside the doubt in favor of a certainty and chose stability for the state.

Polonius—as doddering as he seemed—was the mind of the council. His father had declared him to be free of self-interest, and this Hamlet had not only understood and believed but also had witnessed in his time at Elsinore. The old man must have seen some right in it and led the council into its "one accord."

Hamlet knew that in his camp, he had the hearts of his people and could possibly count on the loyalty of a good portion of the royal host. Yet those knights and men-at-arms who did not stand with him would likely be following the legitimacy of the council's decision. To dispute the succession would not simply split the nation. It would trouble the conscience of its better citizens and cause some to stand against him on the basis of legalities and in spite of their affection. He was loathed to turn Denmark against itself.

Next, his thoughts plumbed to the depth of his heart. There had always been the awful and tormenting question over his suitability for kingship, of his deserts of the honor. Until he could clear up the issue of his thought-life, he feared the risk to Denmark, that it should be ruled over by such a moral ogre, such a potential for evil. Denmark—no one wanted more sincerely to rule in her interest, yet no one had more reason to doubt he could sustain such a noble intent. He felt the pang of a lover who must eschew his own desires and commit his beloved to the arms of the better man.

But was his uncle the better man? Well, for the moment, the more capable man. Something else. Denmark's neighbors, seeing a peaceful succession of the crown into the hand of that more capable man, would not be tempted to try Denmark's strength at arms. It was the thing for which his father had striven: to keep Denmark at peace for wariness of her strength. A contested crown could loose the grips on her vassal states and bring the rest, like vultures, to pick over and batten on Denmark's holdings.

Poor Denmark. Troubles within, troubles without, and troubled in her heart of hearts. And he, by pressing his claim, would be the author of all this. No, he would not. To set all this in motion over a personal disappointment is not the act of a worthy king. Denmark deserved better. The peace of Europe—a particular aim of Sir Hugh's mission of which he had been a part—deserved better. He drew breath, and then he looked his uncle in the eye.

"For the sake of Denmark, I will let the matter thus stand."

His uncle relaxed, smiled even. "I had thought you would say as much. It is the correct decision and commendable in your nature. You will be greatly needed in many offices and capacities here. Your hand will fill a goodly part of the glove of state, I promise you. And... there is your mother and her present needs."

At this, Hamlet started, recalling his near panic aboard ship over her condition. "My mother! How fares she?" He made no attempt to conceal his concern.

"You will see anon. Go to her now. I will attend to Denmark."

*****

"Mother, mother!" Hamlet called, entering her sitting room unannounced and to the sound of weeping. He saw her sitting at her table with her head propped in her arms. Ophelia sat on the floor at her feet while another lady sat across the table from her.

Ophelia's look upon seeing Hamlet was a nearly indiscernible composite of emotions. In it were mingled grief for the king, deep sorrow over the queen's condition—mixed also with despair and bewilderment over what to do for her—and now, joy, relief, deep love, and her own need for comfort. She rose quickly and spoke softly to the queen.

"Your Majesty, it is Hamlet."

The queen looked up. She had thought his approaching call had come from out of her memory. "Oh, Hamlet, my heart is crushed." She also rose and then went to his arms.

"Leave us for now," Hamlet said in low tones to the ladies. "I thank you for your care here. Take your ease, yet I may call you back soon." He tried to split his gaze equally between the two women, but his final glance was to Ophelia. She nodded and sent him a look that said she understood everything he was eager to say to her. They would have their time, but later.

After they withdrew, Hamlet drew back to study his mother. Her skin was pale and her eyes red with crying. The kerchief she held looked soaked. Her nose was red as though she had a cold. "I am here, Mother. And will always be. Unburden your heart and give grief its broadest and deepest exposition. Sit we down and take me in your thoughts wither you will, even to that day."

"Oh, that day!" She sniffed and bit at her lip. "We had our morning visit—your father and I—a sweet last memory. Then went he to the council meeting, and I joined my ladies. We were even in the terraced garden for a time—my ladies and I—the garden that held such sudden death later in that day. There was no sign of evil then. Nor is there breath of it now. There is only somber sad remembrance. You could go there now. Naught is changed. The couch to which he retired and which for a time served as his funeral byre is back in its place. Oh, Hamlet, wherefor has this come upon us? Is it for sin?"

"Hush, Mother. Speak not of sin. It is the hand of God, as all matters are, but unto what purpose, answer have I none. Likewise, how to go about mourning is beyond me. We must teach each other how life continues. It would seem that all our joy is in the past, and to tap it, we must remember. Will there be joy in the future? I cannot say. Will time dull the pain of bereavement? Again, I cannot say. To remember Father is painful. To forget him is unthinkable. Do we carry him, an unfrozen portrait in our hearts? It may be. To think that he is here is to recall that he is gone, naught but a thought and a memory. How do we hold on and for how long? All this must be worked out. I pray this become not a wound that will fester to make the balance of our life one long, prodigious twilight. Sure, the light has gone out. And for the present, I lack the knowledge or the skill or the heart to rekindle it. If eternity be right in our beliefs, we shall see him again, as he was meant to be, and not in mere mortal coil, earthbound, and lusterless. Perhaps this is the hope of joy to which we should cling. What say you to this?"

"Your careful thoughts fall beyond my ken. The stoic philosophy of death is lost on me as on a child who understands only that her happiness is unaccountably taken from her. I simply want to be happy again."

*****

Hamlet found Lady Marta in the chapel at prayer.

"Her Highness?" Her eyes conveyed the full question.

"She sleeps but not deeply. I think it were good you attend her." He looked about. "Where is Mistress Ophelia?"

"I believe she is in...in the terraced garden. I could not, for the life of me, go there. What she does there, I know not."

"Perhaps there is a remnant of gladsome memories to be gleaned there yet. I'll see to her and, if she is composed, will send her up." His mind was already calculating an opportunity to speak with her privately. This suggestion would give them some time for that.

"Thank you, Your Highness." With a curtsy, she departed the chapel.

Before leaving, he studied the rough crucifix above the altar. 'Is it for sin?' His mother's words came back to him. It was the question he had not yet considered. He did so now.

'Are the sins of the son visited unto the father? For aught I know, the Scripture is silent at this, save that Deuteronomy hath it that parents are not to be put to death for the sins of the children.

'And this is no visitation of wrath against Denmark unless I, by an impious stubbornness, make it so by letting slip the hounds of rebellion in advancing my claim. Nay, there is something more to this. This death may have been foreordained and my father's time all spent. 'Tis the loss of a crown that visits me alone with punishment that I may make correction of my faults and suffer the rule of mine uncle in my own person, and Denmark none the wiser for a good ruling of this new king. He may yet rule justly that he is no villain but has with legal leverage merely seized my delay to his advantage, the desire for honor and kingly right being his only fault.

'Is it fault in a man of capable means to desire to try his hand at the helm when he knows himself to be capable? Would I not do the same if I were uncle and he the right-born heir untried, and if I thought Denmark would be the better for it?' He studied the face of the rough-hewn Christ and could see none of the pathos in it that artistry could command. It was wood, lifeless and silent. 'You speak not, Lord. Yet in law silence bodes consent. Therefore, until I hear from you in godly wisdom, must I in this length of time remain content.'

*****

Hamlet stepped out onto the portico and was not surprised to see Ophelia sitting on the steps where they had spoken together just before his departure for Wittenberg. As he had anticipated, she was gleaning gladsome memories. Before he moved to her, he could not resist stealing a glance over at his father's couch. His mother was wrong in part. It was changed. It had been stripped of its cushions and the folded mantle that had always been ready for the king. For that reason, it had lost all sense of the person of his father and reverted to being merely a piece of furniture. As such it may have presented a grimly sad scene, but it held no ominous power over his imagination as he had feared it might. Perhaps someday he would even use it and bring to it some trappings of his character to give it a renewed life. But for now, it must sit and resist any effort to make of it a shrine to the late lamented king of Denmark.

Now to Ophelia. He had stopped short upon entering the portico while he studied the couch. Now he stepped off again but with a slower pace than the one that had brought him there from the chapel. As gently as he stepped, Ophelia heard his footfalls and turned to look up at him. She started to rise, but he waved her back down. It occurred to him that Lady Marta just might be availing herself of the view from the queen's apartment window. He nodded with his head back up that way. She glanced up quickly and indicated that she understood. Hamlet took up his place standing before her as he had that day nearly seven years before. Involuntarily, he also began pacing as before. Neither of them spoke.

Finally, Ophelia asked, "How fares the queen, my lord?"

"Sleeping but not easily. Lady Marta attends her. Has she been weeping this whole time?"

"The first three days visited her with constant weeping. Of late, she sits quietly, taking interest in nothing and eating but little and only when coaxed to it with great entreaties—like an ill child. The weeping comes now in fits, squalls, you would call them. Mostly, these are brought on by a chance remembrance of his late Majesty."

"We may say 'my father' privily, else we shall be overlong in niceties and your presence missed upstairs. For my mother, it would seem the key is to find some diversion to her grief. Could we discover something that would call her away from thoughts of my father? She hath declared she longs to be happy again."

"Her happiness that was lies in his sepulcher awaiting the last trump. What now is there to do for her happiness? I know naught!" Ophelia covered her face with her hands. It was clear to Hamlet that she had been in constant attendance on the queen and was now at or near her own wit's end.

"When did you last take rest, my love?"

She dropped her hands to her lap and reflected. "I was sent home, what is it, three nights back. But I fear for the queen and dare not leave her long. It seems she calls most for me. The other ladies change with the watch and are more rested. We have tried all that comes to mind. Poetry is too bittersweet, stitchery too tiring of her eyes, and talk of fashion merely highlights the futility in the world. The king—your uncle—has offered to take to horse with her on the morrow to view the country and receive the good wishes of the people. The commons have been coaxed to leave off their mourning and cheer the queen's health. It may do."

"Should I ride with them, do you think?"

"I know not, my lord. Your company may be an added measure to her joy. And I think it were good for you to see the love the general populace bears you."

"Aye. I have felt their love before this." His thoughts took a sudden turn back to his uncle. "Yet it is a love I will not employ to gain me a crown."

"Indeed, my lord. How fare you in that matter? I have supposed it to be nearly as much in your thoughts as your father's death."

"On both accounts, like you, I know not what to think. Though my thoughts on it abound, I cannot snatch at them to any effect nor hold them to any concerted end. The world's turned upside down, and ideas new-formed slip away, like leaves in autumn, so that I miss a dozen to seize upon the one. This much I will confess. I have just come from my uncle where I have agreed not to press my claim to the throne. Whether I shall continue in that line remains. There is much to consider, the upshot of which is that to act prematurely in this is to plunge Denmark into chaos. And that I will not have. Can you understand this decision?"

"Aye, my lord—and my love."

Her lord and her love, did he deserve that given his tottering forbearance toward the crown? The passion of his self-doubt rose as he spoke.

"And do you not, by reason of this response, perceive your 'beloved' now to be a man of indecision, a wobbly-legged and weak-willed knave, as insubstantial as John-a-dreams, a prince of vapors, a sieve of the realm to let the succession pass through multiplied openings of weakness, and spill out onto poorer ground?"

"Stop!" Her hands flew back to her face as if to shut out the words that had already passed. "I mean—nay, my lord. I have no thought on it. I am troubled for the queen and have no strength for you. If your doubts seek buttressing from my calm assurance, it were a fruitless search. Be a king or remain a prince on the wings of this drama, it is all one to me. It is enough to be glad at your return. In this topsy-turvy world, enough may be let slip that would give us some pause to speak our love-thoughts less privily. 'Tis all the happiness and strength I seek. Ask no more of me but to trust my love to you in these unquiet times and find some peace in your arms. And when the sun comes up again in its right place, I shall by your side be or at your feet kneel or in your arms lie, and whatever you say, it is right. It is right for me, and it will be right for Denmark, if Denmark is still in your heart. And as I pray, if I am still in your heart. At present, I have no heart to bolster yours. So if thou art weak-willed, together we would a weak-willed couple make nor should such a couple rule in Denmark!"

With this, she burst into tears. Hamlet looked up to see no one at the queen's window. Bending, he took Ophelia's hands to raise her up. Then he drew her deeper into the garden, where the boughs hid all from above, and there they embraced with a passion born of pent-up years. Tears flowed freely on both sides, and everything devolved into the desperately needed kissing that lasted until the world stopped spinning for them both.

*****

Hamlet brought a much calmer Ophelia back up to the queen's rooms just as his mother was rousing. For the moment, the storm seemed past for all. Hamlet suggested a game at cards, one that he had learned in Wittenberg. It required some little instruction for the ladies but was not so complex as to dissuade the queen by reason of needing to concentrate greatly. In the essay of the game itself, Lady Marta proved almost comically inept. The foursome thus found cause for laughter. Upon the realization that she was indeed laughing, Hamlet's mother passed him a grateful and loving look. The theme was repeated in Ophelia's eyes as well.

The changing of the watch came, as Ophelia had described their relief by two more fresh ladies. Fortunately, these new attendants had hit upon some court gossip on their way, and its eager delivery allowed Lady Marta to slip away home while Hamlet escorted Ophelia to the rooms she had taken in the keep since the king's death, this in order to be near the queen should she call.

They happened to be the rooms assigned to Horatio during his stay all those years back. For propriety's sake, Hamlet would not enter. But through the open door, he saw again the small window where, on his return from the war, he had first bemoaned the death of Yorick. 'You were supposed to live forever' echoed as a whisper in his memory, and he thought again of his father. He forced that sad notion aside to give Ophelia a cheerier leave-taking.

In the half light of the hall, he looked again deeply into her eyes. He saw there still a mingling of feelings. Mostly in the midst of a physical weariness, he saw the seed of a spiritual calm. Whatever was in his own eyes, he knew that the look they exchanged would last them through the night apart. Tacitly, they had hit upon the strategy of taking each day as it came, both for their grief, for the support of those whom they loved, and for the future of their own love. They were about to part with a kiss when the sound of footsteps ascending the spiral stairs pushed them apart and broke the contact of their hands.

Hamlet could tell these were not the steps of a servant. A servant would tread lightly so as not to disturb. These were noble footfalls. So he was not overly surprised to see Laertes appear.

"Laertes!" Ophelia rushed to his embrace. Her brother looked from her to Hamlet.

"I have just escorted Mistress Ophelia here from our time together with the queen," he explained.

Laertes spoke over Ophelia's shoulder as they continued to embrace. "I was told she had been in constant attendance on Her Majesty and might be found here at this time. I thank you for your care of her." If he suspected anything of the two of them, he did not show it. Then he drew Ophelia apart from him to study her. In her affection for her brother, Hamlet could see old Yorick's description of Ophelia as the "court kitten." If she could have managed a contented purr, it would be about now.

"How now, sister? Thou art pale." Ophelia dipped her head and leaned back into him.

"In our absence, she has been the queen's link with sanity, as you had been mine in all our dispiriting delays upon the road. Your family is a service to all ours and hence to Denmark. But all we are weary, and to wax in your praise here were not enough and out of season. It should be, and shall be, in the hearing of other ears. I will leave you with your sister for there should be at least one reunion this day that hath not the pang of grief to attend it. A good even' to you both." He bowed and started down the stairs. Then he turned and addressed Laertes again. "Shall I send up a meal for you two to share in private?"

"Ophelia?" Laertes deferred to her.

"Yes," she sniffed gratefully. "I only now perceive that I am hungry."

"And I shall inform your father that he may join you," Hamlet added.

"Father sups tonight in late council session. I will bring her down to him at its conclusion for one more merry meeting. I thank you again, Your Highness."

Hamlet left them to order up the meal and then make his way at last to his own room. It was time to think.

\*\*\*\*\*

The weariness of travel and the exhaustion of tangled emotions plunged Hamlet into deep sleep without delay. He awoke refreshed and grateful. After a quick breakfast, he returned to his mother's apartments prepared to spend the hours with her. He found her seated again at the table. Her attention was drawn to a small caged bird that stood perched, almost studying her in return. It chirped merrily, bringing a look of fragile amusement to his mother's countenance. Ophelia was there as well. She also looked rested and relaxed at the queen's return from the depths of grief. Hamlet prayed silently and quickly that the morning would remain on an even keel.

"What's this, Mother?" he asked.

Looking up, she fixed Hamlet with a smile that peeled away her years and showed him a glimpse of what she must have looked like as a young woman.

"Your uncle hath sent it up this morning to cheer me. 'Tis a sweet gesture, yes? He will be a good king who can think of one subject's troubles in the midst of all the concerns of state. Come, enjoy the little fellow with us. Ophelia has suggested Sweet Beak as a name for him. What think you? It is a joy to watch him make his birdsong."

"A joy indeed. When I studied in Wittenberg, I had an amsel perched somewhere in the eaves above my window and his song to make me merry." Hamlet took a seat and joined in a scrutiny of the bird. Yet peripherally, he studied his mother. She was entirely focused on Sweet Beak and maintained that youthful aura about her. Hamlet began to hope that diversions would not be so hard to come by as he had anticipated.

After a time, as the new pet had run through its repertoire of song for the dozenth time, Hamlet felt himself restless. It occurred to him that his return home, leaving his mission in Paris to be completed by others, left him without employment for the moment, with no employment but the care of his mother, that is. He marveled at Ophelia's patience and the love that could have kept her in such close attendance on an adult woman with such suddenly childlike needs. With this thought, he studied Ophelia as well. She, too, was enthralled by the chattery feathered creature. He decided that the fellow's tiny size and bright eyes must appeal to the matronly feelings of the two women. Try as he might to attend the thing with their eyes, he found only a sense of the quaintness of it. Additionally, he felt the need to speak.

"Mistress Ophelia, you are looking rested. I trust you and your brother passed a good evening in talk."

"Oh, yes, my lord. He was kind enough to prattle on about Paris though I know it was of little interest to him. He spoke well of your work with Sir Hugh and of your contributing interest in their work at the embassy."

"To men, a well-oiled contrivance—to this I liken the embassy—is as much of interest as your Sweet Beak here is to you and all womanhood. And I have learned much that would help me on the… throne." He fought back a short ripple of depression. Ophelia dipped her head at this as if averting her gaze from an embarrassment.

They all fell back into silence. Sweet Beak ceased his chirping to assail some bread crumbs the queen had introduced into the cage through a trapdoor. His mother giggled like a child to watch the bird pecking away at its food.

"That's a merry sound," said Claudius, coming to the door. "May I enter?"

"Certainly…Your Majesty!" said the queen as they all rose. "We were enjoying your sweet gift."

"Splendid. Good morning to you all." He motioned them to resume their seats. Then stooping slightly toward the cage, he studied the bird. "In truth, I came to make a point of this cheerful creature. Two points."

"A point?" the queen asked.

"It seems to me that a merry heart should not be kept thus encaged."

"But he is your gift."

"An earnest of better things and, one hopes, better days. Let him brighten your own hearts a few days more. But enjoy him with an anticipation to set him free ere long. And follow you as well from this cage of Elsinore to sing among the people, as he will do. They have been too long at mournful looks and thoughtful concerns o'er their queen."

"But I am no longer the queen." Hamlet wondered that his mother could utter that realization without an attendant breakdown.

"Well, our sister-queen then. But to my second point, you have promised to ride with me this morning, a short progress, as much for the hearts of the people as for you. I trust you will find it a gladsome duty."

"Do you think I could?" the queen seemed to falter at the thought of a public appearance. Her tone was that of a child seeking guidance—or permission.

"At all hearts, you are queen still, Gertrude, and bred to the stamina of the office."

She managed a grateful smile. "Then give me leave of an hour to prepare. Ophelia?" Ophelia moved to attend her.

"It likes us well. In the interim, I have some office for Hamlet to perform, which will take some short instruction. In an hour then. Hamlet?" He invited Hamlet to exit with him.

Hamlet nodded and followed his uncle out. Outwardly calm, his inner thoughts trembled over one issue: his uncle's use of his mother's Christian name.

# Chapter 19

Hamlet did not join his mother and uncle for their ride. Whether he had intended to or not—and it was still not decided with him either way—Claudius had seen to forestalling him with the task unto which he had appointed his nephew. Hamlet found himself long occupied with Polonius at reviewing the recent expenditures from the exchequer. Though it proved a valuable insight into the daily operation of the keep and opened to him a certain knowledge of some peculiar culinary proclivities among the members of the household, he still felt the pull to be elsewhere. Polonius's long-winded explanations were the icing to a blusterous and anxious tedium.

The task finally completed. Hamlet excused himself and elected to take a stroll on the battlements. His course led him across the yard, up the tower by the postern, along the lower platform, and to the covered stairs where Horatio had so long ago accosted him. He smiled to think of that incident but also sighed to think of that time. He stopped for a moment at the foot of the last turn of the steps to look up at the rectangle of daylight into which Horatio had scurried following his mischievous ambush.

The draft still swept by him coming upward from behind. All was silent except the faint echoing of memory. His thoughts went back to the story of the ghost that had quickened his steps back then. He gave his thoughts on it no form or expression but hung on the sense of a troubled spirit. How did it run, the plot? A knight murdered by a rival at love. That was it. Well, Elsinore boasted no such legend. But the thought of troubled spirits stayed with him. A half-formed question rose up in the stillness, like the updraft, to whisper to his being. Was his father's spirit troubled by any unconcluded worldly matters? Certainly, there was unfinished work for the crown. There would always be that. But in his father's personal life, was there aught to make him unsettled in his sudden taking leave of it?

He thought back to the last memory of his father: the two brothers standing nearly side by side, his uncle perhaps a little behind, his father trusting and unguarded. The younger brother's stance could be read as either protective or menacing. He recalled the chill he had had to stifle at that time as he turned away to begin his journey. Sure, it was prophetic enough to provide a faint hint of the tragedy to which he would return. *The Tragedy of Hamlet, King of Denmark* sounded in his soul like a single death knell.

This time, he did not brush off the feeling. Instead, he began in a strange way to fashion some events into an idea, a theme. He was thinking merely that the story of his father's life and death might provide meet food for the pen and the voice of Master Guilliame on his next visit. Yes, he would like to glorify his father's life. "It must be written down," he whispered to the stairwell, and thought that prayerlike, it carried upward on the draft. Still on the stairs, he heard, but not from memory, a whispered almost response. 'Remember me!'

Suddenly, a figure appeared at the top of the stairs. But it was mortal. Passing out of the sunlight, Hamlet immediately recognized his sword master of old. "Marcellus?"

"He."

"Come you from the watch?"

"Oh, pardon, Your Highness. I did not recognize you at first. I believe this is the first time we have met on stairs. But to an answer, yes. Though it is not a specification of my duties, yet at times will I take a turn to give some soldier a rest and to make good use of a season of solitude. Bernardo hath my place now."

"Have you time?"

"My time is yours, Your Highness."

"Good. Come up with me and help me unbutton my mind. You are not too aged for a second pass at the great tower?"

"A third, my lord, if the truth be known for I found that I had left my cloak up there and am only now returned from retrieving it." He held his cloak up to show. On being saluted, he had stopped only a few steps into his descent of this stairs and remained there but now stepped aside to let his prince pass as Hamlet continued upward. At the conclusion of this—his answer to Hamlet's question—they both came out onto the ramparts and headed toward the great tower. "I have not had opportunity to welcome you home, my lord, sad as that welcome may be."

"Aye. Sad indeed. But thank you." There was a pause as they walked on until they entered the tower. "What intelligence have you of my father's death? Speak frankly, my friend. My grief is composed."

"I know only the main, my lord. The king was at his daily nap and succumbed, it is said, to the serpent's sting. I think he suffered not, or not for any length, for they say his body was found in no tableau of agony but stiffly still at repose."

"And thus, was there no mark or trace or even sighting of this serpent?"

"Nay, my lord. 'Twas thought to be winged and thus to have flown off having delivered of its potent poison, yet I have no knowledge of any such venomous creatures of these parts. Else vipers can fly or drop out of trees, I can foretell no clear discovery of the nemesis."

"But 'tis certain this was no natural demise?"

"My lord, the physician who was called in pronounced a toxic mingled in his blood to carry off the king."

By this time, the two had arrived at the top of the tower.

"Hola, Bernardo," Hamlet greeted his war companion of old.

"Your Highness, 'tis good to see you. It should cheer you some to look about from here and see that despite the gloom of the times, all else is well with Denmark."

"Indeed. 'Twas behind my thoughts to try these heights. And glad am I now for the company of two companions from more joyful times, if open warfare could be said to cosset joyful times."

"Joy and sorrow are dependent on so many things, my lord," said Bernardo. "That their workings, in tandem or abreast, cannot be gauged or gainsaid and must, like the pallet, be left to the individual to savor or to eschew."

"You have become more philosophical. Is't the years at careful watch from here?"

"I think it be just the years, my lord."

"Well, may your years continue in grace and peace beyond counting. I wish that to every man of good will, knowing now what a curtailment of years brings to those who love."

"The sun will come up again, my lord," said Marcellus, taking seat upon a block set along the foot of the battlement for a firing step. Hamlet had waived him to it.

"Those be the same words of Mistress Ophelia, who waits upon the queen." He went to the edge and looked out over the landward side of the castle. "And so it must be for here my mother comes back from her ride and the king with her. She looks the better for it. Why, she even laughs. That is good for the heart." At the same time, he thought to himself, 'Yet my heart misgives the cause of her laughter that it should be my uncle. Is this jealousy?'

"Sure, all may be well, my lord," Marcellus thought aloud, not hearing Hamlet's unspoken doubts. "The winter storms that delayed your arrival here have yielded up to days of sun. And it will be that other storms and nightly cold will ever seek to chill the heart ere return of summer sun that strengthens our resolve to carry on. But love remains to bar the door of final death and warm the heart with inner strength. We have the resurrection of our Lord and the constant earnest of his Holy Spirit to keep us in that hope. I know 'tis easily spoken on my part, who still hath his Da to pass the hearth-warmed night in close company. But that is why faith is faith. It stands against the gloom and the call to leave off hope, to plumb the depths of despair, and to give over to the dulling comforts of this world.

"If we can stand when anticipation fails and disappointment of our dreams is the argument, we will a better song make of our lives than woeful wailing and curses against heaven, whose purpose we know not. Sure, our complaints against the fates smack of the child's tantrum as o'er the careful plans of careful parents to teach with trials the better courses of a life. We must take the bad with as good grace as with grace we accept the good. But all this you know. I speak thus not to instruct but to bolster you in your loss, sire."

"Call you me sire? Do you see in me a king?"

"Aye, my lord. And a king who holds the people in his heart and not within the grip of his sword. And I think 'tis commonly perceived so. Your time will come."

"My time as king. I pray my wits and daring keep me through this soul's dark night and serve me well 'til time shall tell 'tis time to claim my right."

*****

The youthful look espied by Hamlet in his mother's face as she watched her Sweet Beak in song began more and more to strike him as the breathless look of a maiden gone to doting on a youth. His mother's return to happiness outpaced his efforts to lead her to it. It seemed unnatural, and it troubled him. More troubling still was again the realization of the source of this hasty recovery. Claudius had come a courting of his mother. That much was clear. And she, with maiden-like infatuation, responded.

He attempted to sound her out about it once. "The king's attentions come close enough to boarding, Mother." He said this in response to yet another gift he was shown by her from him.

"As I have bespoke, the king is kindly, and his careful consideration is meant to coax me from my cares."

"That's fine alliteration, Mother, but is it meet to close, so close, upon your bereavement? 'Tis not yet a little month since my father, your husband, was laid to his rest."

A cold darkening of her countenance preceded the next. "Teach me not how to number the days, my son. The blood in its heyday flows when and wither it will." The darkness in her look passed quickly, and her tone turned to soft urging, ushered in with a sigh. "You know not the needs of woman, especially in the dark of night, when once she has known the comforts of a pair of arms. But that flies ahead. A woman, any woman, wants to know she still excites, is someone's longed-for dawn, the object of one's waking dreams, the reason for a smile aside while at some other task, the unbidden opportunity for the giving of a trinket of variable worth. It is life to us, as much as manly praise and trials at arms are to you. Without these things, a life is but a pale existence upon a cold and barren moor. Your uncle understands this. And he acts upon it."

"Is this then the happiness you so desired? What if his attentions wane?"

"That's two questions. To the first, it is not *all* my happiness. But his kindness brings me back into the orbit of my other joys. There is you, and remember 'twas your return hath first helped me regain this happy path. You are dear to me as well, my son, the light of all my warmer days and the flesh and blood presentment of my husband who was. Then there are my ladies, whose complex needs are the machinery at which I toil, the measure of my efforts to a peaceful court and the justification of my place in this world. There is the greetings of the people. If I can but be brave for them, as Claudius hath shown me is my duty, they will in their cares subside to make all Denmark a happy state.

"But in all this, the nights are yet empty. And I want them full again. Comes your uncle into this mold? 'I cannot say,' as you have coined it once. But as his kind attentions wax—in answer to your second query—I shall bask in them as long as they remain a comfort to help me fight the pain. And should they wane, well, I know not but hold I tightly to my joys as I proceed through life. Though now a widow, I would again be wife."

*****

Claudius was, in truth, a visible king. By contrast, Hamlet fell to a private brooding. His uncle kept him long at tasks wherein though they were important to the functioning of the crown, yet could he use these to gather no authority nor could he build with them a power base of counter-loyalty. He was being kept busy, and he knew it. What is worse, his natural diligence in keeping to these tasks freed up his uncle for time to spend with his mother. In a sense, he was doing the work of kings but possessed neither the title nor the power nor the rights nor privileges thereof. He "filled the glove" indeed. But his uncle kept for himself the trappings and aired them often to put him out in front of the people. Thus, the unknown brother of the late king swiftly gained the affection of the commons and, with liberal and calculated largesse, also purchased the loyalty of the court.

Hamlet noted as well that though there was no wanton whole-sale lapse of morals yet certain matters under the "Old King" had been relaxed. He remembered his father's mention—almost a proph-ecy—of heavy handed reveling by his uncle in the great hall following the dinner meal. This had grown to a regular observance. The pro-prieties were observed to a point. But with the dishes cleared away, the joviality began. In this issue, Hamlet was not entirely certain of a breach of decorum. Perhaps it was not so bad a thing and only grated against his need to mourn on. Certainly, he could make no specific accusation, put his finger on no misconduct, nor even point to coarser humor for condemnation of the new king and court. But something seemed more lax in the exercise and pursuit of joy among the members of the court. Needless to say, he found himself leaving the hall early after dinner and going up to his room with the noise of laughter dimly following him up the stairs.

Another week, and the queen's heart had been won. She and Claudius had returned from what had become now their daily ride. Hamlet watched from his window as his uncle helped his mother to dismount into an embrace. They followed that up with a moment to study each other. Then she slipped away from him like a schoolgirl scurrying to her next enchanted diary entry. Claudius's brightened countenance was the face of victory.

That evening, Hamlet watched his mother playfully serving his uncle, feeding him morsels with her hands as they sat together upon the dais at dinner in the great hall. Were she not his mother and he not his uncle, they did a loving couple make. But they were whom they were, and he winced to see it.

The meal being concluded, Claudius banged his tankard on the table top for attention. Hamlet wondered if this was some new official start to the "ceremonies of laxity." When all were silent and attendant and all save one sat forward with expectation glowing in their faces, he rose to speak.

"Friends! I call you all friends as one who shares his greatest joy among his neighbors. In this short month that I have reigned, I have the measure of Denmark's greatness taken, to see how well she rises from the ashes of her mourning to resume her rightful place among the states. Resilience is our hallmark as rightly it bespeaks a people ever wedded to the wild and wasteful sea. We have left off our weeping and now move proudly on to a new dawning in her march of kings. For your loving tribute and support, I thank you. And though, like you, I purpose to forget not the greatness of my late kin, whose reign was both the sunshine of kingly glory and the welcome rain of blessings on a worthy people, yet will I not neglect our need of joys that mark us humankind, who can and must from weeping turn in time to dancing.

"But one more joy has been afforded me. And this must I share with you tonight. Nor will I any longer draw it out. Know you all by this that Gertrude here, who once was queen and then, by fate, a widow made, hath consented to keep her station and her title, becoming my queen and wife!"

Everyone went to their feet cheering. Hamlet's mother wept as she smiled. Claudius drew her to her feet, and the two stood together, hands clasped, receiving every ounce of the court's good will. Hamlet, too, rose lest he be seen to be in opposition. Indeed, the look on his mother's face told him her happiness was genuine and coaxed him to a sympathetic, if short-lived happiness as well.

As the cheering settled down, Polonius offered a toast. Hamlet drank their health with the rest but had little heart in their union. The sight of the old minister made him realize that in his brooding through dinner, he had not affected his usual furtive glances toward Ophelia—stolen time it was because he had been unable to find any time with her. It was the old story. As a lady in waiting, she was still kept close and now also gave time to Laertes when both were free of duty. She was, in short, inaccessible to him once again. This, too, fed his agitation and sent him morosely back to the company of the two sisters for solace. This is not to say that she ignored him or had forgotten him. Her looks to him, in those numerous times when her looks sought him out, were pleas for patience and an assurance that she, too, burned to be with him.

Hamlet looked at her now to gauge her reaction to the news. As he supposed, she was so wrapped in the cause of his mother's happiness that her look was as triumphant as Claudius. He noted that Laertes's joy as he stood beside his sister was more subdued. By this, he wondered if he, too, chafed at the short shrift given to mourning after his father. Laertes would be one to hold respectful customs dear and see the hurt to any for whom the memory of the king was not a thing to be let slipped.

When Ophelia finally turned her gaze to him, he caught it but could return only a look that bespoke the confusion in his soul. Again, he received from her that gentle urge to patient endurance, but along with that, a nod toward the royal couple invited him to remember his mother's joy. Perhaps, he hoped, she thought that with that issue settled—save the flurry over wedding preparations they must surely now anticipate—there just might be some time for them. He nodded his head to acknowledge agreement that with his mother's happiness now firmly the business of Claudius, they could indeed carve for themselves.

As soon as he could, Hamlet slipped away and returned again to his room, where he spent an hour's discourse with the dying hearth fire before turning in for sleep. His conclusion was that some things at least appeared to be settled. Also, in the back of his mind, sprouted a thought that he should like to be away from Elsinore. Paris had an uncompleted mission for him, one in whose work he could lose himself. But the thought of facing once again the royal beauty market soured his anticipation of returning to the "City of Light." Horatio was still in Wittenberg extending his studies. Perhaps a season there with friends and books, where he need not bear the apparent frailty of womanhood, might restore him to better contentment. He would consider it. With that thought, he drifted off to sleep.

*****

That night, Hamlet dreamed of his father. It was a disquieting dream. The latter stood upon the battlements in full armor, save that he wore the beaver of his helmet up to show a face painted in sorrow.

"Father?" Hamlet called out voicelessly.

His father uttered only one thing—and that with a forlorn sigh—and then the dream was gone. 'Remember me.' The words floated away like the updraft on the covered stairs.

Hamlet awoke, rolled onto his side, and wept like a heartbroken child until sleep arrived again near the dawn.

*****

If each of us is tempted to lapse into sainthood upon our time on earth, then Hamlet's test came in the short weeks of preparation for the royal wedding. Out of sensitivity to his nature, he was not asked to do much in these efforts, yet his presence at many occasions was necessary to give the appearance of a blessing to this o'er hasty marriage. Daily, he ran the gauntlet of emotions that pulled at him from nearly every direction.

His mother's joy proved so infectious among her ladies that the days were filled with tittering and cheerfully spoken visions of how the wedding ceremony should proceed. Hamlet found himself unable to stomach it and retreated to his work. Once again, his veneer of diligence earned him praise, genuine praise, even from his uncle. He wondered if he had been fated always to live a double life of outward grace and inward turmoil. Perhaps that was the life of a king: to speak roundly before his subjects words of hope and courage and yet to give no voice of inner troubles in the thin air of sparse companionship that attended royalty.

But time moves on, and so the wedding came. And it was all his mother had hoped for. Hamlet played his part well enough to please but with the one concession that he remain robed in the black of mourning. This was painted by his uncle as a fitting respect to honor the memory of the king who was the "contracted brow of woe," as he had said in his address in the great hall following the ceremony and proceeding the feast.

In the wake of the meal, some minor matters came before the court that needed resolution but did not require the voice or the vote of the council. There was some discussion of what to do over the latest escapades of Young Fortinbras of Norway. Then Polonius advanced Laertes's request to return post haste to Paris and resume his good work there.

But then, bending to his new wife's wishes, Claudius made public the issue of Hamlet's desire to return to Wittenberg and added to it an admonition against his "unmanly" grief for his father. This put Hamlet in a place where he could breed no contention. He was forced to acquiesce and gracefully, only defending the depth of his grief. Having thus gladdened his mother's heart, he excused himself to take up his brooding in a more appropriate setting.

Now he sat on the steps of the terraced garden, reviewing the history of his unhappiness. In this frame of mind, he barely held on to life. 'Self-slaughter' rang in his ears, but he reluctantly cast the thought away as it was the quickest road to damnation. Something told him to hold his life more dearly still. Perhaps there was some purpose to it that he could not yet fathom.

His thoughts kept coming around to his mother and her precipitate abandonment of his father's memory, of how quickly she had turned from grief to…to his uncle. These thoughts then took him to comparisons of the brothers that heated his frustration and brought him nowhere toward any peaceful conclusion in his soul. He kept flinging these thoughts away, but they returned as if pulled into a deep well of gravity.

Then he tried to divert himself with thoughts of Ophelia, but his latest images of her, so joyfully supportive of the queen's behavior, were such that he could not help for the moment but to place her almost in an enemy's camp and lump her with the queen and her ladies together with all womanhood, a womanhood that painted such a sorry portrait of human nature that it made his love a question. Was he seeing Ophelia in a new light of truth and finding there a soured image? Was his love for her souring? From there, he questioned all his love and found it wanting in all aspects.

"What has happened to all my trust?" he asked the incorporeal air. 'Yorick and Father, they failed of the immortality that should be theirs by right of greatness and now lie forgotten and never even approached they the waning years, instead becoming mere men with lives as fragile as the next. Ophelia and my mother make happiness their demigod and go skipping off to modest Bacchanalias of the heart. And how true can friends be? They rightly return to keep their duties. Marcellus hath his pupils to consider and Laertes his complex embassies and Denmark's interest to nurture along. Rosencrantz and Guildenstern, ha! They are not friends but companions for the sunny days, muzzled adders eternally at play, who seek for themselves and would for a ducat forsake their friends, thus runs the world away! I pass them by in my regard of friends. Horatio. Horatio, there's a noble heart at once from me cut off in my promise now to remain at Elsinore.

'Enough! This self-pitying assessment avails me not. But what can I? And where now should my trust reside? These lives who were to me the edifice of all I hoped of life are now a house of cards. It needs but one good blast of the winds of fate to bring all crashing down and set me on the path of lunacy—some fell news to wrest control from me and sweep me on my way. And should I grasp at all the nothings proffered me along this downward course, there will be naught to stay me in such a swift descent. I foresee it. Yet must I face it. But break my heart for I must hold my tongue. There is no ear to hear.'

"Hail to your lordship," came a distantly familiar voice from the portico above and behind him.

"I am glad to see you well." Hamlet had employed this phrase to welcome guests to the wedding. Now he lapsed into it again absently. But then, recognition of the voice made him hastily look up. "Horatio—or I do forget myself?"

"The same, my lord, and your poor servant ever."

"Sir, my good friend, I'll change that name with you. And what make you from Wittenberg?"

# Epilogue

Master Guilliame pulled his cloak about him more closely as he stepped onto the portico above the terraced garden. A weak winter sun cast a ghost of shadows, a web of barren branches upon the ground below. Leaves swirled in listless eddies. No one was about. He stood undecided. Should he depart, or should he await the person who enjoined him to this meeting? A third alternative formed in his mind. He could improve the time composing verses for his audience with the new king of Denmark. Off to the side, he saw a couch, the only piece of furniture about. Something about it looked forlorn, and so, he hesitated. Before he could overcome his doubts, he heard steps coming up behind him from the great hall. He turned to see a young nobleman from the court.

"Lord Horatio?" he asked.

"Aye. Thank you for coming, Master Guilliame."

"Your invitation, sire, in light of recent events, could not but intrigue me."

"I penned my request with that intent. There are some benches below. As this will take some time, it is good for us both to sit."

"As you will. I have brought my lute. You have indicated you have a sad tale to tell surrounding the strange death of King Claudius, his queen, and other members of his court. So have I brought it along by habit. It is my method to cast at chords when I receive the matter of a tale. I pray it will not distract."

"I do not foresee it though you may be called upon to strange progressions and contentious modalities as the turnings of my tale take us along. I have the leave of our new king to use this tale to set to rights the events which have so recently caused disruption to our state."

"Of Fortinbras himself?"

"Aye."

"And was he an actor in this drama?"

"Only lastly did he take his mark upon the stage of it, in time to take his cold election to the throne from a voice but barely silenced by death's fell sergeant—'so swift in his arrest.'"

They made their way to the indicated benches and took seat. The troubadour took up his instrument and gave it a quiet tuning. Then he struck a few chords in a minor progression—a very sad beginning. Looking up, he saw tears starting in Horatio's eyes.

"Forgive me if I proceed through this haltingly. The protagonist of my tale was my dearest friend. I warn you now, 'tis a strange story of ghosts and poisons, of love betrayed and love tampered with, of sudden and undeserved demises, drownings and executions, murder behind the arras, and more I cannot say without you knowing the cause. It twists and turns through mischances to a trail strewn with deaths, none of which but at the beginning and at the end were contrived.

"I have all this from my own eyes and from Prince Hamlet himself, who, sometime before its conclusion, unburdened to me his entire heart. Some portions I must keep back. But there will be enough to tell. It will tax my sanity thus to relate what I must. Aye, wring my heart as I relive it before you. But I have a promise to keep, and so must I draw my breath in pain to tell the story, *The Tragedy of Hamlet, Prince of Denmark.*"

The End

## The Chevalier mal fet

Of heroes of old many songs are sung,
of valor and strength and noble heart,
of mighty feats, and purest love,
and tempered faith unending.
These men, who all their years throughout,
from youth to manhood, birth to grave,
their will did they tune to attain their best,
and gain a fame unending.

So too you gentlemen assembled here,
your minds and arms do labor long,
to steel the heart 'gainst any foe,
and stand though you the sole remaining
among your comrades fallen round,
whose fellowship you cherished,
whose lives, though not their friendships, perished,
and thus, great glory gaining.

You know what 'tis to toil and sweat,
to strive and painfully succeed,
to set the riches of the world at naught,
and seek that fleeting glory
to pursue relentless ever higher
in martial skill and moral might;
'tis you, you men with hearts of oak
will best perceive this story.

The *Chevalier mal fet*, he's called,
but neither village, castle, town, was of this
appellation wary,
nor aught of it knew family, friends, nor mentors all;
'twas in his thinking only.
Though outwardly his talents shown,
his graces and his gifts prevailing.
To others he was blessed indeed,
but inwardly was lonely.

What cause for loneliness was here,
in one so noble and so strong,
in one so fair and full of grace,
whose skill was daily growing?
The "ill-made knight," he styled himself
from self-assessment failing.
A greater doubt than glory spread
from seeds the Evil One was sowing.

Which seeds could so devour a man,
whose valor, strength, and mind were tested,
found never wanting, never bested,
from point of soul unto the hilt,
could so corrode the truest heart,
the noblest aspiration,
such a heart of solid gold,
to heart of wood encased in gilt?

'Twas guilt indeed began its work
when heart was young and hand was soft,
when faith was sure and trust was keen,
and promise still unflower'd.
Th' idyllic aim of this young knight
to see the world before him bright
and live this ideal strong and true;
'twas guilt his hopes devour'd.

Guilt o'er his thoughts of earthly things
that held him earthbound from his flights,
and thoughts and prayers
of true nobility ascending
that pulled him down and held him fast,
'til swelled with anguish, he at last
perceived himself, who should be knight,
into the night descending.

Yet outwardly he shown like light
in strength of arms, in depth of thought,
but humble, for he knew his heart
in private self-cajole unheeding.
Though failed of strength to inward fight,
the outward man rose in esteem
of those who saw not inward strife;
his endeavors all succeeding.

Proceed he then, in double life,
in inward thoughts and outward show,
in anguish, but with placid face,
too weak to fight pretension.
Ever higher rose his good repute
in efforts meant to compensate,
to break through sinful, lustful thoughts,
the heart of this contention.

His Gospel learning deep ingrained
taught him the lustful eye to pluck,
and suffer life the better, maimed,
than whole attend perdition.
And also, he who one law breaks,
the whole transgresses to his loss;
so he believed with breaking heart
stood beyond the pale of salvation.

Compound this with the added fear;
though he his thoughts did not enact,
and only nightly entertained
in private weakness yield to flame,
exposure of his "other man,"
unto a world that held him great,
should such a fall from such a height
lead him to the depth of shame.

The years have sapped his struggling heart
and brought him tearstained to the thought
of what was not but could have been,
a painful lack of fruit assessing.
Could he have caught God's grace and power
to wash the stain to white as snow,
a different song would then be sung:
a song of grace and blessing.

[Here ends the song in the body of the story.]

But God is good and yearns to bless,
with years of peace and fruitful toil,
the weed-choked soil of weary spirits
beset by Satan's strongholds ever.
He understands the heart-wrung hands,
the cries of lonely sin-drowned souls,
the mortal weakness, failed intents,
despairing of the next endeavor.

He understands for he himself,
in human form, 'gainst Satan strove,
to quell the pull of hunger, thirst,
and ran the gauntlet of temptations.
'Twas why he walked among us all,
that we may know he knows us best,
and knows our deeds, and knows our needs,
beyond our deepest contemplation.

It is his love that works this way,
to get beneath the outward man,
with searing light, reveal our plight to inward self,
our hearts made broken and contrite.
'Tis not to hurt nor turn us out,
but like a surgeon, cut away
the death-scarred flesh from guilt-held heart,
to stand unwavering in his light.

The Ill-Made Knight upon his knees,
his weakness and his prayers commingled;
for years his orisons were thus,
his fleshly thoughts could not subdue.
Then remembered he the psalmist's cry
to God and prophet, sin confessing.
Could he a Nathan hope to find,
and in confessing life renew?

The cycle of this malediction
always hung upon that thought,
that fear of scorn, should others learn
the truth, his pretense of nobility.
To break the cycle, speak the truth
to God before a trusted friend,
and psalmist-like confess the shame,
and dissipate futility.

This worthy knight did undertake
to bare his soul to open light,
and found he there not scorn, but love,
from corners of his life untried.
Then grace of God with power and might,
attending with forgiveness there,
the Ill-Made Knight was then made whole;
to him no blessing was denied.

God's floodgates opened full and wide.
Though troubles and temptations came,
he had the power to see them through
to victory and peace of mind.
God means for you the same great things,
the storehouse full, the heart o'erflowing,
the strength to shatter Satan's pull,
and all God's grace and blessings find.

Recall the *Chevalier mal fet*,
when inwardly temptations call
to secret life apart from God,
to shadowed lands of man's desires.
Recall how guilt contrition quells,
and keeps us to the broader way.
Confess and call on Jesus's name,
which power to our holiness inspires.

# About the Author

Julian Marck has this to say about himself:

Born in 1954. I tend to be "old school" about many things; however, allow me to forego a stodgy bio and simply acknowledge here my literary heroes. First is Leo Tolstoy (for introspective characters and historic sweep), then William Shakespeare (for metrical prose; lovely, purposeful syntax; and couplets), Charlotte Brontë (for the width and depth and height of emotional expression contained within right moral convention and for vocabulary), C. S. Lewis and J. R. R. Tolkien (for the license and courage to imagine whole worlds and to fill them with faith), Mary Stewart (whose *Crystal Cave* series did for literature what modality does for music—ages it nicely), Anne McCaffrey (for characters who evoke enduring sympathy—I shall never forget Menolly and *The Ship Who Sang*); more recently, Rick Riordan and Richard Peck (for humor in the midst of pathos) and finally—and most importantly—the forty-odd authors of the Holy Bible (for right handling of the truth of God). These are the spirits who haunt my writing. With "ghostwriters" of this caliber, I hope that I should "a good tale make."

CPSIA information can be obtained
at www.ICGtesting.com
Printed in the USA
LVHW032128310323
742781LV00001B/22